Also by Neville Stocks

The Deciding Votes (Austin Macauley, 2013)

About the Author

Neville Stocks is a South African, living in Cape Town. After studying to be a teacher, he taught mainly English for five years, before entering business and qualifying as a Chartered Secretary. He has had extensive business experience, and has managed both institutional and private investment portfolios for many years.

He always wanted to be a writer, and early retirement made it possible for him to devote time to writing. His novel, *The Deciding Votes*, was published by Austin Macauley in 2013.

Neville is an experienced runner, on track, cross-country and road, as well as in orienteering. He has also been involved in running as a coach and administrator. His interest in the Comrades Marathon dates back to student days in the late fifties, and he has himself completed the race three times.

Neville Stocks

ORDINARY RUNNERS

A CIP catalogue record for this title is available from the British Library.

ISBN 9781784554439 (Paperback)
ISBN 9781784554453 (Hardback)
ISBN 9781784554446 (E-Book)

www.austinmacauley.com

First Published (2005)
Dunford Publishers
South Africa

This Edition Published (2016)
Austin Macauley Publishers Ltd.
25 Canada Square
Canary Wharf
London
E14 5LQ

Acknowledgments

Ordinary Runners is set loosely in the mid-1980's, in the era when the Comrades Marathon was dominated by Bruce Fordyce. This is the story of *a race* in the mid-eighties rather than any one particular real race. However, it is absolutely faithful in its depiction of the Comrades Marathon at that time. I have followed the route of the 1985 up-run very closely, but have changed the distance by 100 metres in order to emphasize that this is a work of fiction rather than of history. I have also taken the liberty of re-arranging the timing of certain background events, most importantly the movement of stock exchange prices and the storm, so as to fall into the period leading up to the race itself.

Ordinary Runners first appeared, in a small self-published edition in South Africa in 2005, under the title *Ordinary Runners' Everest*. I would like to thank all the very professional people at Austin Macauley Publishers for adopting my work and giving it new life in this fully fledged edition. I am grateful to many people, including my family and some friends, who have given me their encouragement, assistance and technical advice in various ways. I would particularly like to acknowledge and thank Joy Whittaker for advice on the Zulu language and related matters; Yolanda Pronk on physiotherapy; and Jens Triebel on legal matters. I would also like thank John van den Aardweg and Cheryl Winn of the Comrades Marathon Association, and also that Association for permission to use and reproduce the official map of the 1985 Comrades Marathon.

The authenticity of my representation of the Comrades Marathon relies not only on my own experiences, but also on the actual official documents (for example, race programmes, race instructions and results) issued by the Comrades Marathon Association and in my possession, as well as numerous newspaper and magazine reports and articles from the 1980's onwards. The Comrades Museum in Pietermaritzburg is a valuable source of information and is also an interesting place to visit. I particularly wish to acknowledge and thank the authors of the following publications, which have proved very useful to me in doing research for this work:

"The Comrades Marathon Story" by Morris Alexander (Juta & Company, 1976; and Delta Books, 1985).

"Comrades Marathon Highlights and Heroes 1921-1999 by Tom Cottrell, Ian Laxton and David Williams (Jonathan Ball Publishers, 2000).

"Run the Comrades" by Bruce Fordyce (Delta Books, 1996).

"Bruce Fordyce, Comrades King" by John Cameron-Dow (Guide Book Publications, 2001).

"The D.H.S. Story 1866-1966" by Hubert D. Jennings (The Durban High School and Old Boys' Memorial Trust, 1966), for Bill Payn's Comrades story in his own words.

While many of the events described in this book were suggested by actual occurrences, and while the names of certain real persons are mentioned, all the characters and personalities portrayed are fictional and are not intended to represent those of any actual person or persons, either living or dead.

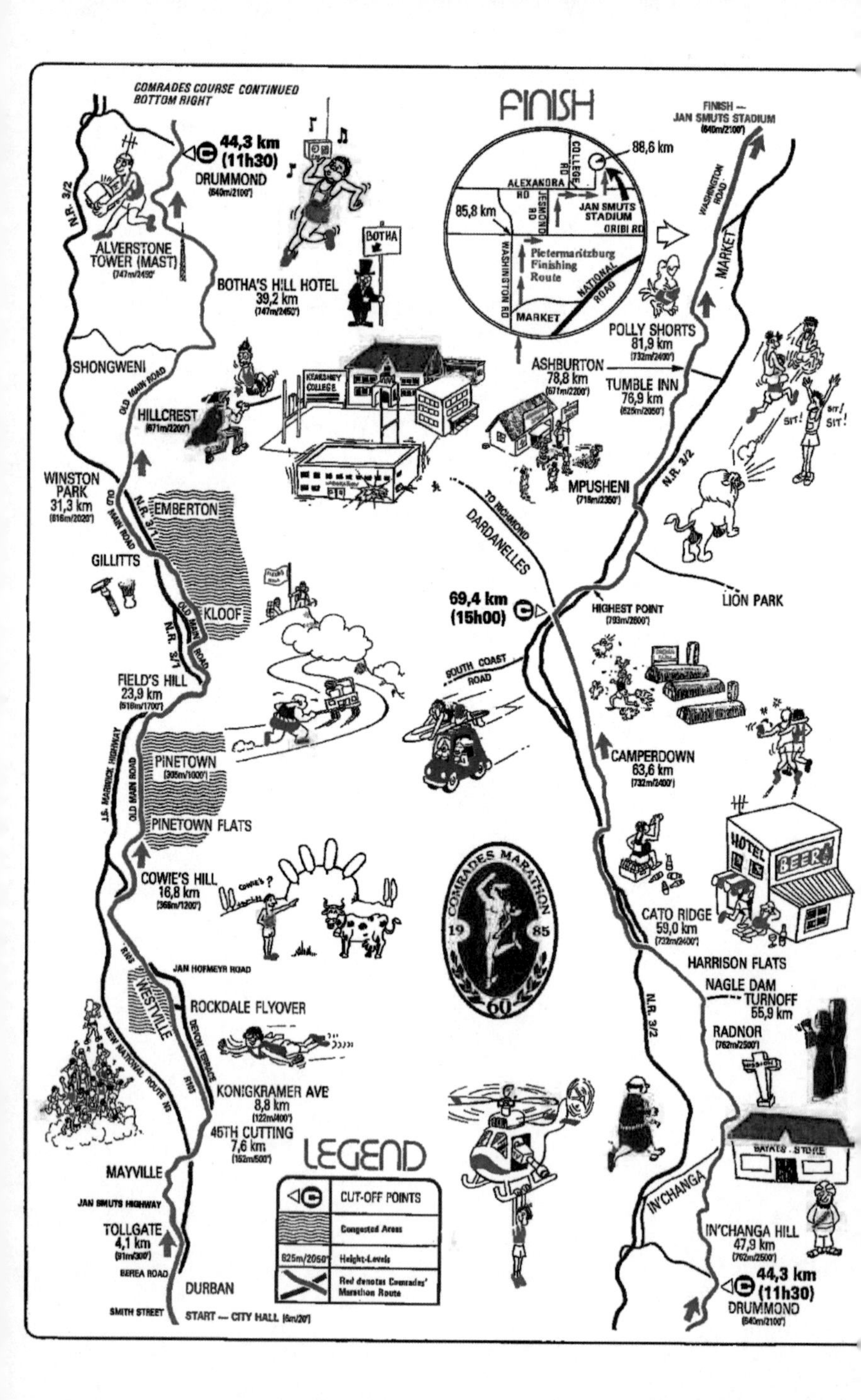

COMRADES COURSE CONTINUED BOTTOM RIGHT
N.R. 3/2
44,3 km (11h30)
DRUMMOND
(640m/2100')
ALVERSTONE TOWER (MAST)
(747m/2450')
BOTHA
BOTHA'S HILL HOTEL
39,2 km
(747m/2450')
SHONGWENI
OLD MAIN ROAD
HILLCREST
(671m/2200')
KEARSNEY COLLEGE
WINSTON PARK
31,3 km
(616m/2020')
OLD MAIN ROAD
N.R. 3/1
EMBERTON
GILLITTS
KLOOF
OLD MAIN ROAD
N.R. 3/1
FIELD'S HILL
23,9 km
(518m/1700')
J.G. STRIJDOM HIGHWAY
OLD MAIN ROAD
PINETOWN
(305m/1000')
PINETOWN FLATS
COWIE'S HILL
16,8 km
(366m/1200')
COWIE'S ?
R103
JAN HOFMEYR ROAD
WESTVILLE
ROCKDALE FLYOVER
DEVON TERRACE
NEW NATIONAL ROUTE N3
R103
KONIGKRAMER AVE
8,8 km
(122m/400')
45TH CUTTING
7,6 km
(152m/500')
MAYVILLE
JAN SMUTS HIGHWAY
TOLLGATE
4,1 km
(91m/300')
BEREA ROAD
DURBAN
SMITH STREET
START — CITY HALL (6m/20')
FINISH
88,6 km
COLLEGE RD
ALEXANDRA RD
JESMOND RD
JAN SMUTS STADIUM
ORIBI RD
85,8 km
WASHINGTON RD
Pietermaritzburg Finishing Route
NATIONAL ROAD
MARKET
FINISH — JAN SMUTS STADIUM
(640m/2100')
WASHINGTON ROAD
MARKET
POLLY SHORTS
81,9 km
(732m/2400')
ASHBURTON
78,8 km
(671m/2200')
TUMBLE INN
76,9 km
(625m/2050')
SIT! SIT!
SIT!
MPUSHENI
(716m/2350')
N.R. 3/2
TO RICHMOND
DARDANELLES
LION PARK
69,4 km (15h00)
HIGHEST POINT
(793m/2600')
SOUTH COAST ROAD
CAMPERDOWN
63,6 km
(732m/2400')
HOTEL
BEER
COMRADES MARATHON
19 85
60
CATO RIDGE
59,0 km
(732m/2400')
HARRISON FLATS
NAGLE DAM TURNOFF
55,9 km
N.R. 3/2
RADNOR
(762m/2500')
BAYAT'S STORE
IN'CHANGA
IN'CHANGA HILL
47,9 km
(762m/2500')
44,3 km (11h30)
DRUMMOND
(640m/2100')
LEGEND
CUT-OFF POINTS
Congested Areas
625m/2050' Height-Levels
Red denotes Comrades' Marathon Route

PART ONE

1

It was a lovely, lazy summer evening towards the end of November. There were no storm clouds in the sky and the air was still and clear. The runners reclined on benches, chairs and lawn in the shade of a great, spreading jacaranda tree in front of the club house of the White Waters Sports Club, home of the White Waters Running Club, to the north of Johannesburg. The waters of the Braamfontein Spruit flowed calmly through trees and reeds along the edge of the sports grounds, slipped over a weir and hurried their then whitened way over and between the rapids and rocks below. The distant complaint of a hadeda ibis cut through the air and briefly ruffled the calm. The runners sipped their drinks, quietly enjoying the feeling of relaxed fatigue that follows the completion of enjoyable physical effort.

"D'you think I could run the Comrades Marathon?"

Melanie looked at Tony as she asked the question about the famous ultra-marathon race which was run each year, in alternate directions, between Durban and Pietermaritzburg in the province of Natal. He was the informal leader of the group which met at the club on certain evenings of the week to train together.

"I think you're capable of it, but I wouldn't advise you to run it yet," he replied.

"Why not?"

"Ninety kilometres is a very long way. You haven't been running for long enough yet."

"I've been running for more than a year. I only started because I wanted to run Comrades. I have a special reason."

The ensuing conversation revolved around the challenge of completing the race, which would be held again as usual on 31st May, within the time limit of eleven hours. The next race would be an 'up' run from the coastal holiday resort of Durban to the provincial capital of Pietermaritzburg at an altitude of 650 metres, but with the highest part of the course 870 metres above sea level. They talked of the long distance (usually around ninety kilometres), the fearsome hills and famous landmarks on the course, the need to qualify for entry by first running a standard marathon in under four and a half hours, and the kind of training necessary to complete the event. It transpired that several of the group were toying with the idea of taking up the challenge of the Comrades Marathon. This was surprising for an informal group of mainly social runners, but was symptomatic of the hold which the race had upon the imagination of runners and the public in the marathon-mad country as a whole. To the layman, and to many runners as well, you were not a runner at all until you had 'completed Comrades', until you had accepted and survived its challenge, until you had endured in it the seemingly unendurable, achieved the well-nigh impossible, and so climbed your own personal Everest. Of the group, only Tony had completed the race and he found himself answering many questions.

Melanie persisted with her questioning and appeared determined to run in the race the following May.

"You need to consider what your aims in running are," Tony advised her. "Do you want to develop your potential as a runner, or is your real – or only – aim to complete Comrades?"

"What potential? You must be joking," said Melanie. "I'm nearing forty and I have a mission to complete Comrades as soon as I can. Will you help me?"

The question was echoed by several others, and before long, Tony found himself agreeing to help them where he could. He even began to turn his mind towards the idea of running it again himself.

2

"We are nearly all lonely or unhappy or looking for something more in our lives," thought Tony.

He was thinking of the group as he drove home that evening. It had started almost by accident and was quite informal. As in all large clubs the members of the White Waters Running Club formed themselves into groups and sub-groups of different abilities, interests and persuasions. These groups grew and declined, coalesced and divided over time. Their memberships changed as people came and went, ran socially or seriously, were fit or injured or convalescent, and became friends or fell in or out of love. Some moved from group to group, some belonged to several groups, but there was usually a hard core of members of each surviving group around which others swirled and eddied.

Tony Drummond had started running from the club in the evenings after work a few years before. He had met one or two people who had come to inquire about running or to look for somebody to train with, he had made them feel welcome and had invited them to run with him. They had brought others and so the group had grown. It was never formalized in any way, but it became known that anyone was welcome to join Tony on his training runs on Monday and Thursday (and most other) evenings. He found himself trying to arrange his work programme so that he could be there, and he arranged for someone else to take the runs when he knew that he would not be able to do so. As many beginners came, and as a wide range of abilities came to be represented, the runs were organised to cater for them all. Usually the faster runners would go ahead, and either stop and wait for the slower ones, or run back to join them before going ahead again. Many women joined the group because they felt safer than running on their own, and they soon learned that they would be looked after and not left behind. The group came to be called 'The Toddlers' or 'Tony's Toddlers' by some who scoffed at its nature and approach and at those slower runners who found themselves at home there.

The reasons for starting out in running were many. Some began to jog to keep or get fit, and some to lose weight and firm up thighs. To some it meant added variety in an exercise programme or the laying down of a stamina base for another sport. Some ran to relax and to release tensions at the end of a working day, some merely to escape from home or their daily responsibilities for a while, and others to embrace the challenges they saw in it. They continued to run because they found these things and more: lives a little less grey, a point of light at the end of the day, exciting but non-essential challenges to meet, and the joy and freedom of movement which only the fully fit can know. Above all, they found comradeship – contact with people, to share time and experiences with one another in a close, companionable, uncomplicated and undemanding way. So it was that many who were lonely or unhappy or without direction elsewhere in their lives wandered into running, and into the Club, and stayed to enjoy the companionship and contentment and sense of direction they found there.

"And even I," thought Tony, "who have run for so many years, so often on my own, and who have found so much joy in it, even I treasure increasingly the evenings at training, and the times at races, for the companionship, the acceptance, the feeling of being wanted and liked and loved, and of being valued. These times have become the high points of my days, to be looked forward to, and (dare I think it?) after which I go home with apprehension and gloom."

3

It was about seven o'clock when Tony arrived home. His wife's car was in the driveway, so he knew that she was still at home, and his easy mood gave way to a conscious effort towards maintaining calm and control. Nora emerged from the house as he closed his garage door, and she hurried to her car on her way to an evening appointment.

"Your food's in the oven," she said abruptly as she saw her husband. "If it's spoilt don't blame me. You want to run every night."

Tony watched her leave and then went inside to find his supper and a drink, his mood gradually lightening.

Nora was an attractive woman in her forties, of medium height with a good figure, grey eyes and fairish hair artfully lightened to blonde. She and Tony had met at university, where she had studied law while he pursued economics, accountancy and other commercial subjects. They had married young, with the love and joy and hope of youth, and had had their two children soon after. Unfortunately, that, and their further part-time studies, had added to the existing financial constraints on the young couple, so they had not prospered as quickly as had many of Nora's private-school former classmates, of whom she became very jealous. She was very ambitious, and, unable to work herself until the children were reasonably able to be without her for at least part of the day, she had been disappointed at the merely steady progress of Tony's career and earning capacity. She gradually became discontented, resentful of her husband and her lot, and compensated by becoming more and more absorbed in her children, whom she adored and influenced. When she returned to work, it was as an attorney with a leading law firm which was enlightened enough to allow her to work on a part-day basis, and also from home at times, so she could also spend time with her children when they needed her. Tony came merely to be tolerated for much of the time, their good income being below Nora's expectations and ambitions, and their comfortable house and respectable address not good enough socially. She was not really interested in sex, and his attentions were generally not welcome, except occasionally in beautiful and luxurious surroundings, as sometimes on holiday or away on business functions or conferences together. However, she was still very attractive and could be very charming and alluring when she set out to be so, particularly with the rich and powerful and famous. She had recently been out at night quite frequently, and Tony briefly wondered whether she was having an affair. That would be unlikely unless something more than sex was on offer.

Thus gradually excluded from the intimacy he would have wished from his own family, Tony slowly developed his own defences to protect himself from emotional disappointment. He lowered his expectations of marriage and family to making the best of the situation, and to carrying out his duties as a provider, husband and father as well as possible. He devoted himself to his work and to his other interests, of which running became increasingly important.

He had started running towards the end of his high school years, and, appalled at his then apparent lack of physical fitness, he had vowed never to become so unfit again. As he came to enjoy running, it had been no problem for him to want to continue with it. The problems had been with maintaining the discipline and arranging his personal and work commitments so that, even in difficult times, he could at least do enough training to keep touch with his previous fitness levels and keep the continuity of his running. On weekdays he had preferred to run in the evenings, as a break between day and night studies as a student, or as exercise to relieve tension after a hard day at work. He had started running on the track as a middle distance runner, and had run many winter seasons of cross-country, so that his perspective on running, when he moved onto the road, was different from most of those who had only done long-distance road-running. Because of continual time constraints imposed by studies, work and family, he had also had to learn to use his limited running time well, and this had also coloured his approach to the sport.

Running had soon become more than a discipline to achieve physical fitness. It also became a challenge, a joy and a way to relax. He delighted in applying his growing knowledge and experience to his limited training time and abilities in order to bring out the best of himself on race days. Running fast and with no apparent effort in beautiful surroundings was the most uplifting, poetic and ecstatic experience. Also, he could either run alone, wrapped in his own invisible cocoon, or have the fun and intimacy of shared experience. When he was tired and emotionally drained, he could go out alone, start slowly, and gradually run himself back to normality and mental freshness. When he was not popular at home, or with his 'superiors' at work, he could go to his Club and to his running group and be surprised and delighted to find that there were after all so many people who really liked him.

He came to depend on his running as a high point of his day, a small space amid all his commitments that belonged to him alone, and a means to help him cope with the rest of his life. As he came to depend on it, and as he defended his right to keep contact with it even while meeting other demands, so Nora resented it. Perhaps she did so because it was a source of strength to him, perhaps because it absorbed part of his time, but, for whatever reason, she resented it much as she would a mistress. In a way she was right, for in running he found a seductive mixture of interest and entertainment, challenge and delight, of being wanted and of belonging, of companionship and love. He did not have a mistress, but he had friends and companions, some of whom he held dear, and at least one of whom he knew he loved.

4

Sylvia Parks taught English at a local high school. She was tall and attractive, with a fuller figure than ideal for running but given proportion and some elegance by her height. She had brown hair, large dark brown eyes and a lovely smile. She had married young, and was subsequently divorced with two sons who were now in their teens and attended a boarding school, in accordance with their own and their father's wishes, during term time. Sylvia had come into running, mainly by accident, about three years before.

One Sunday morning she had been walking with her dog in the nearby Delta Park. That was a lovely, extensive open area, sloping down a hillside to the Braamfontein Spruit, which ran along its lower margin. The park was almost wild in places, but had friendly open grassy areas and patches of forest. A reluctant stream made its way down a valley, supplying a series of pretty dams on its descent. Bird life was abundant and there were hides from which one could watch the different birds over land or lake.

Sylvia was strolling under the trees along the banks of the top dam, watching a family of Egyptian geese which had taken to the water after having received too much attention from her dog, Casper. Suddenly a runner hove into view, moving easily and rapidly along the stream to the head of the dam and then along its shore. Casper gave a yelp and transferred his attention from geese to runner, racing towards Tony (for it was he) in a half-friendly, half-threatening manner. Tony stopped in his tracks, as he did whenever he was charged at by a dog while out running, keeping his hands to his sides. Casper stopped uncertainly just in front of the runner, then jumped up and pawed him, scratching him in the process.

"Casper! Casper! Down! Down! Come here!" screamed Sylvia at the disobedient animal. "Oh, I'm so sorry!" she wailed as she brought the dog under control.

Tony was surveying his scratches and would normally have been annoyed and would have continued unhappily on his way. However, the lady was so concerned and apologetic that his annoyance faded. Moreover, she was attractive, had lovely dark eyes, and, with the heightened colour of the moment, looked very pretty. He gallantly assured her that he was fine, that as a runner he was accustomed to being attacked by dogs of all kinds, that it was a lovely morning and was she enjoying her walk.

So it was that they began to talk. The subject of running somehow led to her indicating an intention to exercise, and to his inviting her to join him at the Club on a Monday or Thursday evening if she wished. They exchanged names and then went their respective ways.

She did not immediately take up the invitation, but did turn it over in her mind from time to time. She knew that she was overweight, she was smoking, and was drinking just a little too much in the evenings when her school work was done and she had time to feel the loneliness and depression that had followed her divorce. Some exercise would be good for her, and it might lead to some new human contact. Then, a few weeks later, school holidays began and her sons came home to stay with her. They had both become involved with cross-country running at school and she thought that it might be good for them to train with Tony during the holidays. So it was that the three of them arrived at the Club one Thursday evening. The boys enjoyed the run and were enthusiastic about coming again, so a pattern of running on certain evenings was established.

Sylvia did not feel that she could keep up with the group, even if it was organised to help slow runners, so she spent several evenings walking and then gradually jogging around one of the more distant fields, keeping as far from the general gaze as possible. She spent most of her time at work on her feet, so it was not very long after her boys had returned to school that she finally decided to venture out with Tony's group.

In a T-shirt and tracksuit bottoms (to hide her overweight thighs), she felt ungainly and awkward. She struggled and was waited for from time to time, but she was given a lot of friendly encouragement and did well enough to decide to come again.

Soon she felt that she was a welcome part of the group. She gradually became fitter and struggled less. In time she lost some weight, her thighs fined down, and she gradually moved towards her optimum figure, as happens to make most female runners so attractive. Her self-confidence grew as she progressed, and eventually she felt confident enough to run in shorts. She gave up smoking, drank less and felt better about herself.

She also made friends. Her fellow-runners were a friendly bunch, and it was good to have contact with them at the end of the day. They chatted a lot and joked and generally had fun, even as they trained. Sylvia especially enjoyed talking to Tony, who often ran at the back of the pack to encourage and shepherd the slower runners. They were both mature, were comfortable in each other's company, and gradually found that they had common interests and values.

One evening after training, Tony invited Sylvia to stay for a drink with him and a few others who did so fairly regularly. The club had a small informal 'non-smoking' bar, off the main bar. It was a comfortable place to gather and to chat, and they could go there in their tracksuits if they wished, so they used it often, although they were sometimes seduced by a balmy evening onto the shady front terrace. For Tony, and for most of the others, that was usually a brief but relaxed and companionable time, for they all had other commitments and so did not stay long. Tony always left by about seven o'clock in order to be home at a reasonable time. Sylvia accepted Tony's invitation, then began to stay occasionally, and finally became a regular. However, for a very long time she only stayed if Tony was there to escort her as she was nervous of going into a bar on her own.

As she was now spending so much time at the club, Sylvia was eventually persuaded by Tony to become a member. Then she felt that she ought to justify being a member of a *running* club by running 'more seriously' and at least trying one or two races, even if at a slow pace. That she did, and under guidance from Tony, she began to learn how to race, as opposed only to jog or to run. Tony ran with her in a few races, and talked her through some sections, in order to help her to understand how one should think oneself through a race. This helped to bring them close, as they were then thinking and feeling together, but he also found that it was better for her to race on her own, once she understood what it was all about, as she preferred to run without the pressure of his immediate expectations. She became a slowish, competent runner, gradually more experienced, but with no great ambition.

So it was that Sylvia and Tony were gradually drawn together. They enjoyed each other's company and felt comfortable and natural together. They had begun to look forward to their time together and to depend upon it. Almost without realising what had been happening, it dawned upon them that they had grown close, and had become very important to each other.

5

Melanie Singer was very serious about running Comrades.

Tony had discussed broad aims and training programmes with his Comrades candidates. Specific and hard training would only begin in the new year. Although certain broad principles would apply, details would vary from person to person according to their backgrounds in running and current fitness levels. However, he was encouraging his runners to establish a training base of about fifty kilometres a week. Those who were not regularly doing that sort of distance were to increase their training volumes gradually, and so lay down a stamina base upon which to build in the new year.

Melanie was tackling the task with vigour. She had been doing moderate distances in training, and had jumped immediately to the fifty kilometre per week level. Now that she was on her way, so to speak, she trained with an intensity that was alarming. She was doing the distance, adding a little more here and there for good measure; she was speeding up her runs where possible; and now she was beginning to be tired and sore.

Tony had to speak to her. Be determined, but not fanatical. Do not increase volumes and/or speed too dramatically, for that risks injury and excess fatigue. Do not do too much too soon. Alternate hard with easy training sessions to allow some recovery from the hard days.

"I must not fail!" was Melanie's response.

"You won't, if you listen; unless of course you're very unlucky with illness or something we can't control. But even illness is less likely if you build your training sensibly."

"I must not fail!"

"Why are you being so serious?"

Then she told him her story, and why she felt she had to finish Comrades.

Melanie lived on her own in a suburb not far from the Club. She worked as an Investment Adviser at a branch of one of the major banks. She was good at her work, for she was intelligent, well qualified and attractive. She was short, but with a lovely curvaceous figure, honey-coloured hair and striking amber-brown eyes. Although not yet forty, she was a widow.

She had married her husband, David, when they were both about thirty years of age, and she had loved him very dearly. He had been a fanatical runner, even when they first met, and he eventually ran nine Comrades Marathons as well as numerous other races. She did not share his enthusiasm for running, but had accepted him as he was, and had tolerated it. In particular, she had become resigned to their life together being partly or largely suspended for the first five months of each year as he prepared for the great race. He was fanatical in his approach. He trained for long hours, especially at weekends, was continually exhausted and often moody, needed much moral support and understanding, and was generally almost entirely focussed on the race until the end of May. Fortunately he more than made up to her, for all her tolerance and support, during the remainder of the year.

David had run nine Comrades, and was looking forward to his tenth. If he completed that he would join the relatively small select group of runners who had done so. He would be awarded a green race number in recognition of his achievement, and his number would be preserved, for him alone, in perpetuity. It would be the culmination of ten long years of striving. He would run this, his tenth, Comrades with the yellow race number, issued to those who were 'going for green', pinned to his vest. Although struggling more than usual with his running for some unaccountable reason (was it hard work, over-training or the start of flu lurking in the background?), he qualified for his tenth Comrades by satisfactorily completing a standard marathon race (42.2 kilometres, or 26 miles 385 yards) during January. It had always been his practice to 'qualify early', and he had also promptly sent off his Comrades Marathon race entry form.

He found it more difficult than usual to recover from the qualifying race, and his health began to deteriorate. At the end of February he was diagnosed as having an aggressive form of cancer, and by end-April he was gone. Soon after, a still grieving Melanie opened an envelope from the Comrades Marathon Association containing David's race instructions and yellow race numbers, to be worn on the front and back of his running vest.

"Oh my poor David!"

She sat for a long time with the envelope and its contents on her lap, thinking of her once fit and active husband flying along the road. This should have been his time, with his race preparations nearing completion and all the excitement and anticipation as his tenth Comrades came ever nearer. How he would have loved to be here now and to be in that race! Eventually she placed the contents back into the envelope, and put it aside.

She may not have looked into it again. Despite her sorrow, there was much to be done as a result of David's death, and she also had to return to work as soon as possible. She was aware of the growing excitement as Comrades Day, 31st May, drew near, for the newspapers were full of what was an important national sporting occasion. She tried not to notice, and resolved not to watch the television broadcast of the race.

Alas! Race day was a holiday, so the bank was not open, and there was no one she could visit that morning. Her thoughts were full of David, and her heart was heavy. She went for a walk and bought herself a cup of coffee, but the time dragged, and she wandered home. It was hardly past eleven o'clock. She turned on the television.

There was great excitement, as the race was nearing its climax. The leader was climbing painfully but steadily up the famous (or infamous) 1.8 km Polly Shorts Hill. The cameras showed the spectators waiting beside the road at the top of the hill, with the refreshment tables and their attendants, and young ladies dressed in blue. The lead vehicles in front of the race began to crest the hill and to appear through the heat-haze which quivered above the hot surface of the tar road. As they did so, the television began to play Vangelis's opening music to the film, 'Chariots of Fire', which has captured so wonderfully the freedom and joy and spirit of running. Then a head of long golden hair bobbed briefly above the crest of the road through the haze, and soon it became a figure in blue and gold. Bruce Fordyce was leading the race. As he reached the top of that last major climb, he punched a fist into the air and strode out like a god, blonde hair flying, and to the strains of Vangelis's music, to Pietermaritzburg and another victory some six kilometres away.

Melanie was in tears. All the emotion of the past few months blended with the emotion of that wonderful moment, so beautifully captured on film and in music. There was grief and there was joy at the same time. David should have been running and was not there, but now she understood the meaning of it all. She understood the wonder, the beauty, the glory, the freedom, the joy and the ultimate fulfilment that was possible in running, and which was the aim behind all the striving. David would never have won Comrades, but she now understood the nature and importance of his own goals. She knew then why he had wanted be part of that great race, and what a tenth Comrades finish would have meant to him. She found the envelope and took out the yellow race numbers. She held them to her face as she wept.

"I will run the tenth for you, David. I will do it for you!"

The next day she started to train. She did not tell anyone the true reason why she had started to jog. She needed to lose weight, she was so unfit, she needed to get out into the fresh air, and she needed to do something since she was on her own. Any excuse was good enough. The real reason would have sounded too unbelievable. She had serious doubts herself once she tried to run.

She sat at her desk in the bank for most of her working day and she was basically very unfit. She found that she could hardly run at all for more than a few metres, and was forced to walk for several weeks before she could start to introduce a little slow jogging into her training. It was difficult to make the time to train and to find places to walk or jog where she felt safe on her own. Injuries (which eventually led her to go to a specialist running shop to purchase a proper pair of running shoes) and illness (mainly winter flu) set her back, as each time she had to regain lost ground. The weeks and months went by with frightening speed and she began to despair of ever running competently, let alone nearly ninety kilometres. She would certainly not be able even to qualify for the next Comrades, the 'down run' from Pietermaritzburg to Durban. She decided to work towards the following up run. That would give her a year longer to prepare, and she told herself that David would possibly have preferred the up run, as the one he had missed, to be their tenth.

She persisted, and made slow progress. She tried an occasional fun run in the area and was rewarded with some hard won finishes, which initially included a lot of walking. Eventually she felt she was ready to join the White Waters Running Club, in whose colours David had run. There she found a home in running, being welcomed not only by friends of David, but by others as well. She found a comfortable niche for herself in Tony's group where she could run with others in a safe and friendly environment on a regular basis. When she felt that the time for serious Comrades preparations was approaching, she had asked Tony to help her. Now, for the first time, she had told her story, and revealed why she was running. She had made a promise to David, and she intended to keep it if she could.

"I must not fail!"

6

The headquarters of National Insurance Group Limited (known commonly as 'Nigroup') were in National Insurance House, a pleasant modern building set in its own gardens in the leafy suburb of Parktown, just north of Johannesburg's central business district. Tony had a comfortable office, looking down onto the fountain and gardens in the inner courtyard of the building. The top floor had extensive views to the Braamfontein Ridge on one side, and over the lovely green northern suburbs on the other. It was very luxurious, was known as 'Quality Street', and was where Andrew Duke, the Chief Executive Officer (or 'CEO'), and his chosen elite were situated. As head of Investment Management, Tony could almost certainly have commanded a seat there, but he preferred to be close to his team of portfolio managers, research analysts, dealers and administrators, and so he sat with the Investment Management Division. That was probably another career-limiting move, as Nora was quick to remind him. However, it kept him in tune with, and an effective part of, his investment team, and helped him to avoid much of the inevitable politics that swirled around inside the Group.

Tony was usually at his desk early each morning. In that way he could avoid the peak hour traffic on the roads, and do much of what he called his basic investment work without serious interruption, while the offices were quiet and well before the various financial markets opened for the day's trading. There were nearly always newly announced company results to review, as well as the latest political, economic and market news, all of which could affect overall investment policy, or investment activity on behalf of the Group or its policy-holders, whose investment portfolios were managed by Tony's investment team.

Tony was busy at work when his secretary, Mary Hanson, brought him a morning cup of tea, as she usually did soon after she arrived at work. He had never asked her to do so. She simply did it because she wanted to, and he appreciated it. They were very fond of each other and happily exchanged greetings and briefly caught up on each other's news.

Mary was of medium height, with an attractive figure tending to roundness, a round face, dark hair and brilliant blue eyes. She had a clear voice, full of joy and light, particularly when she was happy, and that was a great asset when dealing with people on the telephone or face-to-face. She had worked with Tony for a number of years. He remembered interviewing her for the then vacant position. She seemed to be likeable and competent, and as the interview progressed he found himself trying to persuade her to accept the job. She had done so, and proved to be skilful, organised, friendly and tactful. They developed a wonderful working relationship, a close partnership that was efficient, communicative, and with a clear understanding both of what had to be achieved and of each other's strengths and weaknesses. On a personal level their relationship was one of platonic love, based on mutual attraction, perfect trust and respect. Early on they had considered having an affair, but had decided against it, as it would complicate their working relationship, and could possibly hurt Tony's marriage. Mary was now, herself, happily married, and this was a joy both to her and to Tony. They continued to care for and to support each other, as they had done through many difficult times in the past.

"Jane has just phoned," announced Mary, speaking of the CEO's secretary. "Andy called her to say that he wants you to be at a meeting at nine o'clock in his office."

"Damn! There goes my morning. I'll have to ask George to take the morning meeting."

Every morning at nine o'clock the key people on the investment team met briefly to review the latest company, economic and market developments, and to exchange information about their business activities, in order to keep all entities suitably informed. George Jones was head of Portfolio Management and Tony's most senior assistant, while Andy was the Chief Executive Officer of the Group.

Andrew Duke was in his early forties and had been in his present position for five or six years. He had been with the Group for a long time, having started as an actuary in National Life Limited (or 'Nilife'), which was the life insurance company owned by Nigroup and by far its most important and largest operating subsidiary. He was a pleasant-looking man of above medium height and build with sandy hair and grey eyes. He liked to be known as Andy, and cultivated a friendly and apparently informal manner. He was, indeed, very good at moving amongst staff, clients and in the business world at large, showing a friendly face and becoming generally well regarded. His image was very important to him. He worked on it assiduously, especially in public. Every speech he made was rehearsed, down to the smallest nuance and tiniest spontaneous gesture, with a voice and speech consultant who was always on call. A member of the Public Relations Department was employed solely to manage Andrew's image, and to ensure that no-one else in the Group obtained more media exposure, measured continually in television and radio minutes and in newspaper column centimetres. For, despite his calculated affable manner, Andrew Duke ran Nigroup as his personal fiefdom. He wanted the world to believe that Nigroup was his creation, that it depended upon him above all else, and that it was he who should rightly bask in the glory of its perceived success. As it grew so he saw himself realising his ambition to be recognised as a major player in the financial services sector and in business at large. Internally he brooked no opposition, and kept near him only those who would tell him what he wanted to hear and who would do his bidding without question. Even the Board of Directors was effectively in his pocket. He had influenced a number of appointments, cultivated friendly relationships with all Board members, ensured that the value of their shares and options rose by continually monitoring the share price and where possible influencing it upwards, and he carefully regulated the flow of information or misinformation to the Board.

At Nigroup everything revolved around Andrew Duke. To Tony a good manager behaved and operated in such a way as to facilitate the work and productivity of his staff and contacts. That was something that Andrew did not even consider. Everything had to be arranged and continuously re-arranged to suit him and his whims. His colleagues were constantly changing plans, altering schedules and inconveniencing customers and business contacts in order to fall in with their boss's changing demands. So it was that Tony appeared in Andrew's office at nine o'clock that morning while his team met without him. It was a room that was both extensive and expensive, with furniture, carpeting, paintings and sculptures all supporting its occupant's desired image. The Group's financial director, head of strategy and certain other key senior executives had also answered the summons to attend.

"Hi, Tony. How are you?" was the greeting from Andrew.

"Good morning, Andy. Did you have a good run this morning?"

Andy was fanatical about fitness, and was in fact a talented sportsman, although he now confined himself to running and an occasional game of business golf. He usually ran early in the morning before breakfast and work, and his secretary was careful to organise his diary so as to allow him to train and race when he wanted. He competed in the colours of the large and well-known Sandown Runners Club, for many years a rival of the White Waters club. Like Tony, Andy was built more like a middle distance runner than most successful marathon runners, who tended to be small and light and emaciated when fit. He had, however, run the last down

Comrades in a respectable time, and was already training hard for next year's up run. The aggressive, hard-running, fit and trim executive was an attractive part of the Andy Duke image.

After the initial pleasantries Andy got the meeting down to business.

"I met Joe Anderson at the Country Club last night. They have a parcel of shares in Golden, which they want to place in friendly hands. I told him that we would want to look at it, and that we would probably take them." Joe Anderson was the respected Chairman of Golden Bank, one of the larger institutions in the country. "For about three hundred million we could own another three percent of Golden."

"What would be the purpose of that?" asked Tony as the chorus of interest and assent died down.

"We talked about forming a special relationship between the two groups. We already bank with them, and we have about one percent of their shares in our portfolios right now. They should be able to put business our way. They have an awful lot of clients who need life insurance, for example."

"But they already have a life company within their own group," countered Tony. "Most of their business would surely go there. And four percent isn't all that much to base a special relationship on. In any event we'll need to pay for the shares. We don't have cash, and even if we issue shares to raise the money, we already have far too much invested in banks and financial services. We are already simply carrying far too much risk there."

This was a matter of great and increasing concern to Tony. About four years before, Nigroup and an aggressive and promising young merchant banking company, Enduring Bank Limited, had exchanged shares in such a way that each came to own about one-third of the other. For Nigroup the deal had been structured so that the interest in Enduring was held in Nilife, its life insurance company. Those shares had immediately formed an over-large proportion of Nilife's investments, but it had been anticipated that Nilife would grow much faster than Enduring and that the position would rectify itself. The contrary had happened. Enduring had grown very quickly, so that it became an ever increasing proportion of Nilife's assets.

At the same time, the cash flows into the life company, mainly insurance premiums from individuals and contributions of members into the pension funds which Nilife managed, were being used to further the ambitions of Andy to grow Nigroup into a major player in the financial services markets. Numerous investments had been made in banks, insurance and other financial services companies. They had been made mainly on an opportunistic basis, without any clear idea or plan as to how the various pieces would or could be put together as part of a coherent strategy. These investments had now far outpaced the inflows into the life company, so that other investments (both shares and bonds) had had to sold, sometimes urgently and at below fair value, to help pay for them. All that had led to a distortion of the asset structure of the life company, which was now heavily over-invested, not only in shares, but particularly in shares of financial services companies. Though the investments had done well in favourable share market conditions (which had encouraged Andy and the Board to become complacent), Tony and his professional colleagues believed that the stock market prices of shares, and financial shares in particular, were now very expensive and were vulnerable to a fall. In short, they were concerned that the life company had too many investment eggs in a financial services basket which could drop at any time, putting all its stakeholders, including policy-holders and pension fund members, at risk.

"Tony, get off that bloody hobby horse of yours," said Andy angrily, "and stop being negative. You know as well as I do that our financial services interests have done very well for us. We've declared really good bonuses and dividends over the past few years. Golden is doing well, and a special relationship with them will be good for us. If you don't have cash, sell some assets. Sell some bonds. You can do that quickly."

"We've already sold more than we should have," Tony responded. "We need them in the portfolios. Also, interest rates are high and bond prices are low."

The meeting went on. Eventually it was agreed that the Golden shares should be acquired, subject to Board approval which Andy was confident he would obtain at once by making a few telephone calls. Tony was instructed to find the necessary cash, by selling assets if he had to.

"What's wrong?" asked Mary as Tony came back to his office. She could sense his every mood.

"They want to make another so-called strategic investment in financial services. As you know, we simply don't have the cash, and we already have far too much in banks and insurance companies. We shall have to sell assets to raise the money, and that will only worsen the position. Where it will end I do not know. I can't get them to listen. We are simply carrying too much risk."

7

It was a warm, November, Monday evening, a lovely time to be out in the open and away from work and other worries. Although there were clouds in the sky, there was no threat of rain, and the air cooled and became more pleasant as the sun dipped towards the west, promising another glorious highveld sunset. In Delta Park the east-facing slopes were in welcome shade after the heat of the day. Tony ran at the back of his group of runners and watched them straggling up the hill, passing the dams filled by the little stream that dropped gently down the valley. The faster runners were flying ahead, while Tony encouraged the stragglers and tried to help them improve their running technique. Tony, and the more experienced of the group, did quite a lot of coaching, especially to help the newcomers, but nearly always on an informal basis.

"Take shorter steps when going up a hill. It's like changing into a lower gear on a bicycle or in a car. Take the hill in little pieces. Lean forward a little and use your arms to pull you along. Run steadily, concentrate on your rhythm, but keep your speed just slow enough so you do not run into oxygen debt and have to stop."

The runners regrouped at the top of the hill, next to the top dam, and then jogged along its eastern side. The dam was in shadow, the surface very still and reflecting the green of the tall trees growing around it. A pair of geese left V-shaped wakes behind them as they swam gently towards the little reed-covered island near where the stream entered the dam.

"It's like something from a summer night's dream, our Dream Dam," said Tony to Sylvia who now ran next to him. "Do you remember how we met, over there? I'm eternally grateful for that."

The runners crossed the little stream at the footbridge above the dam and ran along the other side, gradually accelerating across the level, and then stringing out again as the leaders plunged downhill at great speed. Tony was again helping those at the back.

"Take longer steps going downhill, and let gravity do the work. Lean forward a little. The feeling is of just pushing your chest out a bit, and allowing yourself to flow down the hill. Revolve your legs and use your arms to help keep your balance and rhythm. You should be able to go very fast with almost no effort. Gravity should do nearly all the work."

Tony had promised that the Monday and Thursday runs would continue as before, even though several of the group were now aiming at the Comrades Marathon. Those days would cater for the less serious runner as before, and could also be used as easy or 'play' sessions for those training very hard in the coming months. They would continue to be conducted on a fartlek basis. That word was derived from the Swedish, meaning 'speed play', and denoted a training session based on relatively informal variations of pace and terrain. The faster parts would be beneficial for all, serious and casual runners, helping them to avoid falling into a monotonous one-paced routine and promoting faster leg speed. That was important to Tony.

"We're going to do a lot of long, slow distance running in the months ahead," he told his Comrades hopefuls, "but we're not going to become one-paced. We are going to follow, in part, the teachings of the great German coach, Ernst van Aaken. His method is based on long, slow distance running, but with between five and ten percent of every session at a faster speed. So, if we do ten kilometres in a session, we'll do at least five hundred metres faster than our usual pace. We'll vary that from day to day as we please. For example, one day we could do a sustained five hundred metres fairly fast, another day we could do five efforts of about one hundred metres each spread out over the run, or three times two hundred metres, and so on. The variations are endless."

Tony had outlined broadly the shape of their training for Comrades over the next few months. First of all, a base of about fifty kilometres a week was being established in the weeks remaining to the end of the year. That would be followed by a specific period designed to ensure the completion of a qualifying standard marathon in early-March. Then a few days of recovery would be followed by a period of about seven or eight weeks of very hard long distance running, and, finally, a three or four week tapering off period to the race itself at the end of May. All this would be adapted according to the progress, setbacks and abilities of those in what he now regarded as his Comrades team.

While certain of Tony's coaching was formalized, and tailored to each individual, much of it was informal. This consisted of talking on the run or at the Club, answering questions and dealing with problems as they arose, all the while trying to help his runners to absorb the principles and be able to think and adapt them for themselves. That would enable them to look after themselves in the future, and to help others. Above all, they would be able to take decisions in races, when they would be all alone, though in a crowd, and everything would depend on the runner only.

8

One evening, Tony arrived at the Club to run to find, as sometimes happened, that someone new was asking for him, with a view to running with them. On this occasion the stranger was a tall, lean, dark-haired man, probably in his late thirties. He was striking to look at, with a long face, hollow cheeks, dark deeply set eyes, and straggly moustache and pointed black beard. To Sylvia he looked like a saint painted by El Greco, but in running shoes, white gym shorts and a plain white T-shirt.

"Good evening. I am the Reverend Joshua Barnard. I have just joined the White Waters Running Club, and I've been told that you might let me run with you. I've been training on my own, but I need some help and I would appreciate the company."

"Of course. You are very welcome," said Tony. "Folks, this is the Reverend Joshua Barnard who has come to run with us. You can introduce yourselves to him on the way."

"Hello!"

"Hi! What do we call you? Reverend?"

"Or Joshua?"

"Josh," said a voice before the newcomer could say anything.

"Hello, Josh."

"Hi, Josh."

So the Reverend Joshua Theophilus Barnard became Josh. Slightly taken aback by this egalitarian approach, he set out amidst the cheerful group for his first run with his new club mates. He managed fairly well, but was grateful that the runners, whom he had feared would run away from him, regrouped every now and again. He felt awkward at first, but soon found friendliness and interest from a number who introduced themselves to him and chatted on the way or when stopping to regroup. At first he was particularly disturbed by the women, who were indeed in a majority, as he was not accustomed to being surrounded by so many beautiful naked legs and attractive figures. They also seemed to be frivolous, or at least full of fun, and irreligious too, as it appeared that they ran long distances on Sundays. However, it seemed that they wanted to be friendly, without showing any tendency towards leading him into temptation.

He enjoyed his run, though he was tired at the end, and promised to come again. He told Tony that he had started to train because he wanted to run the Comrades Marathon next May, and that he would appreciate some advice about training. Tony introduced him to some of the others who were also aiming to run Comrades, and undertook to help him if he could. So Josh settled in as a regular member of the group. They gradually came to know him better, and they learnt his story.

Josh was born into a conservative, religious family of modest means in a small country town. Religion had always played a very important part in his life. He was still a young teenager when his parents allowed him to go to the coast with a church youth group for a week of healthy physical activity combined with religious teaching and worship. There he saw the sea for the first time. There too he knelt alone, on the cool sand near the gently breaking waves one clear moonlit night, and pledged his life to God's service. After many hard years of devoted study, both at home and, with the aid of a church bursary, in the United States, he was finally ordained a minister of The Lord's Church. He served the Church, which was locally a relatively small but active denomination, in various capacities in different parts of the country. During this period he married his dark-eyed Maria, whom he had known since school days, who shared his devotion to the Lord, and who proved to be an ideal companion and source of strength and support. At last they were offered and accepted the challenge of establishing and ministering to an entirely new congregation, in a developing part of Randburg and only a few kilometres west of the White Waters Sports Club.

The Church had acquired land in a quiet semi-rural area beside the rocky, thorn-tree clad Boskop hill, which formed a backdrop. From the site one could look out over the valley to the east, where extensive new housing development was taking place and from where it was thought that the bulk of the Church's new congregation would come. With some Church funds, a few key donations, and much fund-raising, a functional church hall, and a modest dwelling for the minister and his wife and two small children, had been built, in part by Josh with his own hands. A small and growing congregation had been gathered, and soon it was hoped to build a church alongside the hall, which would then be retained for Sunday school classes, meetings, wedding receptions, socials and the like.

Having progressed so far, the building of the church was now Josh's burning ambition. An architect, who was a member of the congregation, had already produced a beautiful and practical design and drawings as a donation to the Church. Every day Josh carried in his mind a vision of the completed building, a beautiful, serene and holy place of worship, and a lasting tribute to the Lord.

As usual, money was the main problem. Fund-raising had been going on for some time, with the guidance of a Church fund-raising committee and the support of the congregation, but there was still not enough to be able to commence the building work. Between leading his congregation in worship, trying to spread the gospel in the community, administering to the sick and those in need of consolation, and being a good husband and father, money and how to raise it were never far from Josh's mind. That was the background to his unusual decision to run the Comrades Marathon.

Early one evening at the end of May, Josh had just arrived home from a visit to a parishioner who was in hospital. Maria was busy with her evening routine of bathing the children and preparing supper for the family. The doorbell rang and Josh found two little girls from the new local primary school, spruce and smiling, on the doorstep. They were helping to raise funds to supply the endless needs of a young school. The school would soon be holding a Big Walk for its pupils, who had each been asked to try to obtain sponsorships from friends and the public, at so much per kilometre completed by him or her in the Walk, for school funds. Josh explained that the Church also needed funds, and so could not sponsor them, but he sent them on their way with some kind words, a smile and a small personal donation.

"I wonder whether we could do something like that," he thought as he went to the kitchen and made coffee for Maria and himself.

He took his coffee to the lounge and sat down to relax for a moment. The television had been left on and he was about to switch it off when he heard music that he recognised. It was the opening music to the film, 'Chariots of Fire'. He watched and listened. The Comrades Marathon would be run the next day, and the television station was previewing its planned coverage and showing highlights of the broadcast of a previous race.

The leader was nearing the top of the famous Polly Shorts Hill. The lead vehicles appeared through a heat-haze, which quivered above the hot surface of the tar road. Then, to the wonderful, uplifting strains of the music, a head of long golden hair bobbed briefly above the crest of the road through the haze, and soon became a figure in blue and gold. Bruce Fordyce was leading the race. As he reached the top of that last major climb, he punched a fist into the air and strode out, blonde hair flying, to another victory as Vangelis's music continued to play.

It was a magical moment, and Josh was sufficiently impressed to watch parts of the race broadcast the next day, when his duties and the calls on his time allowed. Fordyce won again after a stirring battle, but Josh was also greatly impressed by the efforts of the tail-enders to beat the eleven-hour deadline to finish the race. He had, of course, read about it before, but only now appreciated the struggle of those everyday people who had risen to the challenge of the Comrades and, after nearly eleven hours on their feet, were dragging their weary bodies towards the finish. He was completely caught up in the emotions of it all, especially at five o'clock when the official at the finishing line turned his back to the runners, raised a gun and then fired it to signal the end of the race, exactly eleven hours after the start. Some desperate lunges allowed two or three to cross the line as the gun went off, but some, who were only a second or two late, were not allowed to finish even though they were so close. Others stopped in despair in the finishing straight as they heard the sound of the gun, while many were still on the road outside the stadium.

Josh wondered whether there was a lesson for him, or a sermon for his flock, in all that he had seen and felt.

"I wonder whether I could do it under eleven hours," he thought. "But I could not spare the time to train. My time is the Lord's, and I could not waste it on a running race with a clear conscience."

That night he sat at his little desk, as he did when the children were in bed and the house was quiet, to read the Bible, to meditate and to think what he would say to his congregation on the following Sunday. He drew his Bible towards him and opened it at random. It fell open at the fortieth chapter of Isaiah, and some words seemed to leap from the page as his eyes fell upon them.

"But they that wait upon the Lord shall renew their strength; they shall mount up with wings as eagles; they shall run and not be weary; and they shall walk, and not faint."

Surely this was a revelation, and an instruction. The events of the last two days could not be mere coincidence, the fund-raising, the Marathon and now this text. Surely he was being directed to run the next Comrades Marathon. He would run for sponsorships, given and obtained by his congregation and their fund-raisers. He would capture their imagination by running this amazing race, and together they would bring in money to build their church. The training he would need to do would not be wasted time. He would be running for the Lord. He would run and not be weary. He would finish the race. They would build that church.

He prayed about it, and was all the more certain. He discussed it with Maria, who was astonished but sympathetic. It was a long time since her husband had dabbled in middle distance running at college. He spoke to the chairman of the fund-raising committee, who promised support. That Sunday his sermon was based on the text that had so miraculously been shown to him a few days earlier, and he announced his intention to run in the next Comrades Marathon for the glory of God and to help raise funds to build His church.

So Josh began to train, and so a whole new fund-raising campaign around his intended race began to be planned. He was reasonably fit in a general sense, for he had done a lot of physical work in building and maintenance on the church site. He also helped dig and plant to support the volunteer gardening committee to improve and beautify the once barren church grounds. However, he had not run for many years, so he began by walking, gradually doing longer and longer distances, and then introducing jogging as part of each training session. He trained mainly in the early morning, setting out in the freezing winter cold, before his morning duties and the likelihood of any call upon his time. He had setbacks, colds and flu and aches and pains, but he persisted into the spring and early summer and made slow progress. Was it too slow? He was determined not to fail, and he also believed that what was done for the Lord should be done well. He decided that it was time to join a running club and seek help. So it was that he began to train with Tony on certain evenings at the White Waters club.

9

The period leading up to mid-December was usually a frantic time in the investment and related fields. Summer holidays began in earnest with the public holiday on 16th December. Towards the end of November all manner of business people woke up to the reality of unfinished deals, and targets and resolutions not yet achieved, and frantically demanded and attempted completion or fulfilment before the holiday period. It was a frenetic time for the weary after a long year, but also one of anticipation of a quieter period not far ahead, even for those not actually going away on holiday. For Nigroup it was also the time for announcing salary increases for the new calendar and financial years which began on 1st January.

On 15th December Tony informed his most senior managers of their new salaries and arranged for them to communicate with those on their respective teams. He was also able to inform Mary that the salaries 'had been approved as recommended', and that included her well-merited increase in remuneration.

"Thank you very much," said Mary. "I hope they've looked after you as well."

"Not really. I'll be worse off after taking inflation into account."

"That's not fair."

“You see, I’ve been labelled as negative. They don’t like the fact that I’ve been fighting about our asset structure problems. It’s beginning to cost me to be the one man out of step.”

“It’s so unfair! Why don’t they understand the risks involved? I understand perfectly. Don’t they even realise that you’re only doing it for the good of the company and all concerned? It’s not a selfish thing.”

“I don’t know. I shall have to re-assess where I am and where I’m going. I can’t fight a war forever. But there are a lot of people out there, many of them widows or orphans or elderly, who may be very badly hurt. I must try to help them. The trouble is that I’m now starting to doubt myself. When you are told so many times that you are wrong, when you know that you are out of step with everyone else, you begin to doubt. Am I really right, or just stupid and arrogant? I’m sure that it would be easier to ‘go with the flow’ as they say.”

“Don’t doubt yourself. I know you are right, and so do your staff. Our clients are also very happy. Don’t let Andy and his gang get to you.”

10

On Christmas Eve the Nigroup offices were relatively quiet with so many people away on holiday. So too were the financial markets, with not many players wanting to take positions before the holiday weekend. Most businesses would close before lunch, and overall, a relaxed and happy mood prevailed. The large investment administration office was cheerful with streamers and tinsel, and even Tony's office was decorated with the colourful seasonal greeting cards received from the many brokers and others with whom they did business. Fruit-mince pies had accompanied morning tea, and as the necessary duties of the day were completed, various members of the investment division gathered for snacks and a drink before leaving for home or some last minute Christmas shopping.

Mary and Tony had exchanged gifts early that morning after they had arrived at work. They had also arranged to have lunch together. After joining the gathering of their colleagues, and the general exchange of good wishes, they spent some time finishing certain work items which could not be left over to the following week. They then drove to a nearby restaurant where they had a quiet, comfortable table next to a window with a wonderful view across the wide green northern suburbs to the Magaliesberg Mountains in the distance.

Mary wore a blue dress and sapphire earrings, both of which emphasized the deep blue of her sparkling eyes. Her dark hair shone, smiles played about her soft pink lips, and her face was as full of sunshine as her voice. The food was good, and the wine sparkled through the crystal of their glasses. They could relax and enjoy one another's company for a brief interval, knowing that work could be forgotten for a few days. Tony only mentioned that he might have to leave Nigroup if matters did not improve. He was toying with the idea of starting his own investment management business. He would need the right kind of help, and wondered whether she would consider joining him as his secretary and assistant.

That aside, they talked of everything and of nothing in particular. Mary was excited about spending Christmas day with her husband and his family, and she also had other plans for the rest of the weekend. They exchanged thoughts on all manner of topics. It was simply wonderful to be close in an uncomplicated way, confident in each other and quietly rejoicing in their mutual affection.

It was mid-afternoon when they left to take up again the other parts of their lives. Their farewell hug expressed in compressed form all they felt and wished for each other.

Tony drove unhurriedly to the Club. It was almost deserted when he arrived there, with most people on holiday, at office parties, doing their final Christmas shopping, or going home early. The sun was still shining and it was hot, but great cumulus summer clouds were building up in the sky. To the south and to the west it was dark with an approaching storm. Tony had arranged to meet Sylvia earlier than usual, but it was still too early for her to arrive. He changed into his running kit, put his clothes into his car and sauntered down to the adjacent running track. He began to jog gently, feeling full of lunch, but of happiness also. His happiness was deepened when he saw Sylvia hop-skipping down the grass bank onto the field, arms spread to keep her balance, in her joy at seeing him and at being able to spend some precious time with him on this most blessed of days. To her this *was* Christmas, for her boys were away and that night and the following day would be a combination of duty and loneliness. She ran into his welcoming arms and they hugged tightly and laughed with delight.

Ignoring the approaching storm, they made their way onto one of the trails that ran down the Braamfontein Spruit. There had been good summer rains, so the river dived into the waterfall made by the weir below the Club grounds, then rushed its white and turbulent way over rapids as it twisted through the high rocks and cliffs beyond. Soon, however, it slowed and flowed almost black and mirror-like, with two black ducks serenely afloat, between green banks with willow trees on one side and a great eucalyptus on the other. Then the river widened and revealed sandbanks, despite the recent rain, where Sylvia and Tony disturbed raucous crowned plovers and hadedas, tink-tinking blacksmith plovers and a silent, stately heron as they ran past. So they enjoyed the changing face and moods of the river, gloried in the easy rhythm of their movements as they ran, and rejoiced in each other's company.

The sky grew darker as the heavy clouds closed in from the south and the west, lightning flashed ever nearer, and thunder rumbled and roared closer and louder. Tony and Sylvia reached their cars just as heavy drops of rain began to splash down. They grabbed their tracksuits and ran for the clubhouse, arriving damp but happy. They put on their tracksuits and went into their accustomed but now deserted small bar and ordered drinks, a glass of dry white wine for her and a beer for him. They clinked glasses and drank to each other's happiness. Sylvia's hair was damp and dishevelled after their run, but her dark brown eyes glowed deeply in the subdued light and her face was lit by that lovely smile that had first attracted Tony.

After the rain had stopped, they went out to their cars in the car park next to the running track. The air was fresh and clean after the storm, which had moved towards the east, trailing clear blue sky behind it. The trees on the eastern rise across the Spruit, showed their many shades of green, though darkened by the rain still falling over there. It was time to part, and Tony and Sylvia exchanged the gifts which they had brought for each other. As they held each other closely in a farewell hug, the sun suddenly came out from behind the retreating clouds and a glorious rainbow was magically arched across the dark eastern sky behind them.

Nora arrived home just as Tony was closing the garage door. She swept down the driveway, parked her car in the garage, and emerged, briefcase in hand, to give him a brief kiss on the cheek. She was smartly dressed in a light grey suit, which looked businesslike, showed off her figure and emphasized her now cool grey eyes. She looked at his tracksuit, damp running shoes and sweaty hair.

"You'll need to have a quick bath and get dressed," she said. "We're going to have dinner at the Barlows' tonight. We're due at half past seven." Larry Barlow was the senior partner of Merchant Attorneys, the large and leading firm of which Nora was now a partner. He and his wife, Louise, entertained extensively for both social and business reasons.

"I thought we were going to have a quiet evening at home. You know that's how I like to spend Christmas Eve. Tomorrow there'll be plenty of partying. And this is very short notice."

"Louise phoned me this afternoon. Obviously I agreed. I tried to get hold of you but didn't manage. I don't know where you were."

"Someone probably let them down and they have two places to fill."

"Don't be difficult. I can't refuse. *I* need to look after *my* career."

Oh the difference coming home makes! thought Tony.

11

It was Christmas Eve. Sipho Khumalo had spent the day knocking on doors and stopping passers-by to ask for work or for a room to live in in exchange for gardening or other work. The suburb through which he was now passing had many new houses, so he hoped to obtain work as a gardener in some of the many gardens that were being established by the new home-owners. Unfortunately no one seemed to be interested in offering employment when their thoughts and preparations, and what little spare money they had, were all concentrated on Christmas and the holiday season. Building work had also stopped for the holidays so he could not even apply for that at this time.

It had been a hot day and he was feeling tired and depressed. Huge cumulus clouds had been gathering in the sky and their shadows had brought some relief from the heat. Later in the day they also brought thunder and lightning, and some heavy rain. Sipho found shelter in the shell of a partially built house, waiting for the builders to return in January, and he drank the cool drink and ate the sandwiches that a kindly lady had given him at one of the many houses he had called on that afternoon. It stopped raining, but the sky remained very dark in the east. A low sun came out, and there was suddenly a wonderful rainbow, bright against the dark cloud. It did not seem like Christmas, but, despite his weariness, he was moved by the sight. Could it be a good omen?

He had been born in a small village in KwaZulu, or Zululand as the white people called it, in the south-eastern part of the country. It was a beautiful area, with rolling hills that were green at this time of the year, being the rainy season. The people were poor, for jobs were few and there were many mouths to feed. When Sipho was still quite young, his father had gone off, far away to the north, to work deep under the ground as a gold miner. He sent them much-needed money, but unfortunately they did not see him very often. Sipho's mother looked after him and his brothers and sisters, and together they grew vegetables and looked after their small number of animals, a precious cow and a few goats and hens. The children were fortunate that in the area there was a school run by missionaries. Those good folk saw that the children were able to obtain a good basic education, as well as religious instruction. Sipho was good with his hands, and also found the opportunity to learn some woodwork, and to gain a basic knowledge of some aspects of building (bricklaying and plastering and painting), while the mission complex was being extended and work and training were offered.

The time came when Sipho could find no more work in the district. There was not much food, and his mother had many mouths to feed. He needed to find a job, but did not want to work on a mine as his father did. He decided instead to go to iGoli ('the place of gold'), as they called the big city which white people knew as Johannesburg, which had been built where gold had been discovered many years before.

With the aid of a testimonial from the head of the mission school, he had been fortunate to find work as a labourer on a large construction site in the city. The project had been a big one and he had had a secure job for more than a year. Then the work was complete, and he had had to look for another job. Every now and again he had managed to find short periods of work on building sites, being taken on for a day at a time, and having to be at the gate very early the next morning to be sure of securing another day's work. In between he sought gardening work at private homes, and somehow managed to keep himself, and even at times to send money to his mother.

Finding somewhere to live had proved to be an enormous problem. For a time he was given lodging in a tiny, crowded house with a fellow worker, but after some months he had had to leave. He had to make do as best he could. Sometimes he found somewhere to stay for a while, but often he slept out in the open, wherever he could find a relatively safe and sheltered place. In winter it was bitterly cold, and in summer it was wet and thundery.

Now he was both homeless and jobless, and he had spent the last of his money the day before. He had been sleeping at night beside the small stream, which ran through the valley, in an open area beyond the new housing development. Two evenings ago, as he was warming some food over a small fire made from twigs and the wood of a dead branch he had scavenged, the area had been raided by police who had been detailed to remove vagrants. Fortunately he had seen them at a distance and had just had time to grab the bundle containing his few belongings and escape into the dusky evening. He was afraid to return, and had spent two uncomfortable nights curled up half-hidden next to a hedge beside a quiet road. However, the owner of the property had found him early that morning and had chased him away.

Sipho continued his search for work and lodging into the dark, but eventually gave up. There was none to be had. Also, people did not like strangers knocking on their doors at night, and dogs somehow seemed more savage in poor light. Desperately weary, he began to look for a safe place to spend the night, with no idea of how he would get through the next day. He had gradually moved up out of the valley. Nearby he saw the dark mass of Boskop, a deeper dark against the sky. Then, beside the hill, he saw a grassy plot with a fairly large building on it, and, set back to one side, a modest house with lights shining through some of its windows. The large building, which looked like a meeting place or hall, was in darkness save for a single light on the entrance porch, where a cheerful Christmas tree had been placed. Despite the poor light Sipho was able to read the lettering on a large signboard near the entrance to the plot.

THE LORD'S CHURCH

Welcome

Surely this was a friendly place where he could lie down for the night. Surely they would not chase him away. A quick survey showed Sipho that most of the plot was too open to provide shelter. He walked around the building, which was locked and which he now realised was a church hall. The porch gave some shelter, but was too risky as it was lit and was also visible from the road. One side of the building afforded no shelter, while at the back there was some unfinished building work. On the side next to the road there was a narrow length of lawn between the building and a bed of hydrangeas, which grew closely together and could hide him from the road while he slept. Here he lay down to rest, and curled up on his side, a folded jersey under his head and the remainder of his belongings in a bundle held in the protective curve of his body.

Sipho was awakened by a bright light shining in his face and a shoe prodding him in the back. He was on his feet in an instant, holding tightly onto his possessions. When the person who had roused him lowered the torch he was carrying, Sipho was able to make out a tall, thin man with a long face, and with eyes and a beard that were dark in the dim light.

"Who are you? What're you doing here? Go away!"

"Mnumzane! Sir, please don't chase me away! I have got nowhere to go. I am Sipho. I am looking for a job and for a place to stay. Have you got a room for me? I will work for you."

The couple had moved towards the front of the building as Sipho desperately gabbled out the words. Maria glanced out of a window of the house, knowing that her husband, Joshua, was doing his accustomed rounds of the property to see that all was safe before retiring to bed. She saw the two dark figures in the dim porch light and immediately hurried out to see if her husband needed help.

"What's the matter?" she asked as she drew near to them. She saw a young, dark man of medium height, strongly built but with a gaunt, hungry face and frightened, pleading, dark eyes.

"Please, madam, let me stay. I am Sipho. I'm not a bad person. I need a room. I will work for it. Please help me. It's Christmas. I know about church. I went to mission school. Let me show you."

Sipho fumbled in a pocket and took out a soiled and much-folded piece of paper. Josh, for it was he, took it to the light and he and Maria read what was a testimonial written by Father Jones, the head of the mission school Sipho had attended. The couple hesitated and looked at each other.

"We don't have a place to stay, and I'm afraid we don't have money to offer a job," said Josh, more kindly. "I'm building a room for a servant, and a storeroom, but they're not finished yet."

"I'll help you finish them. I can do building – it says so in that paper. I can sleep on the grass."

"Have you got food?" asked Maria.

"No, madam, it's all finished, and my money too. It's hard to find a job."

"Joshua, we can't send him away on this night of all nights. Remember, she 'laid Him in a manger, because there was no room for them in the inn.' I think 'Sipho' means 'gift'. Maybe that is a sign."

"The storeroom isn't finished, but at least it has a roof," said Josh. "Sipho, you can spend the night there if you like, but it won't be comfortable."

"Please, sir."

"I've got some soup I can warm up," said Maria. "And there's bread and cheese, and an apple. Joshua, you show him where he can sleep. There's a tap there too if he needs it."

With the food Maria also brought out an old blanket, and Sipho slept on it on the concrete floor of the unfinished shell of what would become a storeroom at the back of the church hall.

Christmas Day dawned clear and beautiful. Josh and Maria were woken up by two very excited little girls, who dragged them into the lounge for the opening of the presents placed at the foot of the Christmas tree. It was a cheerful, happy, family scene. Josh loved Christmas, which was one of the happiest days in the church calendar. Morning service was only at ten o'clock, so he had the leisure to enjoy the early morning with his family.

After the rustling and tearing of wrapping paper, and the excited squeals and exclamations, had died down, Josh was surprised to hear scraping and tapping noises from outside. He went out to investigate. To his amazement he saw Sipho, trowel in hand, tapping a brick neatly into place on one of the unfinished walls that Josh had been building.

"Happy Christmas, sir!" was Sipho's delighted greeting, his dark face lighting up and his teeth showing a brilliant white as he smiled.

"What are you doing?"

"You helped me last night, I help you now. I said I can build, now you see. I can help you."

"That is very good of you. But I can't let you work on Christmas Day. Just finish that bit, then you must stop. The church service is at ten o'clock and people will be coming."

"Can I come too? To sing and listen to you? I think you are the minister."

"I'm afraid that I can't let you come to the service. All of the people are white, and they're not used to black people in their church. I need their help, and their money, if I'm going to build a proper church for the Lord – over there where it's all grass now. I can't upset them so they decide to go away. I'm sorry. But you can stand outside and listen if you wish."

"At the mission everyone could go to church. But then most of the people were black. I will listen outside. I will help you build your church, then maybe I can go inside."

"Sipho, help me finish this room and you may live in it. You may help us here if you want, with building, gardening, cleaning, on certain days for your room. We can't pay you much, but we'll give you food. On other days I'm sure you'll find work in the area. There are many new gardens for a start. If you find a better job you can move on. Until then, let's see how you do here."

Now it did indeed seem like Christmas to Sipho.

PART TWO

12

New Year is always a time for new resolutions and new beginnings. Runners are no different from other mortals, being full of hopes and plans and good intentions for the coming year. So it was also at the White Waters Running Club, and indeed all around the country, with potential Comrades runners in particular looking forward in earnest to the great race now only five months away. Many came together at the first club night of the year which was always an exciting occasion. Some were already too eager, having recently had the time to cram in enormous distances in training, others had taken a more balanced approach and were reasonably prepared for the hard work ahead, while yet others were emerging from an inactive few months to begin all over again.

White Waters held an official 'club night' every Tuesday evening, commencing after most people had finished work. While the runners trained at the club or elsewhere at other times, a great many made a point of attending club nights if at all possible. There they could run in either of the five or eight kilometre time trials on offer, and they could socialise, communicate conveniently with the club administration, and keep themselves well informed about club and running matters and forthcoming events.

White Waters was a large club by running standards, and much of its success could be attributed to the enthusiasm and strong administration which had been provided for a number of years by Victor and Trixie Pots. Victor was the Running Club Captain and Chairman of its Committee. He had pale blue eyes, a freckled skin and red hair that was now both fading and retreating. He was of above average height and was rather too heavily built to be better than a good marathon runner. He was fanatical about running, and about the success of the Club. The winning of individual prizes and team trophies, by those competing in the Club's now famous colours (sky blue with a flowing white 'W W' on the front and back of the vest), was his unfailing passion. On this first club night of the year he was excitedly moving around, shaking hands, welcoming members and newcomers alike and talking of victories to be won in the coming year.

Trixie was Victor's wife and the Club Secretary. She was small, bright-eyed, enthusiastic, dynamic and determined. She had never run much, but had been involved in administration for many years. The growth of the Club had been built in no small measure on the efficient and reliable organization she unfailingly provided. The Running Club had a small clubroom, serving as office, meeting and general purpose room, just off one end of the terrace in front of the clubhouse. In good weather Trixie and her helpers set out tables on the terrace immediately in front of that room, providing easier access for the members, and enabling her to enjoy the beautiful evening and soak up the lively club night atmosphere. There she sat now, smilingly taking in money, accepting and renewing memberships, giving out running license numbers to be worn on the vest in races, and exchanging friendly words with all comers, nearly all of whose names and circumstances she knew.

Tony arrived to a busy and colourful scene. Last minute arrivals were hurrying to the changing rooms to change from working clothes into running gear, and others, in a motley array of shorts, running vests and T-shirts, crowded around the tables on the terrace and spilled onto the adjacent sports field towards the start of the time trials. He saw Sylvia in the crowd and joined her as they walked to the start. All around them was animation, with people exchanging greetings and good wishes for the new year, as well as news about themselves, families and friends, fitness levels and goals for the time ahead. Regulars were delighted and amused to see faces which had not been there for many months, some since the last Comrades. To Tony the conversation seemed to continue all around him, not only before the run, but also more breathlessly during it, and afterwards as the pleasantly tired and showered or sweaty runners enjoyed a cool drink on the grass or terrace in the cooling, soft, summer twilight.

"Hello! How are you? Happy New Year!"

"Hello, Beth," greeted Victor. "And Mandla! Good to see you! I hope you're both fit. We need you for the teams. This year we want even more wins than last year." Mandla and Beth were two of the Club's more promising male and female runners.

"Hello, Tony! How's your jogging group doing? Did you say going for Comrades? You must be joking."

"Ken, my mate, I'm going for silver this time. Last year it was nine hours, so now it's under seven and a half for a silver medal. I've done a fantastic amount of training on holiday in the Cape. It was hot, but I ran for hours every day."

"Kobus, I'm with you all the way. This year we're going for silver. I stayed at home, but I've been doing my highest distances ever. I'm feeling really strong."

"Yes," from Johan and Simon, "this will be our first Comrades, but we've been training very hard and are very fit."

"Yes," said Bill, "I'm going to try again. I hope I make it this time." Bill had had a major operation and had been recovering his strength.

"Can you believe it? My wife is going to have a baby at the end of May. Of all times to choose!"

"Who can you blame for that? Surely you could get your timing better."

"Hello, Fred! Good to see you again! How's the training? Sorry about that. Will you still be there on 31st May? Will it be medal number twenty-six this time? Good luck!"

"Hi, Tony! I saw your friend Andy at the coast. He's training like a lunatic. Says he'll kill us at Comrades."

"My esteemed boss. Maybe he'll be over-trained by Comrades, or injured."

Tony was also glad to see a number of those from his running group, which was slowly growing back to full strength as people came back from their holidays. He spent time with them, catching up on their news and talking plans and training schedules.

Josh had not been away, but he was as eager as any one and his austere face almost carried a smile. He was achieving the training distances Tony had suggested, and was feeling fitter than he had for years. He was looking forward to the harder training that lay ahead. He was also pleased with the Christmas and New Year period at the church. The services had been well attended and a number of new faces had appeared in his growing congregation. He was also finding that he and Sipho worked very well together. They had made good progress on their building work, and Sipho had proved to be well capable of working on his own when Josh could not be there with him.

Melanie was glad that the holiday season was over. This had been only her second Christmas without David and she had felt very lonely, especially in the general air of joy and celebration all around her at that time. At work the bank had been quiet and she had had little to do. She had trained hard and was doing quite a bit more than the fifty kilometres a week prescribed by Tony. She was feeling strong, though a little jaded, and was looking forward to keeping her promise to David. The atmosphere of excitement and anticipation was infectious, and, as she watched and listened, tears came to her eyes as she thought how David would have loved to have been there as one of them.

Sylvia was still enjoying the school holidays, although they would soon be coming to an end. She had also been lonely at times, as her children were still with their father, and she had only been able to see Tony when he had not been involved with his family. That of course meant that at important times, like Christmas Day and New Year's Eve, she had been on her own. She was glad that they were now again into their regular routine, and indeed meeting Tony was even easier than usual as she was not yet bound down by her own teaching duties. Now she was glad to be by his side, enjoying with him the lively mood of optimism and comradeship that prevailed. For a long time now, she had felt that she was very much a runner and a member of the Club. However, as she listened to the talk of Comrades, and as she felt the excitement and anticipation, she could not but feel a small twinge of regret that she would not be running on that day, and that to that extent she was on the outside looking in.

13

After New Year, business activity picked up slowly, but regained full speed once the schools had re-opened and the summer holidays were over. Merchant Attorneys were doing an increasing amount of business with Nigroup, and Nora was rightly given credit for extending the legal firm's relationship with, and business flow from, that very active and acquisitive institution. She had advised Nigroup on a number of matters in the past and had therefore formed excellent business relationships with Andrew Duke and certain of the other senior management there. Her good looks and charming manner had helped, but her legal work was also good. She was particularly careful to develop her relationship with Andy, whom she met both in the course of her work and at business and social events associated with both organizations. As their relationship developed so did the amount of work that came to Nora and Merchant from Nigroup.

Andy had recently been divorced, and Nora was one of many women who were happy to console him following that event. She was attracted to him, but especially to his wealth and power. She was alluring, obliging and very determined. He liked blondes, and was accustomed to getting what he wanted, so he was quite happy to entertain her attentions. She had the great advantage of genuinely being able to understand and to share his passionate business ambitions. Before Christmas, at the Nigroup end-of-year party, which Nora had attended as Tony's wife, more than a few had noticed that Andy had danced with her more often than formality required. She had danced with obvious admiration and interest, gazing into his grey eyes, her smiling lips parted, and keeping close to him so he could feel her curves and know her interest.

Andy had gone to Cape Town, as was fashionable in certain business circles, over the Christmas holidays. He had socialised with other chief executives, or sat amongst them on Clifton Beach, hatching deals, trying to outdo one another with the importance of their current business activities, and pestering their offices with unnecessary phone calls. All of that was proper and normal behaviour. What was more unusual was that he had continued to train hard every day. Indeed he increased his running distances as there was more time to train over the holiday period.

About the middle of January, Nora and a colleague were working on an urgent legal opinion for Nigroup. Andy suggested that they visit him that evening to present their opinion to him at his home, which was in the beautiful and luxurious northern suburb of Hyde Park. This they duly did, sitting comfortably in the balmy summer air on a wide, covered balcony overlooking a large illuminated swimming pool, the magically lit lower garden, and the now dark but leafy and opulent valley beyond. When their business was concluded and Nora and her colleague had finished their drinks, Andy hinted that he had another matter to discuss with Nora and that he wished her to stay on for a while. As her colleague made ready to depart, Nora saw Andy's hungry eyes as he prowled around them, before finally ushering her companion out.

Andy returned and poured each of them another drink. They talked casually, gazing out into the open. Nora remarked on the lovely situation and the beauty of his home. Privately she compared it with her own more modest abode, and felt how good it would be to be mistress of this magnificent place. She had been there before on certain formal occasions, and had only seen the public rooms, which were opulent and ostentatious with much marble and glass, costly furnishings and some quite good paintings and sculptures. Not all was to her taste, but there would be money aplenty to make whatever changes a future mistress would desire.

"Yes, I like it," he said. "It's taken a long time to get it just right. We did quite a lot of building and renovating, as you know. You haven't ever been shown around, have you? Let me take you."

"Of course I do rattle about in it now that I'm on my own," he continued as they began their tour.

She looked and admired to his evident satisfaction. On the upper storey there were several family and guest suites and rooms. She glanced into the bedrooms without allowing herself to be manoeuvred inside. On this first occasion it would seem too easy and too cheap.

"I mustn't stay too late," she murmured. "I must still finish that job for tomorrow's meeting."

But when they parted, her look was admiration, her lips were soft, and her embrace was close enough to feel and fuel his desire and to offer him definite hope.

14

It was another beautiful Thursday evening in January. The scattered summer clouds were soft and white in an otherwise clear sky. They presaged no rain, but promised another serene and beautiful sunset. The air was still and warm, as the crocodile of runners in Tony's group streamed across the sports fields and onto the Braamfontein Spruit trail, disturbing a silent white egret, and sending a complaining group of crown plovers scattering out of the way. One of the slow starters, talking to Tony at the back of the bunch, had one of those familiar faces which, until the first Tuesday of the year, had not been seen at the White Waters club for a long time. He was Frederick Current, known as 'Fred', or 'Old Fred' for he had been around for as long as anyone could remember. He had emerged from a period of isolation on the first club night of the year, and had had a gentle jog over the time trial course. That evening he had told Tony something of the lonely struggle to run which he had had over the past few months, and Tony had invited him to join his group whenever he felt that the way they were training, and the company, could help him. Fred was too experienced to need coaching, but some friendly company could be welcome to him at this stage of his recovery, and his knowledge of running could be very helpful to those in the group.

Fred was in his late fifties, with greying hair, large green eyes in a weathered face, and was small, lean and wiry. He lived for Comrades. He had completed the race twenty-five times, a feat then surpassed by only a small handful of runners. He had won a gold medal for finishing in the first six when the race was smaller and he had been younger and faster, and he had also won numerous silver medals for finishing in less than seven and a half hours. Now he was beginning to feel his age, and in the past few years he had been content to finish comfortably under the cut-off time of eleven hours. Even that had been difficult last year, as a long-standing heel and Achilles tendon injury had left him struggling. After the race the injury had not healed properly and he had even found it difficult to jog for short distances socially. His job as store man in a food company's distribution warehouse involved a lot of time on his feet, and even that had become uncomfortable. So Fred had taken medical advice and had undergone an operation to his troublesome left heel and Achilles tendon.

The surgeon had told him that he would probably be running again in six weeks, but the operation had been more extensive than anticipated, and after four weeks, Fred was still walking with crutches. In the fifth week he managed to exchange these for a walking stick, and began to learn to walk properly again. He 'trained' religiously every day, but for a month that had consisted only of walking, at first leaning heavily on his walking stick and stopping frequently to rest, going only two or three hundred metres before returning home. The next day he would go about a hundred metres further before turning back, and so on. Once he was able to walk about a mile in that fashion, he began to hold his stick above the ground and walk without its aid for a while. On the first attempt he managed only about fifty metres, but this he gradually extended as he also increased the distance covered each day. After a month he managed to walk three kilometres. During the next few weeks he started introducing small amounts of slow shuffling jogging into his walks. At the end of the fourth month he managed to shuffle a whole kilometre, without stopping or walking, in just under eleven minutes. In November and December he had made steady progress, but they had still represented a few more long and lonely weeks, as he gradually increased his distances, improved his times, and attained something of his normal running gait. Now he was beginning to feel that he might still be able to run another Comrades, if he could maintain his progress and become fit enough to run a qualifying marathon before Comrades entries closed on 9th April.

"I'm sure that now you're running normally, all the years of training will be apparent, and you'll manage very well," Tony had said.

Fred was a survivor, and he believed that Tony was right. After all the patience he had had to exercise, he was determined to succeed.

15

It was Tuesday evening: club night, and time trial night. The weekly time trials were incorporated into the training programmes of Tony's runners, as of many others. The faster running, on an accurately measured course through the neighbouring suburbs, was an important element in their training. Runners could run either an eight kilometre or a five kilometre course. As each kilometre mark was painted on the side of the road, and as most runners wore watches on their wrists, it was easy for them to monitor their progress, practise pace judgement, or run thousand metre intervals, alternating faster and slower around the course. The fact that the courses were hilly, as dictated by the nature of the area, meant that they were also both taxing and suitable for practising the techniques of uphill and downhill running. The variations of what could be done on these runs were endless.

The Comrades hopefuls were of course running the longer time trial. Those who were able to leave work in good time were arriving early and running a few extra kilometres before the time trial began, for they were now increasing their weekly training distances. Tony discouraged his runners from running flat out trials, like races, each week, although sometimes they did test themselves and try to achieve personal best times over the distances and courses. He always stressed the importance of knowing the purpose of each training session and training accordingly. On this evening, for example, they had been encouraged to run the first half at a good steady pace, and then maintain or improve the pace over the second half of the run, in order to run the second half a little faster than the first. So they practised pace judgement, avoiding the common fault of running the first half of a race too fast, and the sustaining of a good pace to the end.

The sun was low and most of the field in front of the White Waters clubhouse was in shade. A mellow, golden light dappled the grass in places and gilded the trees and leafy hillside across the river. As the erratic line of hot, perspiring runners passed the finishing point at the side of the field, many tended to stand around, or sit in the shade on the soft green grass in front of the clubhouse terrace. It was too warm to feel the need to fight for showers in the crowded change rooms or to put on warm clothing. It was refreshing to let the still air, as it slowly cooled after the heat of the day, caress the skin.

Bill Ronson had finished his run, and was sitting on the grass amid a jumble of people and tog-bags and rugs spread out for non-running spouses and their infants. He was looking idly at the grass in front of him, when a pair of clean running shoes and white socks came into his field of vision and stood next to a blue tog-bag. He slowly raised his eyes to a pair of well-turned calves, smooth attractive thighs, a shapely bottom just covered by white running shorts, a neat waist, attractive arms and shoulders, and a head of honey-coloured hair.

"Wow!" he could not help exclaiming.

"Did you say something?"

The figure turned to reveal a front view every bit as appealing, while a face with a quizzical expression and a pair of half-smiling amber-brown eyes looked down at him. She saw a pleasant-looking man of about forty, moderately well built, with an earnest face, sweaty brown hair and light brown eyes.

"I said 'Wow!' Sorry! It just came out, but was a compliment. Please accept it as such. You look stunning."

“Thank you,” said Melanie, as she instinctively felt around in her tog-bag, then pulled out a brush, which she proceeded to pull through her hair to tidy it after her run.

They introduced themselves to each other and Bill offered to get her a drink. She accepted, and they sat on the grass and chatted as they sipped their drinks. Others gradually joined them and soon they were part of a merry circle of runners. Some were from Tony’s group, and Melanie suggested that Bill might like to run with them. He had done so on and off in the past, but not for a long time. Now, of course, he promised that he would do so again.

Bill did rejoin the group and he and Melanie began to run quite often together. As they chatted and came to know each other, they found that they liked one another and their friendship grew. They each also had sympathy for the sadness and difficult times which the other had experienced during the previous two or three years.

Bill was one who enjoyed running, and had run on and off for some years without any great distinction. Once he had attempted to run Comrades but had failed to finish. The following year he had begun to train for it again but had not been able to start. He had collapsed one day at work, had been rushed to hospital, and had had a major brain operation. Fortunately the lump that had been removed had been benign. The surgeons had been very skilled, and he had survived, but he had been in the operating theatre for over twelve hours, and it had taken him a long time to recover. Gradually his health had improved, and he had worked persistently at regaining his strength and physical fitness. However, during that long period, his employer had found a reason to make him redundant, and his wife had left him for someone with better prospects. He had been through a very unhappy period. He had survived by eking out his redundancy payment, but his self-esteem had been very low. Then he had found brief spells of temporary work as an accountant or administrator, and things had begun to improve for him. He had not been offered a permanent job because of his health, but his most recent assignment, which was with a good company, had now extended to several months. He knew that his work was good, and he hoped to persuade the company to take him into a permanent position if he could remove lingering doubts about the state of his health.

Now he was once again running as he had been before his operation. He was determined to run the Comrades Marathon in May, for two reasons. Firstly, finishing the race would surely be clear proof that he was now over his illness and could be considered for the job he wanted. Secondly, he had failed before, so he felt that he had to prove, if only to himself, that he really could do it. Success would be even more important to him with the background of his other recent 'failures': his health, his job and his marriage.

16

It had been another very demanding and disillusioning day at work. Tony had arrived at the Club feeling totally exhausted and emotionally drained. It was Friday, Sylvia was away, none of his other friends had been there, and so he had trained alone. He had run only briefly, slowly and listlessly, as he had been so tired and depressed. The exercise had helped him to feel only a little better. He sat alone under the jacaranda tree in front of the clubhouse and sipped a beer as he stared over the fields to the green suburbs beyond. The sun had set and the soft pink on the gently drifting clouds turned to grey as the dusk slowly darkened. *Wouldn't it be lovely to have a place to go to, where one could relax and be welcome and loved and simply be oneself*, he thought.

Then he started. Surely such a place was called a home? He sat for a long time and pondered as the darkness gathered around him.

17

Nora lay naked on the soft sheets, sinking luxuriously into the comfortable pillows supporting her head and shoulders. She was pleasantly fatigued and well pleased with herself. She knew that she was beautiful and looking her best, and she enjoyed admiring her own shapeliness, and the subtle colouring of her smooth skin, as she allowed Andy to continue to feast his eyes and sense of touch.

They had arranged another meeting at his home, but this time she had come alone. It had been an unspoken understanding that they would make love and she had come prepared to do so. He had not needed the encouragement she had given him, and indeed, she felt sure that her refusal would have been the end of any future personal or business understanding between them.

She had been wonderful and she knew it. She had wanted to make him cry out for joy, to put her mark upon him so that he would never forget her, and she knew that she had succeeded. He had basically been taking what was offered to him, what he believed to be his right in the natural scheme of things, but she had ensured that his serious interest had been secured.

18

Josh was out on his early morning training run. It was pleasantly cool, and the air was clear and clean after the previous evening's thunderstorm. The suburbs were quiet and there was very little traffic on the roads. Many of his runs took him down into the valley and onto the still undeveloped country area, so he could take the path that ran along the riverside. He enjoyed the feeling of the natural countryside, with the erratic little stream, the trees along its banks, the open grassland and the varied bird life. Here he felt closer to God and to His creation than on the tarred roads. It was a lovely start to the day.

As he ran he could relax and let his mind go into free flow. He could think of anything, or of nothing, but he was still amazed at the way problems were solved without any apparent effort while he ran, as somewhere below the level of immediate awareness his mind seemed to shuffle their various elements until solutions emerged. He found that he could also compose parts of his sermons, or find ideas for them, so his runs no longer seemed to be a waste of time, a personal indulgence, or only a way towards raising money for the church. Perhaps running could have a valid place in his life even after what they now called the Comrades Project.

This morning he was thinking that things were progressing well. He was running consistently and growing fitter and stronger all the time. Sipho had also been a blessing, and was such a great help to him and to Maria that he had been taken on as a full-time employee, though on a modest wage. Two days ago he had moved into his own little room, which was now finished. Sipho's spiritual needs were also being attended to, for he was now allowed to attend church services, sitting unobtrusively at the back of the hall.

Fund-raising was also progressing well. Many people were stimulated to make contributions of money or time simply because of the obvious and infectious dedication of their minister, who was willing to take up a challenge such as running the Comrades Marathon and subject himself to the arduous training and racing involved. Even better, certain members of the congregation, who were involved in the building industry, had been so impressed by his enthusiasm that they had indicated that they might provide some large sponsorships for the Comrades Project. These would not be in cash, but would involve the donation of building materials, and possibly the provision of labour at cost. These were very exciting developments.

As Josh ran along the river he became aware of another runner coming along the path towards him. As the figure came closer he stepped to one side of the path, aware that the black runner approaching would probably do the same. He was always touched and amused by such African courtesy, where each showed politeness by stepping off the path for the other, so that neither actually used it as they passed each other with a smile and a greeting. While Josh was still thinking of that, the approaching bare-footed figure took on a familiar shape.

"Sipho! What are you doing here? I didn't know you ran?"

"At home I ran to school sometimes, when to walk took too long. Now, I follow you."

"Why would you do that?"

"I heard madam say she thought it was not safe for you to run here alone, so I have followed you. You didn't see me before. I run far behind you, but so I can still see you. If there is trouble I am there to help. But I see no trouble and I think it's safe. Today I woke up late, so I didn't know which way round you would run. I chose the wrong way, so we meet here. You are not cross?"

"Sipho, I am touched. It was very kind of you to look after me in that way."

"You help me, so I help you. But I like to run and I am getting strong again. Maybe I can run with you sometimes when you want company. Other times I will run on my own."

So they began to run together quite often. Josh found that at times it was a help to have company, especially on the longer, more arduous runs when it could become boring on one's own. He also found that Sipho was a sensitive companion, who knew instinctively when Josh wanted to be left in silence with his own thoughts. Sipho was young and at least as fit as Josh, especially now that he was eating regularly again. He also did not seem to mind running bare-foot. Soon Sipho began to talk of running Comrades with his employer.

"Perhaps people will sponsor me too, then I can also help make money to build the church," he said.

Josh took Sipho with him to the Club to run on Tuesday evenings, and soon Sipho was part of Tony's running group and a Comrades Marathon hopeful.

"You will have to join the Club and become a registered runner," Tony told him on the first evening. "You will also need some running shoes. It's not easy to run very long distances bare-foot. If you don't have money we can talk to Trixie who is the Club Secretary. The Club has a scheme to collect used shoes. Sometimes they are almost new, but are the wrong kind for that person. We'll see if we can find the right pair for you."

"Thank you, sir," said Sipho.

"Sipho, here we are all runners, not sirs or misters. My name is Tony, so call me Tony as everyone else does."

"Thank you, sir. I mean, Mister Tony … Tony."

On the way home Sipho noticed that Josh was struggling with some train of thought. After a while he spoke, with less confidence than usual.

"Sipho, Tony was right when he said that at the Club we are all runners. At the church I am the minister in charge, but at the Club I am just a runner like everyone else. Everyone there calls me Josh, so if you are at the Club with me, I think it would be right if you also called me Joshua, or Josh."

"OK, Mister Josh."

19

The atmosphere in the small bar at the White Waters Club was cosy, friendly and convivial. The comfortable blue and red carpeting and upholstery, and the deep brown wood of the bar counter and the elegant panelling on the walls, glowed warmly in the soft lighting. The room was occupied mainly by Tony and members of his team, enjoying, as was their custom, a friendly drink between training and going home. Tony and Sylvia sat in corner seats with others sitting or standing in a group. This evening the talk was mainly about progress with training, and their current preparation and plans for running a standard marathon of 42.2 kilometres in under 4 hours 30 minutes in order to qualify for the Comrades Marathon. Most had decided to follow Tony's recommendation to enter the Vaal Marathon, which would be run in the nearby town of Vereeniging, situated beside the Vaal River, on 10th March. The race was usually well organised, and the course was not only pleasant, but was relatively flat and about as fast as could be found on the highveld, where all marathon times were slowed by the high altitude around and above one thousand five hundred metres.

Sylvia sat and sipped her drink, happy to be near to Tony. Her dark brown eyes glowed softly as they took in the happy, eager faces. She listened and pondered as they questioned or commented and as Tony answered, explained and encouraged. Gradually the group thinned out as drinks were finished and people left in ones and twos. At last she had Tony to herself. Even in a crowd, she enjoyed being in his presence, but time alone with him was always precious. Sylvia was quiet for a while as they finished their drinks. Then she made a decision.

"I want you to help me to run Comrades," she said.

"Why would you decide to do that now?"

"I want to be involved. I want to share this with you, not just look in from the outside."

"But it's now the end of January. There are only four months left to Comrades."

"I've been doing the training."

"Not the long runs."

"You will get me there if I work hard and listen to you. I know it. Also, I want to support you. I see clearly that Victor, and others like him, think you're mad to work towards Comrades with a group like ours. They think we're not good enough, and they also think you're far too conservative in your approach. I know you and I trust you. I know you know what you are doing. I want to help you to show them they're wrong. I know I can do it with your help."

"Are you sure?"

"Yes."

"I think you can do it. There's probably just enough time, if we're careful. First you'll need to get into condition to qualify. The Vaal Marathon is too soon, so you'll have to qualify later. In broad terms our plan will have to be something like this …"

20

February was usually a hot month and this year's was no exception. Almost every day dawned fine and temperatures rose into the high twenties and early thirties Celsius. Clouds built up during the day and many an afternoon or evening saw typical summer thunderstorms. Then the gloom was lit by spectacular lightning displays, and thunder crashed all around or grumbled away in the distance, depending on the location of the storms. The heavy clouds deposited their loads in often brief but torrential showers of rain or hail. Those that trained in the early mornings before work enjoyed the delicious early freshness of the day. Those who preferred to train in the evenings had to contend with heat or rain and occasional hail. A wary eye was kept on the progress of the evening storms, but training continued unless lightning close overhead made conditions dangerous and frightening. Races could be held in all conditions, and the athlete needed to be able to cope whatever they were. So one grew in strength and confidence as one ran in heat or pouring rain and still managed to complete the training session, particularly while the more timid stayed at home or retired to the clubhouse for an early drink. However, sometimes the storms cleared or passed on early, and then one gloried as one ran in the damp, clean cool air and marvelled at the changing evening light and the atmospheric effects created by the low sun and the remaining clouds.

Training continued. Many were hell-bent on achieving high weekly and monthly distances, with kilometres covered being the main goal and driving force behind their training. Andy was driving himself each morning, as he did in his work, and was logging impressive distances. He was also racing well on Sunday mornings, and, despite fatigue from his hard training, was recording a series of personal best times. This he was pleased to announce to his colleagues at Nigroup on Monday mornings, and particularly to Tony, who was also training hard but much more cautiously, and who was racing only infrequently and conservatively.

Tony and his Comrades team were also increasing their training distances, particularly on the long runs scheduled for Sunday mornings, but the training load was built up slowly over time, allowing for the runner to absorb and adapt to the load without breaking down. Hard runs were followed by easier ones the next day to allow the body some recovery, and harder and easier training weeks succeeded one another. Each week there was one rest day. All the while Tony stressed the need 'to train, but not to strain'. His runners were to listen to their bodies, not to be hypochondriacs as so many runners were, but to be ever watchful for signs of excess fatigue and over-training, for example a persistent niggling sore throat, continually sore muscles or excessive prolonged fatigue. So far there had been a few niggling complaints, but no one in the group was injured. For most of them this phase of relatively hard training would continue into the last week of the month, and would be followed by a tapering off or reduction in training before the qualifying marathon early in March.

Tony was ever watchful over his group, and his coaching continued all the while. One evening they were running hard along a section of the Braamfontein Spruit on the return leg of an out and back run. Along the left bank was a wide grassy area with a clear path following the course of the river downstream. It was an ideal place for sustained hard running, safe and easy underfoot, but also fast as it followed the river gently downhill. Tony had started this sustained effort with the slower runners and was now moving fluently through the group as he increased his speed. He closed in on Melanie, who was concentrating fiercely, moving as fast as she could with arms pumping, fists clenched and shoulders slightly drawn up and tense.

"Relax, Melanie," called Tony as he drew alongside her and adjusted his speed to match hers. "Relax. You're far too tense. You're fighting yourself. Don't clench your fists. Keep your fingers open and just let your thumbs rest on your forefingers, like this. That's right. Now let your shoulders drop. Pick up your forearms a little and let the weight of your shoulders and arms fall through your elbows. That's right. Now resume your normal action and concentrate on relaxing. Run as fluently as possible, with no tension. That's better. See, you're still running as fast as before, but you're not using nearly as much energy."

The longest training runs were usually done on Sunday mornings, when most runners could find the time for them. From very early, early risers could see individuals or groups of runners out on the roads covering long distances. Many of the groups were informal, but many were supported by their clubs, who designed routes to be run and who arranged for long-suffering officials, spouses or supporters to take drinks and other refreshments out to pre-determined points along the way for the benefit of their runners. Without that support, runners had to carry drinks, buy them on the way, or stop at friendly petrol stations where runners were allowed to 'fill up' at their water taps.

With the running boom of the eighties, road races had proliferated, and there was one within easy driving distance nearly every Sunday morning. Some were standard marathons, scheduled to afford Comrades hopefuls the opportunity to qualify for the great race. Others, early in the year, were shorter, but the distances tended to be longer as the year progressed into early-May. Because of the accurately measured courses, the excellent refreshment points usually provided every three kilometres along the route, and the company provided by other runners, many chose to treat the Sunday races as training runs and so did their long runs in those races. The danger was to be caught up in the excitement of the race and so run too hard, racing instead of training, breaking down instead of building up. One had to define one's goals and discipline oneself accordingly.

Josh could not run on Sundays, so they became his resting days. Not only was Sunday his most important working day, but it was the Sabbath, to be kept and observed as a holy day. He and Sipho therefore usually did their long training runs on Saturday mornings and used their Sundays, in running terms, as recovery days. When they wanted to race they would go north to the Pretoria area, where the stricter observance of the Christian Sabbath was more wide-spread and races were usually held on Saturdays.

At first it was difficult for Josh to accept what he saw as the generally casual observance, or lack of observance, of the Sabbath amongst his new running friends and companions. However, their genuine comradeship, their respect for his views and beliefs, their support for him as a runner and their enthusiasm for his Comrades Project, gradually led him towards a tolerance for the way things were. He made it clear, though, that they would be welcome in his congregation.

With Tony, as his helper and the leader of his running group, he had some interesting conversations. Tony supported Josh and helped to design his running around his religious duties and observances. However, he pointed out that there were many different beliefs represented amongst the runners. Also some of the Christians chose to go to Church later on Sundays, after their long runs or in the evenings. There were also many, like Tony himself, who were religious but did not care for rigid doctrine or formal denominations.

"My religion is always part of me," said Tony. "When I run down the river in the evening or on a Sunday morning, and the world is beautiful all around me, I feel part of God's creation as much as in any church. He is all around me, in the water and the sky, the hills and forests, the grass and flowers and birds. His music is in the rush or ripple of the stream, the birds' song, the wind in the grass and the trees, and even the rumble of the thunder. He speaks to me through the new moon in a clear sky and the rainbow arched against the dark storm clouds. So my running becomes part of my religion. That is why I must try to do it as well as I possibly can, even though I am only an amateur trying to do my best at the end of the day or of the week. And 'well' doesn't only mean winning or quality of performance, it is also in how one does things. It is in one's attitude, one's handling of setbacks and acceptance of victory or defeat, in one's sportsmanship. But one finds many rewards. These are in the joy of doing one's best, in seeing the glow of success on the face of someone one has helped to achieve what he or she did not believe possible, and with the love and comradeship one finds through it all."

With some of this Josh could sympathise. He was certainly also determined to do his best for his Maker, but to him much was missing from Tony's beliefs.

The training continued. Not only were Tony and his runners growing fitter, they were also growing in knowledge and experience of their chosen activity and its many practical aspects. They were learning what to eat and to drink, what clothing and shoes were best for them, about developing practical and sensible pre-race routines, how to manage blisters, to tape or lubricate nipples to protect them from chafing on long runs, and a host of other major or minor matters.

However, as Tony had said, no matter how dedicated they were, they remained true amateurs. They ran with what they had left at the end of the day, at the end of the week, after meeting all their work and family and other commitments. Sometimes they ran well. At other times they had very little left in the way of physical and emotional reserves, and it showed in their performances. This they each had to learn to understand and to cope with, trying to manage their lives in such a way that they could perform at their best when it mattered most.

This was the same for Tony, as for all the others. For him, his work at Nigroup presented continuing problems and a growing burden.

21

Returning from a visit to a nearby client, to whom he had walked as it was a fine Johannesburg day, Tony entered the reception area of National Insurance House. It was large and impressive, with marble and granite and the greenery of indoor plants, and on one side a view of the courtyard with its fountain and gardens. There were several people in the foyer, and as he walked through to the lifts and waited for one to take him to his office floor, he watched those around him.

An elderly gentleman, stiff and erect, shuffled awkwardly with the aid of a younger man, possibly his son. He was dressed in his best to come to do business in the big city, in an old brown suit, red tie and brown hat. Perhaps he was calling to collect his pension, or to make some enquiry about it.

A sad stout widow, dressed all in voluminous black, was accompanied by two young children, perhaps to bring in a death certificate to claim the provision, made by her recently deceased husband, for them to live on now that he was gone.

Tony encouraged his staff to know who their clients were, not just the pension funds with their trustees and consultants, but also the actual pension fund members and individual policyholders and their dependants. Those were the people they were ultimately working for, whose future livelihood, upon old age or death, depended on how well they did their work.

"They are all depending on me," thought Tony. "There are hundreds of thousands out there, richer and poorer, black and white, male and female, who depend on me. What would they say to me if I let them down, if this madness continues without my trying to stop it? Upstairs they are playing financial games with these people's money, so that we are no longer able to invest it wisely and appropriately as we should and as we want to. I must make another, very firm stand!"

Nilife's over-exposure to shares of financial services companies had continued and was worsening, though the stock markets were thankfully holding up, and even becoming more expensive. To Andrew that proved the correctness of his strategies and actions. To Tony the dangers remained, and the financial bubble, which the still rising share prices represented, was growing ever closer to bursting point. He had been debating for some time whether he should take a firm and formal stand on the matter, as all his more tactful approaches and warnings had been to no avail. It would do him no good, but it had to be done.

When he returned to his office, he sat down to compose a memorandum to Andrew and the other executive management. He needed to put matters so plainly that there could be no misunderstanding. He had to make it clear that Nilife had run out of cash; that there was no further scope to sell non-financial services assets to raise cash, as the asset structure was already too lop-sided; that the main life fund (the major portfolio and heart of the life company, where most of the strategic financial services assets were held) was already borrowing money from other portfolios, and so was improperly restricting the free investment of the assets in them; that the main life fund held far too high a proportion of its investments in shares; that it was grossly over-exposed to one company (Enduring Bank), and to one sector of the stock market and the economy (financial services); and that all this was especially dangerous in financial markets where share prices in general, the prices of financial services shares, and the price of Enduring shares, were all very expensive and liable to fall. It should be understood that the financial stability, and the very viability, of the life company were at risk.

He took up his Dictaphone and began to dictate.

“Well, you’ve certainly caused a stir,” said Mary the next day, after the memorandum had been delivered. “If you wanted to be noticed, you’ve succeeded. I’ve just seen Jane, and she says Andy was beside himself when he read your memo. He was shouting and screaming and banging things and saying that if he wanted someone else to run the company he’d ask them. What the hell did you think you were doing, and so on.”

“He phoned me along much the same lines. He was definitely not sunny.”

“Jane says he’s been in meetings all day about the matter. At least you’ve provoked lots of discussion.”

“We’ll surely now have to discuss things at Friday’s strategy meeting. That at least will be something. But I’m not optimistic. Andy doesn’t want to change, and his technique will be to talk and talk until everyone has forgotten what the issues are, or whether there even were any issues. I’m also not sure whether anyone will be willing to stick out his neck and support me. Politically it’s not good to be out of step.”

Andy and Nora had arranged another of what promised to be regular meetings between them at Andy’s home for early that evening. Andy was still angry when Nora arrived, and immediately launched into his story of Tony’s memorandum and of his sins in general.

“I nearly cancelled our meeting, but then I thought how nice it would be to be in bed with his wife.”

“Was that good?” asked Nora softly some time later. “Are you feeling better? You see how good I am for you?”

“Yes, but you’ll have to get rid of that man of yours. He’ll also have to leave the company soon. I can’t just fire him. The

Board won't let me without good reason, because – I hate to say it – he's good at what he does. He's just too damn cautious and too damn independent. I'll have to find a pretext to get rid of him, or somehow force him to resign. But I can't get closer to you with him in the background."

"I want to be close to you. I want to be with you so very much. Surely you can see that now? I will leave him if you will take me. I'll divorce him."

"Let's think about it. Seriously, I mean. But if you are going to divorce him for me that will be another reason why he will have to leave Nigroup."

Nora turned these things over in her mind as she drove home. She was pleased with the fact that Andy was prepared to consider a firm future relationship with her. That was good progress. However, she was far from certain of him yet, and she was angry with Tony for muddying the waters before things were settled, and so putting at risk her plans for the future. She also did not want to give up her life with Tony until she was sure of something more desirable. Any change must be for better and not for worse.

"Why have you been causing trouble again at Nigroup?"

Nora confronted Tony soon after she arrived home. He had come home at his usual time and, finding a message to say that she would be late as she had to see a client, he had made supper for them and had just finished eating.

"I had a meeting with Andy today," she continued. "He nearly cancelled it because he was so angry. He told me all about it. I had quite a job to calm him down. Soon he'll be taking business away from me if you're not careful."

"I dare say that Merchant and you will both survive if that happens. I'm not sure that these incestuous business relationships are correct anyway. I can't do my job on the basis of the work that Nigroup gives or does not give you."

"But what about your own future? You're continually damaging your own progress. Why do you always have to be the one man out of step? Why can't you simply go with the flow like everyone else?"

"Nigroup is sailing into dangerous waters. You know my views. I can't let it crash onto the rocks without trying to save it. There are too many people out there who will be badly hurt if things go wrong."

"But Nigroup is doing well. Andy is doing a fantastic job. He has built up the group and will continue to do so. Everyone admires him for it. I admire him."

"We are simply taking too much risk. We may get away with it, but we may not. We will only know some time in the future. But it is not my job to gamble with other people's money. I must do well with it and we have done that, but now things have got out of hand. I know that markets do not go up forever, and we are not positioned to survive a fall."

"You're far too conservative! Look at Andy. He is bold and aggressive, and see what he has achieved and is still doing. He has read the markets correctly. He is a winner, while you are a loser. See where he is, and see where your conservatism has got you. You think that you are being prudent. He thinks you are negative, and I agree. You might think you are full of courage to be fighting this personal war, to be marching to your own drum, but you are only pulling yourself down, and I don't want to fall with you."

22

Tony was fortunate to have, in his running, an interest away from work and home. He was also very fortunate to have the love and support of Mary while at work, and of Sylvia in the evenings and sometimes on Saturdays and Sundays. Together they sustained him and helped to keep him sane and motivated.

On most evenings Tony and Sylvia ran with their training group, or in the Tuesday time trials, but on Fridays they often ran alone together. For many, Friday evening was a social time and Friday a resting day from running, but Tony was loath to take it as a regular rest day for himself as he knew that he could always be robbed of other training days by work commitments. So he tended to take those lost days as running rest days and work his own training around them. As there were few runners at the Club on Friday evenings, Tony and Sylvia could go out together and simply enjoy one another's company. These Friday runs were always very relaxed and casual, at the end of a week of hard work and solid training. They usually ran along the river and relaxed. They enjoyed the coming of the coolness of the evening, the lessening of the light as the lengthening shadows drew together into dusk, the stream with its rapids and pools and sandbanks, the darkening of the green of the grass and trees, and the birds hurriedly preparing for rest. They could speak or not as they wished. Silence was always comfortable between them. It was lovely simply to be together, in perfect trust and harmony, as the tensions of the day seeped away and relaxation crept in.

On Sundays, Sylvia and Tony had no formal arrangements unless they were going to a race together. Family or social commitments made any such arrangements impractical. Also hard training was done on Sunday mornings and they trained separately. Sylvia frequently ran in the organised Club runs, but Sunday was one of the days when Tony usually trained on his own, doing what he felt he needed purely for his own running, without having to adapt to the needs of his group. However, each of them occasionally did have an easy extra run on a Sunday evening, perhaps to escape from tensions at home in Tony's case, to cover a few extra kilometres, to enjoy the beauty of the evening, or simply in the hope of meeting one another. Out of that they developed an arrangement that, for any Sunday evening run, they would go to Delta Park so they might meet. They had a four kilometre circuit there which they often used, and they arranged that one would always run clockwise, and the other anti-clockwise, around it on such evenings in order to improve their chances of meeting.

One Sunday evening Tony was nearing the end of the circuit, and was concluding that Sylvia would not be there that evening, when he was delighted to see her running towards him.

"I'm tired, but I so wanted to see you," said Sylvia as she neared him. "Which way shall we go? Let's not go far. I had a hard run this morning, then marked English essays till I fell asleep. I was hoping you'd be here. I need your company."

Tony turned around to retrace his steps and join her in the direction she had been going. They jogged slowly and chatted, both glad they had met that evening. They soon came to the top dam which Tony called their Dream Dam and where they had first met. The surface was very calm and was given the illusion of depth by the long, clear reflections of the tall trees all around it. It did, indeed, look like a scene from a mid-summer night's dream. They stopped there, as they often did, to take in its beauty. Two coots floated gently on the water, but the Egyptian geese, now a family with six growing youngsters, were on the bank and took to the water as the two humans approached. A tall grey heron stood silently next to a clump of reeds but did not move. Tony and Sylvia crossed the stream above the dam, jogged along the other side and followed the little river down the hill as it filled a series of smaller dams. They left it at the bottom of the hill and ran along an open grassy area to what they called 'Our Garden'.

That had possibly once been the garden attached to a prosperous home, but it had been incorporated to form a little corner of the park. There was always a cool, friendly gloom under the canopy of the tall old trees. Numerous yellow woods had been planted, one day to replace the pines and other non-indigenous trees, but they were still small. The flowerbeds were full of greenery, but with many bulbs which flowered at different times. A complex of little twisting paths wound through the garden. In a clearing there was a lawn with a bench or two, and in another a little pond with water lilies and a small fountain where Sylvia and Tony always paused for a few moments. For whenever they were near this almost secret place it drew them inside. So they would stop running and step into the hushed coolness under the canopy. It was natural to hold hands and to walk in a kind of wonder along the winding paths until one took them out on the other side. Then they would resume their run, somehow always calmed and soothed in body and in soul.

Tonight, when they emerged from 'their' Garden, they decided not to run any further. They walked back to where they had parked their cars by the most direct route, crossing the lower dam wall, then walking up the hill beside a long line of poplar trees, enjoying the ever-widening views as they climbed.

The parking area was quiet when they reached their cars. Most of the Sunday evening walkers and their dogs had gone home. Having put on his tracksuit, Tony sat on the low log fence that separated the car park from the park itself. He watched as Sylvia pulled her tracksuit trousers over her long, smooth thighs. She arranged her clothing, and pushed a hand through her hair to tidy it. On an impulse she sat down, facing him and astride his thighs. He felt her oh so close to him and her breath softly on his face as she spoke. Their intimacy was emphasized by the enfolding dusk.

They were alone, and soon it was dark. It was time to go. They held each other in a last embrace, kissed, and went to their cars.

23

The glorious highveld summer continued and so did the runners' training. Sore muscles, niggling tendons, aching knees, blackened toenails and general fatigue were now commonplace and had to be dealt with. The trick was successfully to walk (or run) the tightrope between training hard and breaking down. Some found it difficult to push as hard as necessary in the tougher sessions. However, the more highly motivated found it difficult to ease back on the planned easier days, to take rest days, or to hold back when the warning signs were flashing that injury was imminent if excessively hard training or racing continued. A high degree of sophistication was needed to find the correct balance. Some never acquired it, others did and succeeded, while yet others were learning, from their mentors or by making sometimes costly errors.

Tony was trying to help his runners to find and follow the balanced approach. Some, like Sylvia and Josh and Sipho, were content to follow his advice closely. However, he was worried about Melanie who was probably training too hard and was in danger of pushing herself over the brink. She was also tending to pull Bill along with her as they now often trained together. Old Fred was a good example, whenever he joined them, for his long experience had taught him to be wise and balanced in his build-up. Without that he would probably not have survived so long in running. He could also give advice when needed, and he helped them to cover the training kilometres more easily by entertaining them with stories from the past. He told of races won and lost, of close finishes and amusing incidents, particularly from the Comrades Marathon and its history, which he loved so much and of which he was so much a part.

"The very first Comrades was run in 1921 with only thirty-four starters and sixteen finishers. It was a down run. The winner was Bill Rowan, in just under nine hours, but conditions then were very difficult as much of the course was on rough dirt roads. The race was the idea of Vic Clapham, who was an engine driver in the South African Railways. He fought in the First World War and afterwards had the idea of such a race, partly to remember the spirit of comradeship amongst the soldiers in the war. The race was held initially under the auspices of an ex-servicemen's organisation called The League of Comrades of the Great War, hence the name Comrades Marathon."

As the runners became more fatigued, so they found it more difficult to maintain their pace and form. Tony suggested they concentrate on rhythm, fluency and relaxation.

"I like to concentrate on my rhythm," he said. "I align the rhythm of my breathing with the rhythm of my running, of my legs and arms. I learn to know the rhythm of the speed I want to run, and try to maintain it even as I grow more tired. Simply concentrating on that takes the mind away from how tired or sore one is feeling and helps one to keep going at the right speed. The danger is to tense up and so waste energy by fighting to move one's own tense muscles. So I also tell myself to be relaxed and fluent in my running. I say 'relaxed, fluent, rhythm' to myself. I repeat it over and over again, while trying to do just that – relax, flow along with no unwanted movements to waste energy or throw me off balance, and run rhythmically.

"Why don't you try it? Like this. Two steps to each word. 'Re-laxed flu-ent rhy-thm re-laxed flu-ent rhy-thm…'"

One Thursday they were doing a fartlek session along the river and in Delta Park. The slower runners had just caught up as the faster ones had walked through the tall eucalyptus trees below Tony's and Sylvia's 'Our Garden'. Tony was giving instructions.

"OK, we're going to cross the road, then as soon as we hit the grass we're going to do a long fast effort down to the little bridge. That's very fast downhill. But then we're going to cross the bridge and carry on uphill for a couple of hundred metres. Try and maintain the effort all the way. Let's go."

He ignored the chorus of moans and groans as he stepped off the road and accelerated over the grass. He startled a number of hadedas, which flew off in all directions with an ear-splitting chorus of protest.

"Ha! Ha-ha-ha! Ha! Ha! Ha-de-da! Ha…"

Tony stopped, laughing. He turned to the other runners who also stopped.

"They sound just like you lot. What a bunch of moaners and groaners! You're just like a lot of hadedas."

They all laughed as they watched the large grey birds fly away, still complaining and calling insults to the runners.

"Maybe that's what we should call ourselves," said someone. "I would like to move like that." The birds were already some way away and were swinging off into the distance. "It's better than Tony's Toddlers or the Housewives' League or whatever else they call us."

There was a chorus of assent, and so they became the Hadedas. Someone later had the idea of printing T-shirts with an emblem of the bird on the chest, and they wore them proudly.

Tony was aware that, particularly in the context of the Comrades Marathon, some of the Hadedas were unhappy that they were looked down upon by many who considered themselves to be more serious runners. Good-natured chaffing was not a problem, but some of the more fanatical runners at the Club made it clear that they thought the Comrades ambitions of the Hadedas to be a joke. They could simply not be taken seriously, and Tony was doing his charges a disservice by leading them towards Comrades ambitions. The fact that Tony's relatively easy Monday and Thursday sessions still included his mainly social non-Comrades runners reinforced that view, as did their long-time designation of Tony's Toddlers.

Amongst the more 'dedicated', 'serious' and fanatical runners there was much talk, and not a little boasting, about the high distances they were clocking up in training, daily, weekly and monthly. Many were racing well and to them that proved the correctness of their programmes. The Hadedas heard and observed, and some had niggling doubts, about their own abilities, whether they were doing the right training, and whether they should be racing more. Was Tony right? Was he well meaning but badly out of step? Two or three moved away to run 'more seriously'.

Little incidents highlighted these things. One afternoon Tony and some of the Hadedas were setting out for a run. They saw Johan and Simon, a couple who were training for their first Comrades Marathon, also setting out onto the road to train.

"Come and join us," invited Tony.

"How far are you going?"

"About ten K's."

"No, we want to do some real training, probably fifteen or sixteen. Bye."

Of course, Tony also had the example of Andy always before him. Andy boasted continually of the distances he was doing in training, the races he was running and the times he was achieving.

"Mind you don't overdo it," cautioned Tony. "There's still a long time before Comrades."

"Huh! You're just as wet and conservative in running as you are in investments. Wait until the race and we'll see who's right."

Tony urged his runners not to be affected by all of this. He emphasised that quantity was not all. Quality was important, as well as how one planned one's running and racing and resting. It was also necessary to proceed from where one was to where one wanted to be, in running training as in life. His runners did not have the years of training background and build-up which allowed the top runners to cope with the great distances and speeds they ran. His Hadedas would simply break down if they tried to do too much too soon. It was important to keep focussed on their goals. For the Comrades Marathon there were three main ones: to qualify, to get to the start well prepared, healthy and fresh, and to complete the race as fast as possible and in good form. Without good sense his charges would not achieve these. Some might not even reach the start. Some might start and not finish. They could fail to climb their own personal Everests, which loomed before them in the shape of the Comrades Marathon, now only three months away.

24

The warm summer weather, with its clear bright mornings, afternoon thunderstorms and glorious sunsets, continued into March. The runners still enjoyed or coped with the conditions as they changed during the course of each day. On the whole they were fortunate to be blessed with such a wonderful climate, but, as the year neared and then passed the equinox, they noticed that daylight came later each morning and the evenings were closing in earlier than before. Soon they would be training increasingly in darkness. However, at the beginning of the month the Comrades hopefuls amongst the Hadedas, with the exception of Sylvia who would qualify later, were all tapering off their training in the last few days before the Vaal Marathon on 10th March.

Tony's training was progressing reasonably well, but he continued to be troubled by problems at work. No real effort had been made to address the concerns he had expressed about Nilife, the group's life insurance company, but he faced increased hostility from some quarters because of the stand he had taken. Share prices continued to be firm, and that of Enduring Bank was now even more expensive. Tony had been refused permission to realise some profits, by selling some of Nilife's shares in Enduring, as that was regarded as a strategic investment. Meanwhile, to Tony, all the classic signs of a stock market bubble were there. Shares were now trading on very expensive ratings that suggested that investors believed that companies would increase profits annually by enormous percentages for decades to come. There were increasing numbers of highly priced new issues onto the Stock Exchange, as well as large numbers of takeovers and mergers and other corporate activities, which provided business for merchant banks such as Enduring and legal work for firms such as Merchant Attorneys. Even more worrying was that great numbers of people usually far removed from the financial markets, clerks and hairdressers, typists and factory workers, were professing to be experts on shares, and were risking their small savings, or borrowing money, to buy expensive shares on the Stock Exchange. Nora was unsympathetic and appeared to be very busy. She worked long hours and was often away until late at night. Tony was continually thankful to have Mary and Sylvia in his life.

Sylvia was training well, but accumulating fatigue made it more difficult to deal with the stresses of teaching and of a school term which would only close towards the end of March. However, she was seeing Tony regularly and was happy to be part of the long build-up to Comrades.

Melanie was very busy at the bank where she worked, as so many of her clients wanted to benefit from the stock market boom by putting money into equity unit trusts or insurance funds investing in shares. She heard Tony's cautious views, but was not sure whether he was right. Share prices continued to rise, and there were few cautioning words coming from the bank's investment experts. In any event it would have been difficult to instil caution into determined would-be investors who would simply take their money to the rival institution across the road if they were not satisfied.

Melanie had to fight more than usual fatigue as she coped with her work, for she was training very hard. She listened to Tony's advice and then did more than he suggested. She was all too aware of the huge distances some of her club mates were doing in training, and she remembered how fanatically David had trained during these months before Comrades. Certainly, he had had many more years of training to build on, but she feared that Tony, on the other hand, might be a little too cautious. So she did extra training when and as she could as a kind of insurance. She could not fail David, she kept telling herself. She was also planning to run the 56km Two Oceans ultra-marathon in Cape Town at Easter, as David had always done. To qualify for that race she would need a standard marathon time of less than 4 hours 15 minutes, which was even faster than she needed for Comrades. However, her training was now often made to feel easier by the presence of Bill, who appeared to be growing fond of her, and who seemed to enjoy running with her.

Melanie had certainly brought an added dimension and a new joy into Bill's life. She was beautiful and attractive and he increasingly enjoyed her company. While she did not give him great encouragement, she was certainly happy to train with him, and they liked having a drink or a chat afterwards. It helped Bill's own training to be able to look forward to, and to have, attractive and interesting company during the long hours of running. He felt more and more that he was leaving his past life, particularly his operation and his marriage, behind him, and that new ways were opening before him. He was growing fitter by the week, he had a developing friendship with Melanie, and his job was continuing with no sign of his contract coming to an end. His employer had even shown interest in the fact that Bill was preparing to enter the gruelling Comrades Marathon.

Josh was also training well. He made a point of going to the Club for Tuesday time trials if at all possible. Occasionally he also went there on other evenings, when his pastoral duties permitted, but it was easier for him to train in the early mornings when his time was still his own to command. Sipho sometimes shared these morning runs, but they always ran together on Saturdays when they did their long weekly training runs. It helped to have company to make the long distances less lonely.

Josh was also growing more and more excited about the fund-raising Comrades Project. Plans were developing well, though it seemed that more support would be apparent once Josh had actually qualified to enter the Comrades Marathon. His qualifying race, near Pretoria on Saturday, 9th March, was therefore very important. Sipho had been adopted into the Project, and plans were advanced to raise sponsorships related to his Comrades run as well. A local businessman, who had recently joined the congregation, had donated a small family motor car as the first prize in a competition which was being planned. Entrants would need to forecast the time that Josh would take to complete the race on 31st May. With such an attractive prize, tickets could be extensively sold, and arrangements were being made for sister congregations around the country to be involved as well. Tickets would be printed as soon as Josh had completed his qualifying race. In addition, Josh's finance and fund-raising committee had suggested that certain of the already accumulated Church funds, that were waiting on deposit, should be placed in shares listed on the Stock Exchange to benefit from the ever rising prices. This had been done and Josh was now eagerly watching the business pages of the newspapers each day to see the value of these investments growing.

Sipho felt more and more accepted in his new home. He was trusted and liked by Josh and Maria, by the Minister and his wife. He was contributing to the Church by his work, and soon would be part of the fund-raising Project. He was also becoming known to many of the congregation who appreciated and responded to his cheery smiles. He usually went to the Club with Josh on Tuesday evenings, but somehow managed to get there to run with Tony on many other evenings as well. Often he ran the seven kilometres or so to the Club and then also ran with the other Hadedas. Usually he refused when Tony invited him to join them for a drink after the run. Tony was never sure what he did or whom he met while they had their drink, but when Tony was ready to go, Sipho would suddenly materialise before him and ask for a lift home. Although it took him a few kilometres out of his way Tony was always glad to oblige.

25

Tony had just returned from an early morning meeting with the Trustees of a large pension fund whose investments were managed by the Nigroup Investment Division. He stopped as he reached Mary's desk, next to his own office. She paused in what she was doing and looked up at his approach. They greeted each other warmly, for they had not yet seen one another that morning. Tony noted that she was dressed in a lovely royal blue, which enhanced the deep blue of her eyes. As usual she seemed to exude calm and cheeriness at the same time.

"How did it go?" she asked.

"Very well. It was a good meeting. They're very pleased with what we are doing."

"Are you feeling strong?"

"Why?"

"I had a call from Jane. Andy is speaking at a business conference tonight. He wants a whole lot of economic and investment stuff for his speech, by lunchtime. Last minute as usual. I wonder how long he's known about this engagement."

"Damn! There go my plans for today."

"I gave the details to Joe. He's already working on the economic part."

"Well done. Surely Andy could have given us a little more time."

"I hear that he'll be rehearsing his speech with Gillian this afternoon in the auditorium." Gillian was Andy's speech and voice coach.

"Well I'd better get together with Joe at once. Try to keep us from being interrupted until we've finished this job."

Later, with Andy's speech having been attended to, Tony again passed Mary on his way back from the office of Joe, the economist.

"It's not your day," said Mary. "Rita wants to see you. She's very upset. Andy's been shouting at her."

Tony turned around and went to the dealing room, where the dealers in the various financial markets, equities, bonds, money market and the like, sat in front of their computers and traded, mainly on behalf of Nigroup's clients. Rita was the chief equity dealer, and very astute and competent at her work.

"What's wrong, Rita?" asked Tony as he entered the busy room. "Do you want to come to my office or can we talk here?"

"It's OK, I've calmed down a bit now," she replied, though Tony could see that she was still flushed and somewhat upset. "But I still think you should know that Andy has been screaming at me. I mean that literally. He phoned me and gave me absolute hell because our share price is down. He phoned early this morning to say he wanted it to close at 550 or better today. Apparently he's giving a speech tonight, and you know how he likes to boast about the share price performance. He said that Noel at Enduring would be buying and I was to watch the market. Then later he saw on his screen that the price was down to 540. He phoned and screamed at me. What the hell was going on? He'd given instructions, and so on. I'm sorry to trouble you, Tony, but you know we can get into serious trouble if we try to manipulate the share price. I found that Noel did have some orders to fulfil, but then sellers came in and the price is still at 540. It's not the first time this has happened. All Andy seems to worry about is the share price."

"Thank you for letting me know. I'll talk to him about it. I learnt, and I'm sure you did, that if we look after the business the share price will look after itself. Try not to let it upset you. If it happens again, be polite and let me know. Of course we can't manipulate the share price. Your job is to execute genuine, legitimate orders only. Make sure you know their origin and that they are properly documented, even if they come from Andy. If you are not sure of anything, call me at once."

26

"I remember my mother telling me that it was dangerous to drink when you were hot from exercising. Some runners also believed that and ran, even long races, without drinking."

Fred had joined the Hadedas for a drink after sharing their evening run. They were all in the Club's small bar, which Tony and his group now called the Hadeda Bar as they frequented it so often. Appropriately enough they were talking about drinking, about what to drink on the run, and Fred was reminiscing about the past.

"When I first started marathon running," he continued, "you were not allowed to drink in a race before you had run ten miles, that's sixteen K's. After that you were only allowed to drink every five miles. Nowadays we have drinks tables every three K's and the scientists are telling us to be sure to drink a litre of fluid every hour. The old-timers used to mix their own special concoctions. Arthur Newton, who still rates as one of the greatest of all long distance runners, used to add lots of sugar and a little salt to tea, or sometimes to lemonade. Today there's so much advice, and so many products on the market, it's quite confusing."

"We're trying to keep it simple," said Tony. "Water and Coke are provided at the drinks tables, so we drink a 'half and half' mixture of the two. We can vary the proportions if necessary, like taking more Coke towards the end of a race if we need extra carbohydrate. It works quite well and we don't have to carry sachets of corn syrup or whatever with us."

"I'm not sure about this litre an hour business," said Fred. "I've tried to be careful to drink that much. The scientists should know after all. But I found that I was wasting a lot of time passing water in the bushes beside the road. Also, last year near the end of the Korkie ultra-marathon I was on my hands and knees puking pure water. I've cut back again to between half and three-quarters of a litre an hour, depending of course, on the weather conditions and whether I feel thirsty. I'm sure the scientists will one day find out that it's possible to drink too much."

"I've had similar experiences and have come to the same conclusions," agreed Tony. "It's essential not to become dehydrated, especially in hot conditions, but I've also heard of one or two cases recently of slower runners becoming very ill by apparently drinking too much. It also seems that Newton and the old-timers were right about needing to replace salt lost in sweat in very long runs. I understand that it's to do with the proper regulation of the level of body fluids. In my experience, salt also plays a part in relation to certain types of cramp, although I know that the scientists are not quite sure about that as yet. For Comrades we'll each carry some salt tablets in case we need to top up."

Of course what to drink on the run was only one of the many things that the Hadedas were learning and thinking about as they graduated into long distance running and began to focus on what was, for most of them, their first marathon.

"What should we eat?"

"Basically what your body tells you it wants. Emphasise carbohydrates in your diet in the three days before a race."

"What shoes are best for me?"

"Buy the best you can afford with the advice of an expert at a reputable specialist running shoe shop."

"What clothing?"

"Club colours, of course, in a race. But cool and comfortable, and nothing that chafes. For ladies, also a good sports bra to control breast motion and prevent discomfort or injury."

They also learnt to settle all details before any important race, so that experimentation was done only in training or in unimportant races. They also discussed matters such as 'tapering' or reducing training before important races, pre-race routines, race strategies and pace judgement while they prepared themselves to qualify for the Comrade Marathon.

27

After all the preparation, the excitement and nervous apprehension, qualifying was almost an anti-climax.

Josh and Sipho drove to Pretoria very early on the Saturday morning for their marathon race on the western outskirts of the city. As with the other Hadedas, they understood that the qualifying race was to be only that. They were to start slowly, maintain a steady pace and be sure to finish inside 4hrs 30min. They were to have a good solid run, but were not to race all out unless for some reason they needed to in order to finish under the qualifying time. With hundreds of others they set off in the early morning coolness. They started comfortably enough together, and helped one another to keep going as the journey grew long and the day became uncomfortably warm. Tony and Sylvia drove to the finish to show their support, and Tony was delighted when Josh and Sipho entered the finishing area, still side by side, to finish with nearly twenty minutes to spare. They were tired and sweaty, but very happy with their efforts. Josh was already preparing to inform his congregation and the fund-raising committee that they had qualified and that the Comrades Project could go ahead. Tony drove home glad that the first two of his charges had safely qualified.

Road races were usually run in the early mornings, in order to avoid as much as possible of the heat of the day, with its inherent dangers in prolonged, intense physical activity.

When Tony's alarm clock went off at three-thirty on Sunday morning he thought how uncivilized their sport could be. He was planning a solid but not all out performance, but as always he followed his pre-race routine. At home that involved being awake for about forty-five minutes before leaving for the event. That gave him time to wash, shave and put on his running clothes and shoes. He would also have something to drink and have a light 'breakfast', which for him consisted of a high carbohydrate liquid meal such as Sustagen, and for others might include fruit and/or toast and honey. It was also important for him to wake up sufficiently for his bowels to work, so he would not need to queue up to use usually scarce toilet facilities at the race venue. Soon after arriving at the venue, he would attend to the formalities of entering or registering for the race. Then he would spend time warming up, which had its own routine adapted to the conditions, and which included jogging, stretching, faster running and finally relaxing just before the start. All the while his mental focus narrowed until everything was excluded except his concentration on the race itself.

This morning he left a sleeping Nora and made his way out into the early morning darkness. The race would start at six o'clock and there was an hour to travel to Vereeniging to the south of Johannesburg. He picked up a sleepy Sylvia, who was waiting outside her front gate, and they set off. Sylvia was to enter the race, but cover only about thirty-two kilometres in a training run using the refreshment points along the route.

Tony saw Bill and Melanie in the throng of runners as they moved towards the starting point. The two were planning to run together and hoped to finish in less than 4hrs 15min so Melanie could qualify for both the Two Oceans and the Comrades Marathons. He saw Fred, chattering away to old friends, and looking forward to his first marathon since his foot operation. There were also a number of others in the sky blue colours of the White Waters Running Club.

There was much excitement as some two thousand runners were set off on their way by the firing of an old cannon, which had been brought there for the purpose. With ears ringing, those in front got off to a fast start, while those behind began to walk, then to shuffle, to jog and finally to run at their planned racing pace. Tony had just begun to run when he found himself pushed aside as a runner in the red, white and blue of the Sandown Runners Club thrust himself between Tony and another runner. It was Andy, in a hurry.

"Probably arrived late," thought Tony, but he ignored his boss who disappeared into the crowd ahead of him. Tony was not there to race, but to have a good sustained run. If Andy finished in front of him so be it. There was a more important contest to come at the end of May.

The course was pleasant and fairly flat, winding along tree-lined suburban roads and through treeless open country. Tony set a relaxed pace, which he maintained throughout, to finish comfortably in just over three hours. Andy had finished about ten minutes before him. When Tony congratulated him, Andy was tired but clearly gloating over another personal best time, and victory over Tony and certain other rivals.

After a quick drink Tony made his way to his car and then drove back along the route to pick up Sylvia, who would have started walking at the thirty kilometre mark and who would be looking out for him. They shouted encouragement to friends and club mates they saw along the route, especially to Bill and to Melanie who were wet and hot and appeared to be tiring. Tony and Sylvia returned to the finishing stadium, for they could not coach runners from a moving car, and watched the remainder of the race, mentally ticking off the names of their running friends as they came in to finish. Fred arrived safely in about 4hrs 10min, shuffling along in his characteristic, slightly stooping style. Tony grew anxious as the quarter hour approached, for he knew Melanie wanted to finish before then. However, just as his watch read 4hrs 13min 30sec, Melanie's short, curvaceous, blue-clad figure hove into view, with a taller figure in blue in the shape of Bill a metre or two behind. Melanie looked serene and confident as she strode around the stadium track to finish just fifteen seconds under her 4hrs 15min target. When Tony complimented her on how well she looked in the finishing straight, she remarked:

"You only have to look good when you start and when you finish. Nobody's there to notice in between."

There was much happiness amongst the Hadedas as all their Comrades hopefuls, except for Sylvia as planned, had now qualified. They had done so relatively comfortably, but they had all been very tired at the end of their qualifying marathons. After the initial euphoria of finishing had worn off, their unanimous reaction was:

"Whew! I am so tired. How will I be able to run twice as far, and then still go on for a few more kilometres?"

28

For most of the Hadedas the week after qualifying was scheduled as a 'play' week. It was a time to recover from the worst of the fatigue and soreness of their marathon runs, and a time to relax mentally after the intense focus on qualifying. After a day or two of rest, they did begin to train again, but easily and light-heartedly, assisting the body and the mind to recover rather than applying stress. Some began by walking for a day or two. Some jogged gently in pleasant surroundings enjoying one another's company. On Thursday evening most came to join Tony's regular run, knowing that it would be playful and relaxed.

The talk in the Hadeda Bar afterwards naturally turned towards their future training. Tony had of course discussed individual plans with each of his Comrades runners, but the basic principles were the same. After this easy week they would begin a period of eight weeks of hard training, which would be followed by about three weeks of tapering towards the big day. In a sense the really hard running was about to begin. There would be an increasing emphasis on distance, but the build-up would be sensible and their other training principles would not be forgotten. They would still regularly do faster running to avoid becoming one-paced and to maintain leg speed. The 'hard-easy' principle, where a relatively hard session or week would be followed by a relatively easier one, would still be followed. However, a lot of training would be done at their respective planned Comrades Marathon running speeds, in order to accustom their bodies specifically to the future demands to be made upon them in the race. With the increasing training loads they would gradually be assuming, it remained vital to listen to one's body, to avoid breaking down into injury or illness if at all possible, and to reduce the load or even rest if necessary. Tony warned that setbacks could occur, and that work or other demands could intrude, so that their running programmes should be flexible enough to adapt to any problems as they arose.

It was clear, however, that some were still troubled by the question of how they would manage the huge step up from the standard marathon of 'only' 42.2km to the Comrades Marathon of around 88km. They had felt really tired at the end of the marathon.

"Are we going to run an ultra?"

Ultra-marathons are those long distance races that are longer than the standard marathon. Several, usually between fifty and sixty kilometres, were held around the country during this period, many as preliminaries to the Comrades Marathon but some with their own special qualities and traditions.

"I'm not planning that," said Tony. "We only have a few weeks left and I think we would do better without one. To run an ultra soon would involve a short taper, the physical and mental demands of the race, and then some sort of recovery before heavy training could resume. The main benefit would be in knowing that you had run more than 42km, but even 56, for example, is still a long way off the Comrades distance."

"Most people say you should do at least one ultra before Comrades."

"I know. But there are many ways to train, and to prepare for Comrades, and many of them work successfully. Some have more volume and less quality. Some advocate running several marathons and ultras. Some people have more time to train, and more years of running behind them, than most of us here. One needs to be faithful to the method one is following. If you follow me, please trust me. I have proved that it is not necessary to run an ultra."

"Fordyce does."

"Yes, but he has great talent, and years of hard training behind him to support what he is now doing. Also, watch carefully and you'll see that he's not racing hard. He is training, not running flat out, even when he is running times which most of us only dream of doing. He'll be ready for a full effort on Comrades Day."

"Do you think he'll win?"

"Yes, unless someone else of equal potential trains as cleverly as he does. He'll get to the start fit, but relatively fresh and not over-raced as so many others will be. They will not beat him until they learn to do as he does, which he even teaches in his book and elsewhere."

"But how will we do ninety K's without having raced further than forty-two?"

"Remember how easily you ran forty-two when you'd not gone further than thirty-two before? Remember how you also finished in front of some of the 'serious' distance runners who'd done much bigger training volumes?"

"Yes, I remember passing Johan and Simon, who wouldn't train with us because they wanted to do some 'real training'. They couldn't believe it."

"I passed Ken and Kobus at thirty-five K's and had the same reaction," continued Tony. "Also Beth, who was looking very tired. Victor was trying to pull her along to help win the ladies' team prize. They think we don't train, but we do. But we also need to train sensibly and do what is best for us as we are now. If we try to train like a Fordyce or an Alan Robb, we will simply break down.

"Remember too that our training has a cumulative effect. That is what most people forget. Soon you will run for four hours or more on a Sunday morning. On Monday you'll have an easy day, but by Tuesday when you tackle the time trial, and possibly more, you will still not be recovered from Sunday's run. So it'll go on. We'll be carrying a lot of fatigue, and will still be running. Our problem will not be to do enough. Our problem will be to avoid doing too much, to avoid breaking down.

"Then don't forget that we'll also taper off our training before the big race. We'll take the pressure off and allow our bodies to recover. We'll arrive at the start both fresh and well prepared. We will also set our sights, or perhaps I should say our minds, so we'll be prepared for the distance. Our bodies will be ready and so will our minds. We'll be able to run all day if necessary."

29

Bill and Melanie had been for quite a long evening run together. They had the pleasant lazy feeling that came with relaxed minds and fatigued bodies after a solid but not too hard training session. They had bought drinks in the clubhouse and had taken them outside as the evening was pleasant. They were now sitting some way from the buildings, on a bench under a fine spreading pin oak tree looking out across the deserted main field. The air was soft and cool after another hot day, and a gentle breeze played with Melanie's honey-coloured hair. A squadron of hadedas called stridently from a distance as they flew to roost. In the evening light the place had a pleasant feeling of intimacy. The sound of talking and laughter from the terrace seemed far away, but their own conversation was kept private by their relative seclusion and by the sound of the river rushing over rocks behind them.

As they talked and sipped their drinks, Melanie realised that, almost unconsciously, they had sat close to each other, and they were now leaning shoulder to shoulder in an unselfconscious gently intimate way. It was a pleasant, comfortable feeling.

"What about your wife?" asked Melanie softly. "You've never said anything about her. Aren't you being unfaithful, being so close to another woman?"

"Yes, I am still married, but in name only. Our divorce should be final very soon. She really gave up on me quite a long time ago."

"What happened?"

"Although we shared some good times, I don't think she was ever really in love with me, certainly not after we had been married for a few months. She left me after my operation, when I was made redundant. But the signs had been there for a long time, so it probably would have happened sooner or later."

He paused for a long while, deep in thought, before he continued.

"We waited until we were married to make love in the fullest sense. But somehow she never really seemed to be interested, and that became a problem for me too. It's something one doesn't usually talk about, but there are things I will never understand. You can try so hard to make a woman, this one at any rate, feel wonderful, but she still finds it too much trouble to reciprocate, or even to be available to be made to feel wonderful again. Now is never a good time for her, but at bedtime she's tired, or not feeling well, or there's some other excuse. You mentioned fidelity. There are many ways of being unfaithful in a marriage. You don't only swear to forsake all others when you marry. It seems so easy sometimes to forget your promise 'to have and to hold, to love and to cherish', yet the other party is the one condemned as guilty if he or she looks for comfort outside of the marriage."

"And did you seek such comfort?"

"No, although it was a temptation. I did feel imprisoned though, so I'm glad it has ended."

"Poor Bill. David and I were always wonderfully close, in all ways. That's why I miss him so much. I'm sure he didn't feel trapped or imprisoned. Sometimes in peak training he was rather too tired to think about love-making, but we never had any problems."

They sat silently for a long while, thinking their own thoughts as the gentle evening drew in around them. Then Bill turned towards her, put an arm around her shoulders and a hand on her knee.

"It feels so good to be together. I would like to be very close to you, in every way," he said.

Melanie kissed him softly on the mouth and then withdrew herself a little.

"I feel good too, for the first time, in this way, since David died. I like being with you, and who knows where we will end up? But for the time being let's just continue to be friends. Good friends. I can't go any further at present. You see, I have not yet finished with David. Of course I will always remember and cherish him, but there's more. I promised him I would run his tenth Comrades for him, and until I've kept my promise I can't let him go. Please understand. Let's run together and enjoy each other's company as friends. Then after Comrades let us see how things stand."

She stood up as a cool gust ruffled her hair. He could just see her face, and her appealing soft eyes, in the dim light.

"Of course I understand," he said as they turned towards the clubhouse.

30

As often now happened, Old Fred was helping them over the long, weary kilometres of training. The time always seemed to pass more quickly, and the distances seemed shorter, as they listened to him.

"Of course, the Comrades Marathon has many characters, and there are many interesting stories about them and their races. But my favourite Comrades story is probably of Bill Payn's run in the 1922 Comrades. That was only the second Comrades Marathon, and the very first up run. I met Bill at the D.H.S. (that's Durban High School) Old Boys' Club in Durban a few times. He was a wonderful man, with a great sense of humour and a love of words and their origins. He fought in both World Wars, and was a schoolmaster at D.H.S. for four decades. He was a large man, and a famous rugby player. His Comrades run is almost legend, and I was fortunate to hear him tell the story in his own words.

"He said that there was a huge field that year, as shown by the fact that he wore number 111. But not all those who entered actually started, as usual, and I believe only 26 eventually finished. The cut-off time was twelve hours. Bill says the first thing he realised was that running gave him an almighty thirst, so he was not able to refuse anyone who offered him something to drink. He ran in rugby boots, and at Hillcrest his feet were already blistering. Someone gave him some hair oil, which he smeared on his feet. He then went into the hotel and knocked back a huge plate of bacon and eggs.

"Bill carried on to Botha's Hill. At the top he found another runner, named 'Zulu' Wade, sitting down waiting for his supporter (we would say 'second') and looking in bad shape. The second arrived on a motorbike, with a carrier which held a wicker basket. From that he took out a curried chicken, and what Bill called a huge snowdrift of rice. The two runners shared this meal between them, and then, feeling much better, they set off together for Drummond. There they went into the pub to drown their sorrows in beer. One of the race officials found them there and suggested that they get a move on, as there were only five runners ahead of them. Of those, only Arthur Newton was a long way ahead of the field. Zulu was not going any further, so Bill left Drummond alone for Pietermaritzburg.

"Somewhere on the Harrison Flats he saw a frail little woman with pink cheeks who offered him a tumbler full of her own home-made peach brandy. He graciously accepted, but at once realised that he had swallowed a near lethal dose of the rawest liquid he had ever tasted. Fortunately, he was facing Pietermaritzburg, so he continued in the right direction.

"Just after he crossed the Msunduze Bridge in Maritzburg, he was hailed by his wife's family, who were having tea on a veranda beside the road. He joined them for tea and cakes, and, during that time, two other runners overtook him. So it was that he eventually finished in eighth place. His time was 10hrs 56min. His brother-in-law rewarded him with a bottle of champagne to round off his race.

"Bill says his feet were a mass of blisters. The next day he played rugby for his Old Collegians club team, but he had to play in tackies, tennis shoes, because his feet were so sore."

31

The Pieter Korkie Memorial ultra marathon was being run on 24th March, so there were no standard marathons in the greater Johannesburg area that weekend. So very early on Saturday, 23rd March, Tony and Sylvia drove out into the country and entered themselves for a standard marathon there. Sylvia had had a good six week build-up, and a week's tapering, since her decision to run the Comrades Marathon, and it was now time for her to attempt her first and, she hoped, qualifying marathon. They were joined by other Hadedas who felt that they had recovered sufficiently from their own qualifying marathons to use the country marathon for a long training run with good company and refreshment stations along the way. Josh and Sipho came, as did Bill with Melanie, who wanted to use the race as a last long training run before the Two Oceans Marathon in two weeks' time. By arrangement they ran as a 'bus', a group, driven by Tony with the aim of finishing just inside the Comrades qualifying time of 4hrs 30min. Tony was concerned that Sylvia was not yet ready to go much faster (some cynics at the Club felt that she had no hope at all of qualifying), and the slow pace would be suitable for the others for training purposes.

The early morning was fairly cool and it was only pleasantly warm by midday, the course was interesting and without too many hills, the country people were friendly and encouraging, and Sylvia was touched by the support she had from Tony and her other club mates. For her it was a very long morning and her hardest and longest run yet. However, she was aided by Tony's careful pacing, and, in the first two hours or so, the distraction of good company and cheerful conversation. Her desire to succeed for herself and for Tony was immense, and her concentration intense in the latter stages when she was tired and sore and had to force herself to keep going. She was ecstatic when she stepped onto the grass at the sports ground where the finish was situated and she knew that she would finish with about four minutes to spare. Sylvia was all smiles as she ran the last few hundred metres. Tony was still running beside her, and Josh and Sipho were finishing just ahead of them. Melanie had pulled Bill along a little faster over the last few kilometres, despite Tony's gentle words of caution, and they were waiting at the end and shouting encouragement.

Sylvia threw her arms around Tony and hugged him tightly as soon as they had crossed the finishing line. She was tired and hot and sweaty after the long effort, but there was an inner glow of satisfaction and achievement, which showed on her face and in her eyes, and which remained with her, despite her fatigue, all the way home and into the night.

32

On Monday Tony managed to run a few kilometres alone before meeting his group for their usual training run. Sylvia was recovering from her Saturday marathon and would be having a very easy running week. She had arranged, however, to join him for a drink later, and was indeed waiting for him as the group finished their run. As Tony was putting on his track suit a small dark figure limped past them.

"Hello, Mandla," said Tony. "What's wrong? Did you run Korkie? How did you do?"

"I did run, Tony, but I didn't finish. My Achilles tendon was too sore. I stopped at 39 K's. I was too scared to carry on and do more damage. But it's still very bad. I can't run today."

"Why did you run when you were injured?"

"Mister Pots, Victor, he said I must run for my Club, to help them win the team prize. He wasn't pleased, because I stopped and we didn't win. But I was already battling in the Vaal Marathon, though I did finish and we won that one. It has been hard to train these last few days. I remember you said I must be careful until I was better. Perhaps I should not have tried to run the Korkie, but Victor he says the Club will not help me to go to Comrades if I do not race for them. So I thought it might be OK once I got going, but it was not."

"Perhaps we should have a talk some time, Mandla. Come and have a drink with us."

Mandla Dube was one of the Club's most promising young runners and had already run several good times. He was in his early twenties, and was small, slim, wiry and loose-limbed. He was all grace and fluency when running. He had an oval face with dark eyes, short black hair, a thin moustache and a short straggly beard. Like Sipho, he was born and grew up in a rural area in KwaZulu. He was also fortunate to have attended a nearby mission school for several years. His father had died when Mandla was young, and, after his mother had gone into domestic service in Eshowe, Mandla was looked after mainly by his grandmother. As money and food were scarce, and as there were few jobs to be found in that part of the country, he had eventually left to try to find work on the Witwatersrand, the mining, industrial and commercial area of and around Johannesburg. After scraping a precarious living in various ways, he had at last been fortunate to find steady work as an assistant groundsman at the White Waters Sports Club. His job was to help with the maintenance of the grounds. His wages were very modest, but he was given accommodation in the Club's staff quarters.

Mandla saw the sporting activity continually going on at the Club. He was inspired to try running, which was relatively simple to begin, and which he could fit in around his work. He had run a lot in KwaZulu, not as a sport but as a means of getting from one place to another. He had often run to and from school as a boy, so his running background was good and he soon became fit and showed promise as a runner. He was given encouragement by the runners at the Club and was soon joining in training runs, doing time trials on Tuesday nights, and then racing proudly in the famous sky blue Club colours. He had now been running competitively for nearly three years and was showing real promise. He had begun to finish near the front in some of the road races, helping White Waters to win team trophies and earning small amounts of prize money for himself. He was thus able to supplement his meagre wages in a small way, and hoped that his running would help him to improve himself. He hoped not only for better prize money, which was still very modest in those days, but to become well enough known as a top runner for him to find himself a better job, as a salesman in a running shoe shop, or in a sports company.

Victor and Trixie had made much of Mandla, as an emerging star, and had encouraged him in many ways. However, they were mainly interested in the winning of championships and trophies in the name of the White Waters Running Club, and did not sufficiently take into account the development and other needs of the athlete. Runners were all too often pressured into running races, often with the bait of a free trip to the coast or the countryside, with the aim of winning individual or team prizes for the Club. For Mandla, these pressures from the Club, combined with his need and desire to supplement his income, had inevitably led to his being badly over-raced, and now apparently seriously injured. In less than three months this year, he had already run two hard standard marathons (a 2hrs 24min in January and 2hrs 30min in the recent Vaal Marathon, when he had struggled to finish with an injury), a fast 32km, his abortive 39km of the Korkie, and several half-marathons.

His main aim, however, was to run a good Comrades Marathon, now only just over two months away. This would be his second attempt at the great race. The previous year he had been carried away by the excitement of the occasion, had started at great speed, had run near the front for nearly two hours, and had then faded away badly to finish way down the field. He had been proud to finish, but he had walked most of the second half of the race and it had been a very painful experience. This year he hoped to do much better, but now he was injured and unable to run at all.

Mandla and Tony spoke about all these things, as indeed they had before, most recently after the Vaal Marathon when Tony had warned Mandla against over-racing, and of the desirability of concentrating on his main aims in running.

"Mandla, you now have just over two months before Comrades. I think you will still be able to do well and have a good race, but, if that is still your most important goal, then you will have to be very careful during the next few weeks. The time is short, and in that time you will need to rest and recover from your injury. Then you will have to build up to do some long running without breaking down again, and finally taper down to Comrades so you are fresh when you start your race."

"Will you help me, Tony? I don't have a coach. I'm just copying what I see the others doing."

"I'll help you with pleasure, Mandla, but then you must listen to me and do as I say," responded Tony. "I don't mean that you shouldn't think about what you are doing and change your programme according to how you feel when necessary. But you must understand why we are doing what we will be doing, so you can still be true to what we are trying to achieve."

"I will listen to you."

"Mandla, it won't be easy. First, you will have to stop racing. You have already done too much this year. Your injury is also telling you that. You now need time to recover and prepare for your next big race, which is Comrades. There will be pressure on you to race in other events. Victor and Trixie will want you to run in Club teams. Your friends will try to get you to race, and even to train too much, more than will be right for you at a particular time. You will have to be strong to go your own way. But it will all be worth it if you have the good Comrades that you want."

"I understand. I need a good Comrades."

"OK. First we need to help you to recover from your injury. Ask the barman to give you some ice to put on your heel, several times a day if possible. Make sure you stretch your calf muscles. Tomorrow evening we'll ask Lucy, she's a physiotherapist, to have a look at it and give you some advice.

I'm sure she'll be willing to do that for you. Then how are your shoes?"

"They are just about finished," said Mandla. "I know which ones I need that are the right ones for me. I've been to see Terry who owns the running shop. I've been saving money to buy them. With maybe two more team prizes, I'll have enough. I also asked him to teach me, and to give me a job when he has one."

"We'll go and talk to Terry. I'm sure that between the three of us we'll be able to arrange something about a new pair of shoes for you. Meanwhile I suggest that you rest for a couple of days. Then when you can walk reasonably comfortably, you can start walking on the grass, only as much as you can without hurting your tendon. As soon as it becomes sore you must stop. You'll be able to do a little more each day if all goes well. Keep in touch with me, so we can build a proper programme for you as we see how you improve."

33

At the end of March it was announced to the financial world that a controlling interest in Stella Insurance Limited was up for auction. Stella was part of a larger group which had only recently been taken over by a very substantial company called Growth Financial Holdings Limited, often abbreviated to GFH.

Andrew Duke called a meeting of Nigroup's executive strategy committee the same afternoon. When Tony entered the meeting he found a team from Enduring Bank, who often acted as merchant bankers to Nigroup, as well as Nora and a colleague from Merchant Attorneys, already present. Andy limped in soon after, still suffering from the effects of an arduous run in the Korkie Marathon.

"Of course, we cannot miss an opportunity like this," said Andy as he opened the meeting. "Bids for Stella close on 24th April, which gives us just four weeks. We must certainly put in a bid. The question is at what level, and then how will we pay. I have asked our friends from Enduring and Merchant to be here, so work on our bid can start immediately."

"GFH have just bought Stella. Why are they selling it?" asked Tony.

"They say it's not a core business for their future strategy."

“I hope they did not find something wrong with it after they bought it, and are now passing on the problems. Those guys are quite sharp. We’ll have to do a careful due diligence.”

“They’ll provide all serious potential bidders with what they say is all the necessary information. Hopefully that will be enough to make a decision.”

So the meeting continued.

“Tony, you should be pleased,” said Andy. “You’ve been telling us that we’re too heavily invested in financial services. If we can put the two life companies together, that will have the effect of diluting the proportion of the total assets represented by Enduring and our other strategic financial services investments.”

“That’s so. It’s one of the suggestions I’ve made before. It would help to an extent. But we must be careful not to pay too much, even if we do pay by issuing our own shares. They are quite expensive, even by the standards of the current markets, but so are those of Stella.”

34

Nora and Andy were sitting on Andy's large and comfortable bed, leaning back into the soft pillows. Neither had yet bothered to get dressed. They were well satisfied with their evening's exertions, and were chatting companionably as they sipped the drinks which Andy had poured for them.

Nora was pleased at the way their relationship was developing. Andy was growing closer to her, and was beginning to rely on her at times. He would talk to her about many things, but particularly about Nigroup and his work, which was his great passion after his own image, with which it was inextricably associated. Physically, he was also drawn to her, and she was enjoying their relationship, being genuinely aroused by her growing power to excite, influence and even control this attractive, powerful and wealthy man.

Andy was pleased at the prospect of acquiring control of Stella Insurance and creating a stir in the markets and the country at large. It was good that someone as attractive and obliging as Nora could share his business, as well as his physical, passions. She was a good lawyer and business person and could relate to him with genuine understanding. She was very attractive, attentive and compliant. She was good-looking and well spoken, and could surely support and enhance his public image. He felt that she would also look after and attend to him rather well.

“We should get together. Get rid of that man and move in with me. We can get married, if you want, after you’ve divorced him.”

“Do you mean that I should now consider us to be engaged?”

“If you want to put it like that, yes. I think we’ll do very well together. But let’s do nothing, and keep this just to ourselves, until after the Stella deal has been done. We don’t want any public distractions till then.”

35

There were school holidays in the last week of March and until after Easter, which was over the first weekend of April. Sylvia still had the preparation of lessons and other work to do, but she was free of classes for a few days. She had a small house in the suburb of Parkhurst, two blocks away from the Braamfontein Spruit and not very far off Tony's morning route to work. She invited him to call in for an early morning cup of coffee the first Monday of the holidays. This he did, departing from his usual early start at work.

The weather had continued warm, but it had been dry recently. As Tony drove to Sylvia's home in the early morning, he noticed small signs of coming autumn. The white stinkwood trees beside the road had yellow highlights as some leaves were starting to turn, and the great planes were now just touched with brown.

Sylvia's neat little house was set in a small well-kept garden. As it was a beautiful highveld morning, they sat outside on the front lawn under a large old loquat tree, which spread its dark-leaved branches to provide a perfect open-air shady area. It was lovely there, sitting in the fresh morning air, Casper the dog lying nearby with his head between his paws and eyes on his mistress. It was quiet, except for the occasional call and activity of the birds, Cape robin, olive thrush, bulbul and laughing dove, which only emphasised Tony and Sylvia's all too brief luxury of laziness in one another's company. It was only two days since Sylvia's qualifying marathon. She was a little stiff, but still elated with her achievement. An hour fled by as they talked of the race and made plans for the future. All too soon Tony had to tear himself away, slipping into the morning traffic, just behind its peak, and arriving at work in time for his morning meeting.

"It's good for you," said Mary after he had told her where he had been. "You seem so much more relaxed."

So Tony stopped in Parkhurst to have coffee with Sylvia almost every morning of her holidays. Those were lovely quiet times together for both of them. They were happy simply to be with each other for a few precious quality hours away from the pressures of their normal lives. They talked, or simply savoured the companionable quiet of two people at home in one another's company, eyes on each other or the flowers and trees, and hearing the singing of the birds, particularly enjoying the repeated call note and endless variations of the robin's song.

For them it was a truly beautiful early autumn time under the loquat tree. Tony left Sylvia on each of those mornings, for the frenzy and problems of his work, relaxed, refreshed, and even a little excited. For sometimes she teased him, just a little. One morning she wore a low cut sundress, which showed off her beautiful broad shoulders and back, and which revealed her lovely breasts as she leaned forward to put his coffee on the table. Another morning she was attractive in a silky summer dressing gown. When they hugged, when it was time for him to go, he could have sworn that she wore nothing underneath it.

36

April was usually a beautiful month on the highveld, and this year's seemed to promise that it would be another. However, the weather proved to be more changeable than was often the case. Sometimes it seemed to settle into a normal pattern of calm and pleasantly warm sunny days. At other times it was hot and sultry, with thunder grumbling in the afternoons or at night, as though summer lingered and did not want to go away. As the days passed they grew noticeably shorter and training routes had to be chosen with visibility in mind, as more and more of each session was being run in the dark or near-dark. Early morning runners were getting up in darkness, starting out in the cool pre-dawn and running into full daylight. Evening runners were rushing from work to start training while it was still light, and running mainly in dusk and darkness. The properly prudent were now putting on their white or light-coloured clothing and wearing reflective belts in order to be visible to other users of the roads.

The start of April saw everyone, who was not injured or ill or tapering for the Two Oceans on Easter Saturday, training very hard. Every morning and evening, and often in the middle of the day as lunch hours were used for training, runners were to be seen on the roads cramming in the kilometres they thought they would need for their Comrades Marathons. Some ran to and from work, and came to be familiar sights to motorists on their regular routes each morning or evening. Sometimes they even ran faster than the rush hour traffic as it dammed up in places.

Even Sylvia, after an easy week, had moved into a period of long, hard running. She and Tony managed to train twice together over the four-day Easter weekend. Tony had two hard runs and two easier ones over the four days, the easier ones being shared with Sylvia as her hard runs.

Josh and Sipho were still training well, but could not train over Easter, which was the holiest part of the Christian calendar and a very busy and important time for Josh. However, after the joy of Easter Sunday, they had a lovely, relaxed long run on the Monday.

Many other runners, especially the fanatics, took the opportunity of the four days' holiday to cram in as much training as possible, covering great distances each day. Some coped, and ended up only stiff and exhausted. Others were sore and nearly or actually injured, and were forced, unwillingly, to scale back or even halt their training over the next few days.

Andy had had a hard run in the Korkie. He had probably gone out too fast in the beginning and had paid the price later on, having to hang on over the last few kilometres and finishing exhausted. He limped around for a few days, but still forced himself to do four long runs over the Easter weekend. On the Tuesday he arrived at work tired and sore and highly irritable.

By following good advice, and with the resilience of youth, Mandla was recovering well from his Achilles tendon injury. He had progressed from walking to gentle jogging and by mid-April was training reasonably well again, but without yet doing any very fast or very long running. He felt generally better for the period of enforced rest, which Tony thought might be a blessing in disguise following his heavy racing programme. Mandla's new running shoes, fitted with heel raises to help protect the Achilles tendons, were working well and feeling good. With such an injury, the first step in the morning was a useful indicator. So Mandla monitored his progress by that first step out of bed each day. If his heel was too stiff or sore he held himself back a little in training. If the stiffness was less than before, he knew that the injury was improving and that he was absorbing that level of training.

Melanie was one of those tapering for Two Oceans in the first week of April. She flew down to Cape Town on Good Friday, and the next day ran the 56km race along one of the most beautiful courses in the world. The way along the narrow winding Chapman's Peak Drive was especially memorable. First there was a long climb with the road clinging to the mountains on the right and rocky cliffs plunging into the sea on the left. At the top the road turned sharply to the right to descend in sweeping curves into the village of Hout Bay. Across to the left was a spectacular view across the bay, with its blue sea, colourful little fishing harbour and enfolding mountains. The subsequent climb through Hout Bay and up the winding, tree-lined road to Constantia Nek was gruelling. The distance was long for Melanie's tired legs. The cut-off time for the race was only six hours, which made the task of qualifying for a finisher's medal quite difficult for the ordinary runner. However, Melanie kept focussed and kept herself moving forward. With barely five minutes to spare she stepped onto the grass near the end, and finished, in her apparently serene way, in 5hrs 57min.

She was delighted, but very tired and sore. She remembered Tony saying that everything was stiff and sore after a very long race. Over the next two or three days the body started to recover, and then what still remained painful told of what had really been damaged. As the tide of stiffness and soreness retreated, Melanie's knees continued to be painful, especially the left one. She rested for two days, and then began to train again by walking for two or three days. When she tried to run, she had to hobble to get herself going. Her knees were a little better once she had warmed up, but they still ached as she jogged. Tony advised caution, and walking while she could without pain, until she had recovered.

Unhappily, she was forced to follow this advice for a few days. All the while she walked she fretted about losing training with Comrades only weeks away. Bill, who had continued to train hard but sensibly over Easter, walked with her at times and tried to console her.

"Melanie, you need recovery time. You won't lose months of training in a few days. You must allow yourself to recover, from your injury, and your racing, if you still want to do Comrades."

"I must do it. I cannot let David down." That was her constant thought and motivation and worry.

Fred was happy that he was now running normally again. He had had a steady run in the Korkie, treating it merely as a long training run and finishing comfortably in something over five hours. He still joined the Hadedas for certain sessions, and he continued to keep them entertained.

"There've been some very close finishes in the Comrades, even though the race is so long. In 1931 Noel Burree made up ten minutes on Phil Masterson-Smith over the last ten miles of the run into Durban. They raced each other round the track at the end, changing positions more than once. Masterson-Smith won by two yards with a final desperate surge.

"But the 1967 race between Manie Kuhn and Tommy Malone was the most dramatic. Tommy had won the up race the year before by a big margin. In 'sixty-seven, he was two minutes ahead of Manie at Tollgate, with only the run down into the finish at the Durban Light Infantry grounds at the Greyville racecourse to go. At Tollgate, Tommy was actually given the scroll with the traditional message from the Mayor of Maritzburg to the Mayor of Durban, which the winner usually hands over at the finish. But Manie was catching up fast. The last straight was quite short, and with only about seventy metres to go Manie was only about twenty metres behind. Tommy tried to speed up, but cramped badly and fell just before the finish. He got up and lunged forward just as

Manie swept past him to breast the tape first. It was a wonderful, memorable race.

"I also remember Bob Calder, the president of the Natal Athletic Association, telling me that he had gone to watch the finish and that there had been no finishing tape. After all, who would think it necessary at the end of such a long race? He persuaded the officials to put up a finishing tape, as he said, 'in order to do things properly'. Thank goodness. It would have been awful not to have known who had actually won the race, but fortunately the finish was clearly defined."

37

Entries for the Comrades Marathon closed on Wednesday, 10th April. Many of the more than ten thousand entries reached the organizers, the Comrades Marathon Association in Pietermaritzburg, in good time, but a great many flooded in just before the strictly enforced deadline. As the closing time approached, the organisers were increasingly busy processing the mountains of mail and checking the entry forms for completeness and correctness.

Tony had ensured that the Hadedas had sent in their entries in good time. Soon after qualifying, the details of the qualifying race and the entrant's time had been written onto his or her Comrades entry form. That had then been signed, as required, by Trixie as Club Secretary, to certify that the information was correct and that the entrant was a paid up member of the Club. The entry forms had been sent in by registered mail and acknowledgements had been received from the Comrades Marathon Association.

However, not everyone displayed such efficiency and had the same resulting peace of mind. Andy had given his entry form to his secretary to fill in for him. Jane had done so with her usual efficiency, and had put it in a folder on Andy's desk for him to check and sign and then obtain his club secretary's signature. The folder had somehow become buried under a pile of papers on Andy's desk. On the Tuesday before entries closed, Jane asked him whether he had indeed sent in his entry, as it had not come back to her.

"I gave it to you. Don't tell me you haven't sent it in," cried Andy.

"I put it on your desk for you to sign."

"I haven't seen it." Andy's voice rose until he was almost screaming. "Are you telling me that I've done all that training and you haven't sent in my entry form? Find it, and do it at once. I don't care what else you have to do."

"Andy, you need to get your club secretary's signature. Have you got it?"

"Find the form. Find her. Take it to her and make sure she signs it. I don't care where she is, find her. Then courier the form to Pietermaritzburg. And tell the courier company from me that they'll get no more business from Nigroup if the form is not delivered in good time tomorrow."

For Trixie, as Secretary of the White Waters Running Club, it was as usual a nightmare time. As a large club, they would have several hundred entries, all of which she had to sign. There was always a last-minute rush. Some people were just careless and forgetful. Some had only recently decided to run Comrades, for a bet made in the pub or stimulated by the pre-race media coverage, and then had to qualify before entries closed. Others had also left qualifying to the last minute because they had been injured. Some had travelled out into the country during the past weekend to take part in whatever races they could find that were suitable for qualifying.

At the Club, on the Tuesday evening before entries closed, there was a long queue of people with entry forms waiting to see Trixie. She had also been fielding telephone calls all day from now desperate Comrades aspirants. She had arranged, as she usually did, for a last batch of entries to be taken down to Pietermaritzburg the following morning and handed in to the organisers. She was exhausted when she and Victor arrived home from the Club that Tuesday night.

However, her day's work was not yet over. There were last minute entry forms stuffed into their mail box, pushed under the front door, and even one posted through the open bathroom window.

38

It was Wednesday, 17th April, and the Nigroup executive strategy committee was meeting, with their advisers in attendance, to finalise the details of the proposed bid for control of Stella Insurance. Their proposal would be put before the Nigroup Board of Directors for approval on Friday morning, in good time for the bid to be submitted before the Stella auction closed on the following Wednesday.

"I hear there's a lot of interest in Stella, and I see the share price is doing well."

"There's talk of maybe five or six potential bidders."

"Golden Bank is definitely one of them."

"And I know that Certain Life is too."

"So is Solid Bank."

"We must make sure that our bid is attractive enough to prevail," said Andy.

"Without overpaying," added Tony.

The meeting heard the external and internal experts (accountants, auditors, actuaries, merchant bankers and lawyers) summarise the findings and opinions, which would be the basis for the bid documents, containing the price and conditions of Nigroup's offer to acquire GFH's shares in Stella. If Nigroup were successful, it would have brought about a change of control of Stella, and it would then have to make a similar offer to all the other (i.e. the minority) shareholders in Stella, in order to comply with the relevant regulatory legislation and rules. As the plan was to issue Nigroup shares to Stella shareholders in exchange for their Stella shares, the relative prices of the shares of the two companies was important.

Shares of Stella Insurance had been trading on the Johannesburg Stock Exchange at 450 cents before the announcement of the auction, after which they had shot up and had traded at an average of 500 cents per share over the past fortnight. Nigroup shares had been averaging 550 cents. The advisers recommended that Nigroup offer one Nigroup share for each Stella share it acquired. At current prices, that would mean that Stella shareholders would receive a premium of ten percent over the present Stella share price, and just over twenty-two percent above the Stella share price before the auction was announced.

"All that sounds very reasonable," said Andy, "but will it be enough? What can we do to sweeten our offer so that it becomes irresistible?"

The head of the Enduring team hesitated for a moment. "You could offer a cash alternative, between say 500 and 520 cents. Some might prefer cash to Nigroup shares."

"No!" exclaimed Tony. "We do not have the cash. We cannot make such an offer!"

"The likelihood of paying out much cash will surely be very small," responded Andy. "The stock market is firm and our share price is holding up well. It should even rise if our offer is accepted. It hasn't been below 500 for months."

The exchange between Tony and Andy continued.

"Our shares are expensive and so is the market. Our shares will fall if the market falls."

"If we need more cash than seems likely, we can place shares to raise cash."

"Once the price starts falling that will be difficult, especially in a falling market."

"The market isn't falling. But, in any case, there might be some friendly parties willing, if necessary, to absorb quantities of Nigroup shares in the market just above 500 cents. I have some past favours to be repaid, and who knows when those friends may need our support in the future."

"I don't like that."

"We could borrow cash if necessary."

"A major insurance group short of cash and taking on a couple of billion of debt! That would be bad for us. And debt needs to be repaid."

"Stella has cash. As soon as we take over control we can get our hands on that and repay any debt. I don't think we'll need much cash anyway."

Nora intervened. "We could write into the offer a condition that would give us the right to revise or withdraw the cash alternative in the event of a substantial change in share market conditions."

Nora flushed as Tony turned on her. "You know as well as I do that no-one in his right mind will accept an offer that is not really an offer, a cash underpin that is not one at all. The conditions of the auction are clear that bids have to be firm. No, we must drop the whole idea of a cash alternative."

"Why the hell are you so negative?" asked Andy irritably. "You say yourself that we need this deal to help correct our high exposure to financial services assets. Now all you do is object."

"The markets are vulnerable. We don't have cash. We should not risk it. The risks are far too high. Our structure is already weakened and distorted. We should not take risks that could collapse it."

"I think a cash underpin will make our bid attractive. We will offer a one-for-one exchange of shares, and we will offer a cash alternative at 500 cents. I want that deal!"

White-faced, and grey eyes cold with fury, Nora followed Tony to his office after the meeting. She stormed past Mary to confront her husband.

"What do you think you're doing, talking to me like that in a meeting? And why are you always so negative? Are you trying to scupper the deal? There'll be a lot of work for me if it goes ahead. You just don't care! And why are you so disloyal to Andy, and to Nigroup?"

"Dissent is not the same as disloyalty," responded Tony, keeping calm. "I am loyal to my clients and shareholders and staff. I am trying to stop Andy from steering the ship onto the rocks. He won't see them. He won't even acknowledge that there might be any danger. He only wants to hear good news."

"Which he won't hear from you! Can't you even see that you are destroying yourself here? What are you going to do about it?"

"Soon I may have to think about doing something else. Perhaps I will start my own business."

"Well don't expect me to start all over again with you. You are a loser! Don't be surprised if I leave you." She swept out of the room.

"I suppose you heard most of that," Tony said to Mary, who appeared, eyes wide, a moment later.

"Poor Tony! It can't be nice going home these days. But why is she so worried about your alleged disloyalty to Andy? Isn't she being a rather caring attorney?"

Andy and Nora did not have the chance to see each other alone until that evening at Andy's house.

"That's the last straw. He'll have to go," said Andy. "I'll have to find a pretext."

"He may be happy to resign. He knows that his position is becoming untenable. I told him I would leave him."

"So we'll both fire him. Does he know that you'll come to me?"

"No."

"I would love to see his face when he finds out."

"When shall I come?"

"On Friday. The Board will approve the Stella deal on Friday morning. I don't want any distractions until then."

"I will come that afternoon."

39

Friday, 19th April, dawned clear and unseasonably warm. As Tony made his usual early way to work, it was already sultry and promising to be very hot later on.

"Stand by for fireworks," he warned Mary as she placed his morning cup of tea next to him. "This is really my last throw of the dice. Somehow I have to try and persuade the Board to drop that cash alternative for the Stella deal. I'm not optimistic, but I must try. Then at least I'll know that I've done all I can to stop it. But, whatever the outcome, Andy won't like it."

"I'm surprised he hasn't excluded you from the meeting."

"No, that would cause comment, and perhaps raise questions. I'm sure he feels the decisions have been made, and that only a rubber-stamping is needed. No doubt he has done a lot of lobbying."

The boardroom was on the plush top floor of the building. It had a wonderful view to the north, and was expensively but tastefully furnished, with warm wooden panelling and three valuable, excellent paintings on the walls. The directors arrived, mostly greying, dignified and avuncular, and gathered for tea or coffee and biscuits in the comfortable lounge next to the boardroom before the meeting commenced.

The meeting had been called mainly to discuss the Stella bid, so the initial formalities and certain minor business matters were quickly disposed of. A team from Nigroup, not including Tony, had prepared and rehearsed a presentation about Stella Insurance and Nigroup's proposed bid for control, and this was now given to the Board. After that, a few questions were asked and answered, and then Tony spoke.

"Mister Chairman, I would like permission, please, to say a few things relating to the Group's financial structure and aspects of this proposed bid."

"No," said Andy quietly to the Chairman, next to whom he was sitting.

"Mister Duke says 'No'."

"Mister Chairman, I believe that what I have to say is very important, at least as important as anything you have heard me say at any meeting over the past few years. With your permission, I would like you to hear what I have to say before you make your decision on this matter."

Tony paused. As no one said anything, he took that to mean consent, and so proceeded to present his case. He sketched his concerns about the over-exposure of the group, especially the life company, to financial services investments, and to Enduring Bank in particular. The pursuit of those assets had used up all the cash resources of the group, and had led to a serious imbalance in the asset structure of the life company. The acquisition of Stella could help correct that imbalance, though only partially. However, the cash alternative proposed to be included in the bid was very dangerous and should be removed. If included it would be the preferred alternative if the Nigroup share price fell below 500 cents, which was quite possible if the markets weakened. That would create a demand for cash, which the group did not have. Borrowing to meet a large cash commitment would be difficult or costly in a weak market, and such a commitment would severely stress an already strained asset structure and should not be risked. He also regarded share prices as expensive, and therefore vulnerable. If share prices in general were to fall, or if those in the financial services sector, or even of Enduring alone, were to fall, that would cause a situation from which the life company, as its assets were currently structured, might never recover. It would quickly go into deficit, it would not be able to declare bonuses on clients' policies, and it might even have to reverse bonuses already declared in past years. In those circumstances it would not be able to bring in new business, and it would probably lose business very rapidly even if it did survive.

"Mister Chairman," he said in conclusion, "Nilife is Investment Management's largest client. As investment managers, we cannot tell our clients how to do their business. However, I believe that it would be improper and irresponsible not to point out the risks and dangers that a particular strategy or investment or course of action would involve. That I have tried to do, and I thank you for listening to me."

There was silence as Tony finished. He was well respected and the directors knew that he would only speak as he had done out of genuine concern. Andy began to talk, slowly at first and then gathering momentum. As he did at times, he talked and talked and kept talking, until the issues were blurred and Tony's concerns were half-forgotten. However, two or three non-executive directors were genuinely concerned, and kept bringing the conversation back to those issues. They insisted on a discussion about the risks attached to the cash alternative in the bid, and they asked for more information to be provided, as soon as possible, to enable the Board to evaluate properly the asset structure of the life company and the group.

Eventually Andy prevailed. The Board agreed to allow the Stella bid to go ahead as presented, including the cash alternative.

The directors retired to lunch in the directors' dining room after the meeting closed. As soon as lunch was over and Andy found himself alone in his own office, he summoned Tony to meet him there.

"You're fired!" was Andy's furious greeting.

"You can't fire me, and you know that," responded Tony. "You can't fire me for doing my job, and you can't fire anyone with a record like mine. However, I will make it easy for you. I cannot keep on fighting a war forever. I have done my best and I can't realistically do any more in the present circumstances. If you make it worth my while, I will resign. But I will need money to start out on my own, as I plan to do. First of all, I will need immediately the benefit of all my share options in full."

Andy telephoned Beryl Berry, who was the head of the Human Resources (or Personnel) function, and asked her to join them. She quickly appeared, small and neat and well groomed in a soft pink suit. She looked startled as Andy informed her that Tony was to resign over a difference of opinion about policy, and that her help was needed to agree his leaving conditions. They sat around the table and worked out a settlement. Tony was granted all he reasonably wanted in return for his resignation and immediate departure. Beryl was instructed to accompany him, or to arrange for him to be accompanied, as he packed up his things before being escorted off the premises.

"I suppose I could wish you good luck, for you will need it," said Andy as they stood up at the end of their discussions.

"You will need it more than I. You'd better go down on your knees every night and pray that the markets don't fall."

They did not shake hands.

"If I don't see you before, I suppose I'll see you at Comrades," said Tony as he and Beryl moved towards the door.

"At Comrades you won't see me for dust. With your wishy-washy so-called conservative approach, I'll be in Pietermaritzburg long before you reach Polly Shorts, if you even get that far."

Tony left the office with Beryl. He liked her, and was still able to admire her neat figure as he followed her into her nearby office. He told her briefly about his apprehensions, and the reason for his unceremonious departure, as she listened intently and concernedly.

"You can watch me, or have me watched, as much as you like," said Tony. "I know you must, but no one will stop me from saying good-bye to my staff, and packing up my things and taking them with me."

"Don't worry. I know you well enough. Go and do those things, then call me when you are ready to go. I will see you off, as instructed, and say my farewell then. We will miss you. I'm trusting you, so please don't let me down."

"Thank you."

There was worry in Mary's blue eyes and furrowed brow as Tony returned to his office.

"What happened? Why have you been so long?"

"I am to leave immediately." He told her briefly about his meeting with Andy and the agreement about his departure.

"I'm going to start my own company. I would love you to join me if you would like to. I will need you, and would love to continue working with you. Don't do anything now, but please think about it. I will contact you soon. They may try to retrench you, now that I am leaving and as we are so close to each other. If you do want to leave, don't resign. Rather let them retrench you so you'll get better benefits."

Tony tried to phone Nora to tell her about developments, but she was not at work and did not answer her cellphone. There was no reply when he tried their home number.

Tony went around the Investment Management offices, saying farewell to his shocked colleagues. Then he packed up his few personal belongings, hugged Mary solemnly, and went to his car with Beryl who also wished him well.

40

Nora was a bundle of confused emotions. She was intensely excited that she would be going to Andy that afternoon, but she could not show it yet. She also knew that Tony would be upset when he found her gone. He deserved it, but they had had many years together, including some good times. It did not help that the weather was hot and sultry. She felt vaguely irritable and had a headache. She snapped at her secretary and was almost rude to a client.

She saw two clients after lunch and then left the office to drive 'home', for her home was to change, to collect those of her belongings that she wanted to take with her to Andy's place, *which will soon be mine*, she thought.

The weather was still very hot and oppressive. During the day great white cumulus clouds had been building up and were now combining ominously. Over the city centre to the south, and to the south-west, the sky was now a deep, dark grey, alive with lightning flashes and presaging heavy rain or hail. Thunder rumbled as the leaden mass moved northwards, gathering smaller storm centres to itself as it moved.

The traffic on the roads was even worse than usual. People seemed to go mad as the storm gathered, and drove ever more recklessly and aggressively. She found herself cursing and screaming as vehicles changed lanes dangerously around her or drove too close behind.

As she arrived home, for perhaps the last time, the clouds were low and dark and still darkening. She went in through the front door just as some heavy isolated drops of rain began to fall, and she had to turn on the lights inside in order to see what she was doing. She had already surreptitiously packed some of her things, and she immediately set about gathering the remainder of what she wanted to take with her and put them into suitcases. These she took out one by one and placed in the car. By now the lightning was all around and was frightening. The thunder crashed around her as she ferried her belongings.

She returned to the house for the last time to collect the last suitcase. Before leaving she wandered around the house, taking a last look. There were so many memories. She and Tony should have done so well together. It was Tony's fault that she had had to ensnare Andy. Pent up emotions rose inside her, seeking release. There was a blinding flash of lightning and immediately a fearful, deafening crash of thunder. She jumped with fright. There was a brief stunned silence, a few restless sounds as the first large hailstones fell, and then a low roar as the hailstorm enveloped the house, reducing visibility outside to a white torrent of ice falling and bouncing off the whitening lawn.

Something snapped inside her.

Tony had telephoned Sylvia to tell her that he would be at the Club earlier than usual that evening, so he drove cautiously northwards through the scurrying, frantic traffic, headlights on in the deepening gloom of the gathering storm. It was dark and thundery, particularly to the south, when he arrived and parked his car in the usual place. He tried again to phone Nora but got no reply. Although he was not optimistic about being able to run in those stormy conditions, he changed into his running clothes and returned to his car as it began to rain heavily.

Sylvia arrived shortly after, parking in the adjacent space and then diving breathlessly and damply from her car into his.

They exchanged greetings as she settled herself into the passenger seat beside him. They were cocooned together inside as the rain pelted down, the storm flashed and crashed around them, and the car windows misted up.

After mutual exclamations about the storm, Tony told Sylvia his story of the day's events. She was sympathetic, but had been expecting something of the sort and felt that he would be better off in a new environment of his own creating.

"What does Nora think?"

"I don't know. I haven't been able to contact her. I don't think she'll be pleased."

"Let's go inside and drink to your new venture. I'm sure you'll do very well. The rain's not quite so hard now, so let's make a run for it."

So they ran inside and settled damply but comfortably in the Hadeda bar to sit out the remainder of the storm and to drink a toast to the future.

It was still quite early when they emerged from the clubhouse. The sky was a lighter grey, the thunder and lightning still played, but distantly, to the north. The air was calm and cool and pleasantly moist, and from quite near they heard the liquid, melodious call of a coucal, which some call the rain bird. Then they became aware of a roar of rushing water from the direction of the river.

"Let's go and have a look."

They sloshed their way over the flooded fields and looked in awe upon a raging torrent. The usually small and placid Braamfontein Spruit was now a great river in angry flood. They had never seen it like that before. It dumped itself over the weir from a fearful height, crashed and thundered over the great boulders now metres below the boiling surface, then rushed with terrifying power and flying spray between the high cliffs beyond. They gazed in awe.

"I wonder what it's like higher up." Tony had to shout to make himself heard. "Let's run after all, and go and see."

They ran upstream. The size and force of the river was frightening. Bridges were under water and road traffic was at a standstill. It had obviously rained much harder upstream to the south and all that deluge was now racing downstream in a great rushing flood. At Rattray's Weir the water, usually only a few metres wide, swept over in a torrent across the whole length of the wall. Great branches and whole trees were swept over. Just above the weir the lovely grassy area where they often ran was flooded. At one point the river was fully a hundred and fifty metres wide. Further on they watched in awe as the raging flood waters undermined the riverbank and grasped at a large willow tree. The tree swayed as a powerful current surged at its roots, it swayed again, and then a further great rush of water tore it away. They saw the whole tree turning slowly over and over as it was swept down the white-capped river. It was a demonstration of the awful power of nature, and, thought Tony, of the impossibility of standing up against more powerful forces.

Tony arrived home at about his usual time. He thought Nora was at home when he saw that lights were on inside, but found it strange that her car was not in the garage. He let himself into the house, and was met by a scene of chaos. The lounge looked as though it had been ransacked. Vases and ornaments, cushions and cloths had been swept or thrown onto the floor. Even some of the curtains had been ripped down and left to lie on the carpet. There was no sign of a break-in, but some ornaments had been shattered against the walls and some had been thrown at the windows and had broken panes of glass. A chilling breeze blew in. His study was a mess, with everything swept off his desk, drawers and shelves emptied onto the floor, and some of his papers torn up and scattered about the room. Their bedroom was not much better, with bedding torn off the bed and left on the floor where his clothes had also been scattered. The other rooms were intact.

Tony still could not see any signs that the house had been broken into, and was both astonished and confused. He went through the house looking for clues as to what might have happened. Then, on the mantelpiece above the fireplace in the lounge, he found an envelope with his name on it. He tore it open and took out the contents. It was a note from Nora. It told him briefly that she had decided to leave him, as she had threatened to do. She was going to Andy, whom she planned to marry after she and Tony were divorced. Her decision was final. She wished him well.

Tony put down the note, then surveyed the chaos around him. Everything seemed to be in ruin, as though a storm had struck him and all at once had blown away his job, his marriage and his home. It was dark outside, and the lights inside only illuminated the general mess. Andy, of all people! Perhaps he should have guessed. All those late business meetings! He sat for a long time as he absorbed the reality of what had happened.

He went to the telephone and dialled Nora's cellphone number. She answered at once, perhaps expecting a call.

"Is it true?" asked Tony.

"Yes, it is true."

"Couldn't you have done it some other way?"

She rang off.

Tony sat for a while and thought. Then he dialled Sylvia's number.

"May I come and see you? Nora has left me, and I don't feel like being alone right now. I'll tell you all about it when I see you."

"Oh my darling, of course you may."

"I'll see you in a short while. I just need a bath. I'm still sweaty after running. Then I'll come. Thank you."

After hearing his story, Sylvia made a supper for them, and they sat on a couch in the lounge and ate from plates on their laps. They talked intermittently. It was raining again outside, and they could hear it pattering on the trees in the garden and running off the roof from the gutters through the downpipes, but it was cosy and safe inside. Tony gradually felt more relaxed and soothed. He became aware that Sylvia had for some time been leaning against him, and it seemed so natural and comforting and supportive.

"Thank you," he said softly, keeping close to her.

He kissed her gently and caressed her, softly and a little at first, then more, and gradually more, in a slow awakening. She responded, ever so gently to begin with, and then they kissed, long and tenderly, the expression of love so long restrained.

"I want you," she said.

Tony thought how wonderful it was to be loved and to be wanted. They made love, intensely but tenderly, as they had so far only imagined or dreamt of, in a way which, somewhere deep inside, each had wanted to believe they still could find.

"This is what it's supposed to be like in the real world," whispered Tony, still close in the quietly joyous calm that followed.

"This is the real world."

"Perhaps it could be."

41

Sylvia woke up soon after dawn on Saturday morning. The rain had stopped, and, judging by the strength of the early morning light filtering through the curtains, it would be a bright day. Tony was still asleep beside her, and she looked tenderly at the peaceful face and tousled dark brown hair so close to her. She sat up carefully, without disturbing him, and watched over him as he breathed softly and regularly. She thought about the events of the previous day and night.

She was deeply in love with him, and all the more so after last night. No two people could have been closer. It had all seemed so natural and so right. Then other thoughts and doubts began to intrude. Had she been right to let things go so far last night? It had been wonderful, but had it been wrong of her to take advantage of his vulnerability, even though she had certainly not thought of it like that at the time? Why had Nora treated him so badly, and why had she left him in the way she had? Had she, Sylvia, had any part to play in the break-up of Tony's marriage, simply by being so close to him? She herself had been the victim of divorce after another woman had taken her husband away from her. She had no desire to do that to anyone else. Until last night she and Tony had always carefully observed certain self-imposed, proper boundaries in their relationship. Could his marriage be repaired?

She watched as Tony grew restless, and then awoke. In succession, she saw confusion, then hurt, and then relief and love on his face and in his blue-green eyes, as he quickly re-oriented himself to where he was and why, and as he saw the tenderness in the large brown eyes watching over him.

"Thank you for being so good to me," he said as they embraced. "You have helped me to survive, not just yesterday, but these last two or three years."

They lay together and talked, about yesterday and last night, about each other, and about Nora and his marriage. Sylvia confided some of her doubts and worries.

"Perhaps I harmed your marriage by being too close to you. Do you think it can be repaired?"

"No, my marriage is dead. It would have happened whether you had been there or not. It's been coming for a long time. There have been times, when things were not going well, that I wished she would find someone that suited her, and now she has. But it's all been very sudden and a bit of a shock. I had no idea that she and Andy were more than business associates."

"Perhaps we should not see each other for a while, so you can see whether or not your marriage really is finished, and whether you want to carry on with our relationship when you have got over things."

"I want to continue seeing you. I know my love for you. Where it leads us, we can take time to discover."

"I'll come and help you clean up your home, and we'll think about it."

"Oh my goodness! What kind of hurt or madness would make someone do this?" asked Sylvia as she surveyed the wreckage of Tony's home.

They began to clean up, to make the place habitable, and to do what could not, or should not, be left to Martha, the part-time housemaid, to do on Monday morning.

Soon after, the telephone rang. It was Mary, phoning to ask how Tony was after his leaving Nigroup the previous day. To Tony that already seemed a long, long time ago.

"I'm fine, but Nora walked out on me yesterday during the storm. She's gone to Andy, so that should cause a stir. They intend to marry. She left things in a mess, but fortunately Sylvia took me in last night and looked after me. So I'm all right. She's here now, helping me clean up the mess."

"John is out playing golf. I'll come round at once," said Mary, ringing off.

She arrived a few minutes later, looking very worried. She threw her arms around Tony and they held each other close for long seconds. Then she drew back her head, while still holding him, and searched the eyes and face she knew so well in order to understand his present state. He saw concern and tenderness in her expression and in those deep blue eyes.

"I'm all right. I'm sure it's all for the best in the long run. It's just that I have so much to adjust to all at once."

Mary and Sylvia knew one another and greeted each other warmly. Then Mary perceived the mess that the normally comfortable house was in.

"Oh my poor Tony!" she exclaimed. "What could have caused her to leave like this? I thought Nora and Andy were getting along a little too well, but surely they did not have to behave like this. I wonder if she knew you would be leaving your job yesterday."

"I don't know. Perhaps the timing was co-incidental, but I could not have stayed on in these circumstances anyway."

Mary began to help with the clearing up. Later, while Tony was trying to restore order to his study, she and Sylvia were setting the bedroom to rights, making up the bed and putting Tony's clothes back on the shelves. They both knew of each other's fondness for Tony, and of his for each of them, so Sylvia confided in Mary some of her concerns about her relationship with Tony.

"He asked to come round to my place last night. He was very shocked at first. We had supper, and were very close, and he gradually felt better. He slept over, and we came here after breakfast. You know that we are very fond of each other. I'm afraid that that may have helped cause the break-up of his marriage. Also, he is very vulnerable at the moment, and I'm afraid that one day he may think I took unfair advantage of that if I stay too close to him now. Perhaps I should go away, or not see him for a while."

"No. You didn't cause the break-up of his marriage, and it can't be revived after this. I know that Tony has been very fond of you for a long time, and I know that you also care for him. You must stay close to him, and so must I. We have both provided him with support through very difficult times: I, mainly at the office, and you, outside of his work. We should not take away that support now."

"Perhaps you are right."

Sunday dawned bright and clear, promising to be a perfect early autumn day. Tony opened the bedroom curtains and looked out. The garden was pretty, but had been sadly damaged by Friday's hailstorm. The large trees now rather raggedly showed their autumn colours, yellow, copper and brown with some lingering green, but under the trees the lawn was thickly covered with shredded leaves brought down by the heavy hail.

Tony wandered through the empty house, opening curtains and windows while the kettle boiled. He had just made tea for himself when the telephone rang. It was Sylvia.

"I hope I didn't wake you, but I thought I might miss you if I phoned any later and you were out on your long Sunday run."

"I haven't started yet. I'm debating with myself about whether or not I have the motivation for a long run today. Physically I'm really jaded, and I'm emotionally exhausted after the last few days."

"Coach," said Sylvia sternly, "in terms of your own principles, 'listen to your body', 'take a rest if you are really exhausted', and 'it is good to walk sometimes as most people walk a long way in Comrades', we are going hiking today. Last night I phoned Minnie Dawson and got permission for us to walk at Somerset Farm. I also need a break. I've made some sandwiches and packed some fruit and other hiking food. Can you bring some drinks and pick me up in an hour or so?"

Tony needed little persuading, and so they drove north-west for about an hour into the Magaliesberg Mountains near Hekpoort. Somerset Farm was a large, wild and beautiful game farm, which was managed like a nature reserve. It was very hilly, mountainous in parts, and the vegetation varied from indigenous forest to scattered thorn and protea trees and open grassland. With day packs on their backs, Sylvia and Tony spent hours wandering through that splendid rugged area. They stopped occasionally to drink or to eat, high up on the main ridge with vast views all around, or under the trees in a cosy spot beside a river or a nearly dry streambed. They saw some giraffe, a herd of zebra, eland, kudu, waterbuck and numerous smaller animals. There were also many birds, including literally dozens of Cape vultures filling the sky around and above a vulture restaurant where food had recently been placed.

They spent the day in comfortable companionship. When they spoke it was mainly about what they were seeing and experiencing. They did not talk of the past or the future. By silent consent that time was a complete break from their everyday world and recent events. It was a temporary release, a blessed interval, which would make it easier, especially for Tony, to break with the past and look to creating a new future. They returned home physically tired, but knowing that the many hours spent on their feet were also good for their training, and spiritually refreshed. Somehow the doings and concerns of man, the relentless scurrying after wealth and power and precedence, were put into perspective against the vastness and apparent timelessness of the mountains and forests and veld. When Tony dropped Sylvia off at her home, and left her to do some necessary preparation for the lessons she would have to teach the next day, he felt more able to leave the past behind him and look ahead.

Mary telephoned to ask him to supper, and he spent a quiet, comfortable and happy evening with her and her husband.

Tony got out of bed at the usual time on Monday morning. The house was strangely quiet and empty without the usual morning scramble for Nora and him to be ready to leave for work ahead of the rush hour traffic. He felt hollow and almost without value or relevance in the world. It was strange how people were so often defined, by themselves and by others, by the positions they occupied and the roles they played at work. Suddenly he had no role. Here was Tony Drummond, Head of Investments at Nigroup and responsible for billions, reduced to nothing. There was also no Mary to talk to, and no Sylvia, for they were at work.

However, he was still an investment man. He went outside to fetch the morning newspaper, which was delivered early each day to his home. Then he sat down, as he would do at work, to study the latest company news and results, and to catch up on the economic, political and other news, which would affect financial markets and investment decisions. It was important to keep up to date all the time. Afterwards he began to plan seriously the beginnings of his own new investment and investment management operations.

Meanwhile it soon became known in the financial markets that Tony Drummond was not at his desk, and that he had suddenly left Nigroup. News travelled fast in the closely knit investment community. Rumours began to fly around, including one that Tony's wife had left him for his boss, Andrew Duke. Nigroup's public relations department hastily put out a notice to the effect that Tony had resigned "to pursue his own interests". Tony was well known and highly regarded in the financial markets, and the Nigroup share price began to fall. It started the day at 560 cents and closed at 530.

With time on his hands Tony went to the Club early that evening and ran a few kilometres, finishing at the clubhouse to join his running group for their usual Monday evening run. Almost everyone was there. It was probably the largest group he had ever taken on a run. He was touched to realise that everyone who could be there had made the effort to come out and support him. News had travelled fast here too. Hardly anything was said about his job or his marriage. A hug or a handshake, and their very presence, said it all. He was still their valued leader and coach.

"Thank you all. Thank you very much for being here. Now let's run."

PART THREE

42

On Sunday, 28th April the White Waters Running Club held its annual pre-Comrades long training run. It was usually held about five weeks before Comrades and the distance was about 65km. It was designed as a very long training run for those who wanted to incorporate one into this period of peak training volumes. It was also meant to be a confidence booster for those who ran it to prove to themselves that they were indeed capable of covering the major part of the Comrades distance. A lot of organisation went into the long run, with volunteers manning refreshment stations along the way to provide drinks and sustenance for the runners. For a small payment to cover expenses, members of other clubs were also welcome to run.

For the same reasons that most of his charges would not be running ultra-marathons before Comrades, Tony had severe reservations about this annual long training run. While he accepted that it could be useful for the highly fit and experienced athletes, he believed it was wrong to lure the lesser runners into participating, as they were by the publicity and hype put out by Victor and Trixie in the name of the Club. Tony believed that most Comrades hopefuls simply did not have the running and training background to support such a long run, particularly so close to the actual race. Many would not recover in time to perform at their best on race-day. Some might run themselves into injury, by over stressing bodies already fatigued by their current heavy training loads, and not even recover in time to take part in the great race itself.

However, with a little organisation the long training run could also be useful to those who wanted to run only a part of it. There would be company along the way, the refreshment stations were most welcome, and the regular distance markers along the route were useful for practising pace judgement. So it was that Tony arranged with his Comrades entrants to do a portion of the long run, setting tasks for each of them in accordance with their individual training requirements at that time. Most, including Tony himself, were scheduled to run 40km at their planned Comrades Marathon pace. Mandla, who had been recovering well from his injury and had gradually been building up his training again, was to run as he felt for so long as there was no discomfort, but no further than 40km. Amongst them they arranged transport to bring them all back to the Club after they had completed their runs. Very early on that Sunday morning, Tony left his car at the 40km mark and was driven to the Club by Sylvia in time for the pre-dawn six o'clock start.

The course meandered through the suburbs of Randburg and then out into the pretty rolling countryside to the north-west. The morning was cool and good for running. It brightened as the sun rose and grew only pleasantly warmer. Tony enjoyed his run, the only unpleasantness being when he was bumped by an elbow just after the start and the figure of Andy went past him and gradually drew away into the distance. Tony was weary but pleasantly satisfied when he reached the refreshment point near his car at the 40km mark. He was greeted with a drink and a bright smile by Mavis, who was in charge of the drinks' table and who was also an occasional member of Tony's Hadedas.

"Well run!" she said. "You'll be pleased to know that Mandla seems to have recovered. He's running like a champ. He went sailing on, ahead of the field, a little while ago."

"What? I expected to see him here. I'm taking him back to the Club."

"He did stop, and had a drink. He said he felt so good that he could carry on quite easily. Trixie persuaded him to continue as he's been short of training recently."

Tony nearly exploded. "He's recovering from an injury. I'm going after him before too much damage is done. Mavis, please tell Sylvia when she comes to wait for me here. She'll be expecting me. Tell her I'll be back to pick her up."

Tony sprang into his car and set off to follow the course. The runners were strung out and were few and far between in this the faster section of the field. A few kilometres further on he caught up with Mandla, running at a good speed clear of the rest of the field and approaching another of the drinks' tables. Trixie was following the front runners and at the same time checking that the organisation was working properly as planned.

"Well done, Mandla," she called as he took a drink and swept past the table. "Keep going. You're looking fantastic."

"Mandla, what the hell are you doing?" cried Tony as pulled his car alongside the runner. "Get into the car at once!"

Mandla stopped in his tracks and looked sheepish as he saw Tony leaning out of the car window. He had never seen Tony angry before.

"Tony, I felt so good that I just carried on past 40 K's. I can easily finish. See, I'm faster than anyone else here today."

"Mandla, you promised to listen to me. Get into the car. I want you to run well at Comrades, not now."

Trixie had seen what was happening, and was beside them in a flash.

"Tony, what do you think you are doing? You're spoiling Mandla's run. And how can you talk to him like that?"

"How could you encourage him to carry on?" asked Tony angrily. "I arranged for him to go no more than 40 K's. I'm not spoiling his run. He's in the process of spoiling his Comrades, and risking injury at the same time. I've been rehabilitating him for the past few weeks, after you so nearly ruined him by over-racing. Do you want to spoil everything again?"

"How dare you talk to me like that! The long run is an important part of preparing for Comrades. Everyone knows that. Mandla's short of training. I told him that if he shows his fitness by finishing this run he may still be selected for the Club's elite Comrades squad. He'll get his transport paid for, and also hotel accommodation right next to the start. Do you want to lose that, Mandla?"

"Mandla, you must choose," said Tony. "I said I would help you, if you promised to listen to me and do as I advised. I warned you it would be difficult at times. I'm not concerned about transport and a hotel at the start. I want you to have a good race. If the Club doesn't select you for their elite squad, so be it. I'll help you with transport. You can sleep in my own hotel room if necessary. We will make plans. And they can't stop you scoring for the Club team at Comrades. If you are good enough to run into our first four, you will score for the Club, whether or not you are selected for the elite squad. And even Trixie will be very pleased with you if you are in our top four."

"He won't be if this is the way you advise him," snarled Trixie.

"He won't be if he runs into injury again, or if he leaves the best of his running on the road here today."

Mandla had stepped to one side and was thinking.

"I'm sorry, Tony," he said. "I got carried away, like in last year's Comrades. You have helped me to run like this again, and I did promise to listen to you. Mrs Trixie, I did promise."

"If you don't prove your fitness you will not be selected for the squad. Remember that, Mandla," said Trixie firmly.

Mandla got into the car next to Tony and they drove off together.

43

The hail had stopped, but it was still raining, when Nora left the home she and Tony had shared for so long and drove carefully in the treacherous conditions towards Andy's house in Hyde Park. The roads were white with hailstones, water ran deeply and strongly in many places, and there were smashed leaves and twigs and broken branches everywhere. She picked her way through them, the car's windscreen wipers driving furiously with a rapid restless rhythm in chorus with her own quick heartbeat and panting breath. The weather and road conditions improved as she neared her destination, and she gradually grew calmer. However, as she crossed the Braamfontein Spruit, the river was higher than she had ever seen it before, and it looked as though it might soon be flowing right over the bridge itself.

Andy was still at work when Nora reached her new home, so she let herself in with her own key. She asked the maid to make her some tea, after her belongings had been brought in and taken upstairs. Then at last she could sit in a comfortable chair in the main lounge, safe from the retreating storm outside, and regain her self-control. She was only half sorry for the havoc she had caused. One was not supposed to behave in that way, but Nora had never been one to apologise for her actions. Tony would be shocked at the mess he would find in his once-comfortable home, but it served him right. It was a small revenge for all his faults and inadequacies. The hot tea was soothing, and gradually she felt more relaxed and began to take in the details of her surroundings. This was her new home. In a sense, it was now all hers. She went upstairs and unpacked and arranged or put away the most important of the things she had brought with her. Then she had a leisurely bath, dressed and made herself up to be desirable for Andy. While she waited for him to come home she walked around the house in a proprietary way, approving of what she saw or planning alterations.

Andy came home full of the success of the morning's Board meeting. Though he had been angry at Tony's contribution, he was now well satisfied that Tony was out of Nigroup. Nora was also now his. She hugged and kissed him tenderly. She was soft and perfumed and looked beautiful in a lovely dress. How good it was to be welcomed home by this alluring and sympathetic woman. She poured him a drink and they sat down and exchanged stories about an eventful day.

Nora slept well, woke up late on Saturday morning and had a quiet, lazy day. She needed to rest after the previous day's tensions, emotions, and eventual regaining control of herself in order to be just right for Andy all evening. It was a clear calm morning after the storm, which had not been as severe in this area as at Tony's home. There was little damage to the garden. After Andy had returned from his morning training run, they had a leisurely late breakfast together. They sat on the shady front veranda and chatted, looking idly over the still, clear swimming pool to the lower garden, and out across the widening valley with its opulent homes nearly hidden in leafy gardens. Nora had a satisfying sense of proprietorship. Andy and all of this were now hers.

However, Sunday brought them back to business again. The Nigroup bid for Stella had to be submitted by Wednesday, and Andy had called a meeting of key participants in the preparation of the bid for Sunday afternoon in order to monitor progress. Nora herself was a critical part of the legal team advising Nigroup, and they all worked tirelessly to ensure that the bid was safely completed and lodged in time on Wednesday afternoon.

Nora found that Andy's emotions fluctuated as events unfolded. As the work progressed she realised, more than ever before, that he could be very demanding, inconsiderate and even obstructive. Sometimes the experts had to work around him, in a sense, in order to make progress. When matters were going well, his mood was buoyant. When there was a delay or a setback, he was suddenly down. After the bid had been submitted he could hardly wait until the result of the auction was announced. He spent hours in fruitless speculation about the possible result, and Nigroup's chances of success. He wanted to stride upon a larger stage. He wanted to be on the front pages of the newspapers and business journals as the driver of a successful take-over. He wanted to be interviewed on television for the national and business news broadcasts. All his hopes and doubts were poured into Nora's ears, and his attitude changed continually with his emotions. He was happy and loving, then anxious, doubting, demanding and inconsiderate. He was also training hard, and the resulting physical fatigue only aggravated matters, making him even more irritable and selfish. Nora began to realise that theirs was a relationship that would need a lot more managing than she had anticipated. However, she resolved to be very careful until she was quite sure that he was, indeed, securely bound to her.

On Tuesday evening, 30th April, it was announced that Nigroup was the winning bidder in the Stella auction, subject only to regulatory approval. Andy was ecstatic. He was in his element, being interviewed by television and the press, and the centre of attention of the financial analysts and in his social circle.

The only thing to cloud his triumph was the behaviour of the Nigroup share price. The morning after the announcement was made it rose briefly to 540 cents. Then selling came in as the market reflected on the deal. Were Nigroup paying too much? How much might they have to pay out in cash? Gradually the price came down to 515 cents, and then fluctuated for some days between 515 and 510. Andy watched anxiously, and his emotions changed with the share price. Surely they would not have to pay out cash for Nigroup? Would Tony be right after all? Impossible! The market was still strong and the Nigroup price would recover. It was still holding above the critical 500 level. Nora listened to his hopes and doubts and bore with apparent equanimity his conflicting moods.

Tony had made no further attempt to contact Nora, and they had not spoken at all, since his phone call to her after he had discovered her departure. Nora had, however, seen him twice. On the evening of the Friday following the storm, she had been returning home from an afternoon meeting with a client, when she had seen him out running with 'that Sylvia woman'. The two had presumably just left the Club and were crossing the busy main road. They had negotiated one half, and were stranded on the grassy island that ran down the middle of the road, waiting for a gap in the traffic to allow them to cross to the other side. The two were chatting and laughing as they waited, apparently happy and carefree together.

The next day Nora had gone shopping in the very up-market local shopping centre. As she passed one of the coffee shops that had comfortable tables and chairs set out in the open, she saw Tony and Sylvia sitting at one of the tables. They were in earnest conversation and had eyes for no one else. Nora noticed that Tony looked solemn, and that Sylvia had lovely lustrous hair and large dark eyes. Tony placed a hand affectionately over one of hers on the table between them.

Nora walked on, but the image lingered in her mind, and rankled. She began to feel resentful. It was not right that Tony should get off so lightly, and forget her so easily. He should be punished. He should be made to pay. He should not so easily take up another woman, and be comfortable with her, as he seemed to be doing. She brooded. Then on Monday she phoned Sylvia.

"I'm phoning to tell you that you've been seen going around with a married man. That married man happens to be my husband."

Sylvia nearly choked. "But you walked out on him!" she exclaimed. "I saw the note you left for him. I even helped to clean up the mess."

"Tony and I may have had our problems, but we are still married."

"You can't seriously believe that you two could still get together again?"

"Probably not. But we are not yet divorced. Leave him alone, or I will make things very messy and very nasty for both of you. Divorce settlements can be drawn out, and made very complicated and unhappy. And have you heard of alienation of affection? You have caused the break-up of my marriage. You've been seeing Tony for a long time and have taken his affections away from me. I will clearly be seen as the long-suffering wife in this affair. If you care for him, leave him alone, or things might just get nasty for both of you."

"Your Andrew would not be happy about the drama, or perhaps the kind of publicity, any action of yours against us would create. It would hurt your relationship."

"He sympathises with me. I'm sure he would support me," lied Nora.

The conversation continued for quite some time, until eventually Sylvia put down the phone. She was shaken by the call, and sat alone in silence for a long time and pondered. She did not seriously believe that Nora could have any real case against Tony or herself. Also the manner of her leaving Tony was against her. But then might she not portray that as the ultimate expression of the agony and frustration of an aggrieved wife? Whatever the merits of any argument, Sylvia was quite certain that Nora was very capable of making trouble if she wanted to. That would hurt Tony, and probably also herself. Should she yield to Nora's threats, or should she ignore them?

What Nora could not have known was that she had been playing upon some of Sylvia's own internal doubts. Had she really helped cause the break-up of Tony's marriage? She did not think so, but was she really only making herself believe what she wanted to because of her love for Tony? Tony needed support, but, by staying close to him now, would she hurt him more than if she kept away? She also wondered, as she had before, whether she was not taking unfair advantage of his present vulnerability to bring him closer to her. She loved him and wanted him, but not at the price of causing him hurt, or of his one day perhaps regretting the haste with which he had fallen into her arms on the rebound from the effective end of his marriage.

That evening at the Club, Tony noticed that Sylvia was quiet and strained. She did not volunteer reasons in response to his concerned inquiries. She left after a quick drink, pleading a headache and wanting to be on her own. She also had school work to do.

Sylvia had a restless night, turning these things over and over in her mind. Eventually she decided to go away and think. She needed to distance herself from everything and try to gain a proper perspective, so she could choose a course of action between what she wanted, and what she ought, to do. Perhaps they were one and the same? She could not be sure.

She had leave due to her. Early in the morning she requested, and was granted by a startled school principal, a few days' off on grounds of urgent private business. She phoned Tony that afternoon and told him that she was going away for a while to think about their relationship, and even whether they should continue it in present circumstances. She was greatly pained by his shocked reaction, and felt compelled to tell him about Nora's telephone call.

"She shouldn't have done that," said Tony furiously. "I'll talk to her. She can't hurt us, though she may try. We've done nothing wrong. We have nothing to hide. I'll come and see you now."

"No, I don't want to see you. You'll only persuade me to stay. I've made my arrangements. I need to be alone to arrive at my own clear perspective, so I can decide which way to go. I do love you, Tony, and I believe in the things you stand for, but I'm not sure the time is right for us now. I know I'm hurting you, and I'm sorry, but I'm afraid I may cause you even greater harm. I don't know. I'm so tired and confused. I'll let you know one way or another, as soon as I know myself."

"Where will you go?"

"I'll go and see my boys. Not for long, as they're at school, of course. Then I'll probably go into the mountains somewhere."

"Will you be taking your running shoes with you?"

"Yes. I will keep training, I promise. I still believe in you and your approach to things, including Comrades. I still want to show the doubters that you are right."

In a few hours she was gone.

A cold front moved through from the south overnight and a mighty gale blew for some hours. In the morning Tony went out to run to clear his head after a sleepless night. A cold wind still blew. Without consciously choosing it, his route took him through Delta Park. He stopped, as he often did, to walk through 'Our Garden'. It looked sad and untidy after the overnight storm, with leaves and twigs, blown off the trees, lying everywhere. One of the tallest pines had been blown over. With its roots cruelly exposed, it lay on the ground across one of the clearings.

44

Tony went home and sought refuge from his misery in work. The previous evening, after the stock market had closed, Nigroup had been announced as the winner of the auction for the controlling interest in Stella Insurance. Andy would be in his element. Only regulatory approval was now needed. Tony watched the Nigroup share price rise, and then begin to fall, until it settled around the 515c level. The shares of Enduring Bank, with its large holding in Nigroup, fell in sympathy. Tony knew that that in turn was not good news for Nilife, which depended heavily on Enduring and the performance of its share price.

The business news also confirmed Tony's impression that stock markets around the world, and particularly in the United States, were becoming more and more volatile. There were large daily price movements in both directions. It was a tussle between the market bears, who believed that share prices were too expensive and should come down, and the bulls, who had done so well in the markets for so long that they believed that stock prices would continue to rise. The effects were also being seen in the local markets, which were increasingly volatile. People from all walks of life, with little or no knowledge of financial markets, or even of the companies whose shares they bought, were continuing to trade enthusiastically. Investors were being advised to buy shares whenever the markets fell back a little, in order to benefit from the expected resurgence in prices. Tony continued to worry and be cautious.

He telephoned Mary, and they met for lunch. She was as warm and assuring as ever, and he felt better just being in her company.

"Don't worry about Sylvia," she said. "She'll be back. I know she loves you very dearly. Perhaps it's better that she should be perfectly clear in her own mind before you commit yourselves to each other. I'm sure you'll hear from her soon."

She told Tony of the reactions at Nigroup to the result of the Stella auction. The offices were abuzz, and Andy was euphoric. However, many people were now beginning to wonder about the security of their jobs once the merger of the two life companies was put into effect. As Tony had expected, Mary herself was being retrenched following the departure of her boss, to whom Andy believed she was too close for her to be retained at Nigroup. It was stupid and vindictive, for Mary was an excellent worker and Tony's successor would need a secretary, but Mary did not contest it as she would be well paid to go and she wished to continue working for Tony. She would leave Nigroup in the middle of May, and would then join Tony as his first employee in the new company.

Later in the day Tony received a phone call from Victor Pots.

"Hello, Tony! Are you going to be at the Club tomorrow evening? If so, could you please pop into the office for a while, say at six-thirty. The Committee would like to discuss a few things with you. Just an informal chat."

"Victor, you know that I will still be running at that time. If you can make it seven o'clock I can be there."

When Tony entered the Club office the next evening, having just finished his run and being still sweaty in a tracksuit, he found that only Victor, Trixie and two other members of the committee were there.

"Hello, I thought this was to be a committee meeting," he said as he sat down.

"Well, not everyone could be here," said Victor, who was of course the Club Chairman. "But thank you for coming. We would like to talk to you about a few things that we are not happy about. Firstly, we hear that you were very rude to our Secretary, Trixie here, on Sunday."

"What is this, a disciplinary hearing? Have you come with a whole charge sheet?"

"No, no, no, we just want to have a friendly chat."

"What about? I don't recall having done any wrong, or having done or said anything to apologise for."

"Quite frankly, Tony, we are not happy about your approach to running, and the way you are influencing and coaching some runners in this Club."

"As far as I know, I have encouraged a lot of people. They seem to enjoy their running, and are usually very happy with the way their performances improve. They do not need to heed my advice or join my evening runs if they don't want to."

"But Tony, to take beginners for a jog around the park is one thing. Now you are getting those same people involved in Comrades, and with little or no training. Lately you've also started interfering with Mandla Dube, who is one of our top athletes. What makes you think that you are competent to coach in that way?"

"Years of experience, a lot of study, reading, observing, having made most of the mistakes myself and learnt from them. Hundreds of races on the track, cross-country and road, right up to Comrades itself. Isn't that enough? Besides, I have never coached anyone who did not want me to. My current Comrades group asked me to help them months ago, and we are working to a plan. They're doing well and are very excited about their progress. Mandla was exhausted and almost crippled from over-racing, and he accepted my offer to help him."

"You pulled him out of the long run, and you've stopped him from racing. We need him to be properly fit, and we need him to run for the Club."

"He has raced too much, he has been recovering from an over-use injury, and now he is preparing for Comrades, which is his main aim. Can't you think of the athlete, instead of pot hunting (excuse the pun) for the Club for a while? I am looking after the best interests of the runners who have put their faith in me."

"They are ignorant and misguided. From what we can see, they will have done nowhere near enough training. Some of them will have no chance of completing Comrades, Sylvia Parks for example."

"That is what was said about her before she qualified for Comrades. She supposedly had no chance of completing a marathon. She did decide to run Comrades very late, but we still got her into condition to qualify. Barring accidents, she will be ready for Comrades. In training, some quantity is necessary, but it isn't everything. If it were, all we would need to do would be to run every day until we dropped in order to win races."

"Tony, just because you never really train, that doesn't mean that you can lead others in the same way."

"Well, I've probably only run something over three thousand kilometres in the last year, and by some standards that is not a lot. But with good planning and the right quality work, it can do me quite well. It's not bad for an amateur coping with the demands of my kind of work. For my runners, I plan to take them from where they are to where they reasonably want to be. I cannot destroy a runner by imposing on him the kind of heavy volumes that I believe will only lead to his breaking down."

"Tony, why are you always so sure that you are right?" asked Trixie. "What you are doing is out of step with what most of the best people are doing. Why do you think you are right and the others are all wrong? Wasn't it the same with your work? I hear that you were thrown out of your job because you were too conservative, and stubbornly out of step with the best minds in the business."

Tony wondered who she had been talking to. Andy had been there on Sunday. He remained silent.

"We think you are a bad influence here," continued Trixie. "You were rude to me on Sunday, you are misleading the runners you are supposed to be coaching, and morally you are also a doubtful influence."

"What on earth are you talking about?" asked Tony, astonished.

"You've been rather too close to Sylvia Parks for some considerable time. Word is going around that your wife has left you for that reason. That is not a good influence on some of the younger people around the Club. Some even run with you."

Had Nora begun talking already?

"You make me laugh," said Tony, standing up. "What you say is not true, and it is none of your business. All over this place there are people falling in and out of love and marrying and divorcing. I will not stay to debate such matters. As for training for Comrades, let's see what happens on 31st May. Then we can have another chat if you wish. I will not be leaving the Club, if that is what you are angling for. My friends are here and I intend to stay. I must, however, thank you for keeping this to a friendly chat. I would hate to think what it would have been like otherwise."

With that he left.

Tony tended to deal calmly with matters as they arose, but then afterwards feel the emotions they generated. Despite his apparently calm manner, he was shaken. He bought himself a drink and sat out in the quiet coolness of the main terrace, gazing into the darkness beyond.

The attack had been unexpected, and to bring in his work and his personal relationships had been nasty. Here, as in his work, he believed that he acted with knowledge and insight, and always in the best interests of those who put their trust, through their assets or their running dreams, into his hands. He believed that he acted responsibly, carefully but not over-cautiously. Surely it was not wrong to avoid taking extreme positions with the possible dangers they entailed? Why should one be expected to follow the herd, even when it seemed hell-bent on its own destruction? To act independently seemed only to invite censure and sanction, to put oneself in conflict with the hierarchy. Even here, where he looked for fun and relaxation and companionship, he now felt that he stood alone, being targeted for views that were characterized as too conservative when seen against the fanatical pursuit of high volumes.

He would have felt less alone had Sylvia been there, but she too had left him.

45

The month of May blew in with a cold gale from the south. The weather had been calmer since the big storm, with clear April days and increasingly cooler nights and early mornings, but the cold front that came with the start of May gave warning that winter was near. The nights were also growing longer, with most of the training now having to be done in darkness. The runners were becoming used to that, and white clothing and reflective belts had become normal wear for responsible runners to make themselves more visible on the roads. Now the added challenge of cold, chilly winds and occasional late season rain came to test their resolve. Warm clothing, and woolly hats or gloves, were necessary at times. Autumn was far advanced. In the parks and beside the roads leaves lay in profusion. When dry they crunched underfoot, they formed soggy or slippery carpets when wet, and sometimes they concealed the road surface from the wary runner, who had to feel his or her way when already blinded by the headlights of oncoming traffic.

The fact of the arrival of May brought mixed emotions to runners looking towards the Comrades Marathon. There was excitement because the month of the great race had come at last. There was apprehension amongst those who felt that their preparation was inadequate, and panic amongst the injured or ill who felt they were losing training and fitness and had to recover just to be able to be at the start in a few weeks' time.

The running scene seemed to be full of walking wounded. The period of heavy training still had some days to go, but everyone was now tired. The sensible were monitoring their progress carefully, and just keeping on the right side of breaking down. The fanatics were still obsessed with distance, and were pushing themselves to extremes that found out their physical or mechanical weaknesses and left them injured. Some would recover in time for the race, and some of them would even come to wonder how they came to run so well after being saved from themselves by the enforced rest needed to recover from injury. Some would not recover, and would have to try again another year. The strongest would survive the enormous demands they placed upon themselves, but would arrive at the start tired, and would give tired race performances.

Winter seemed to bring in assorted germs and viruses that manifested themselves in colds and flu, and throat and ear and other infections. Runners who were operating near their limits, and who were becoming chronically tired, were susceptible to these ailments, so that many of them were ill or bordering on illness. They learnt that to be fit was not necessarily to be healthy. Tony had taught his runners to recognise their warning signs, not only sore muscles or tendons or joints, but also niggling sore throats or runny noses, and to cut back on training to avoid crossing the threshold into full injury or illness. Alas, even with the best of intentions and monitoring, it was not always possible to avoid them. Sometimes it was a crisis at home or at work, or even a strenuous piece of gardening that pushed the body over the threshold.

Behaviour became weird or eccentric, and needed huge amounts of understanding and support from families, loved ones, friends and colleagues. Runners who were excessively tired became irritable or moody. As they focussed on their training and the race ahead, they became uncharacteristically selfish and obsessive. Their only subjects of conversation were themselves, their running, training, and Comrades prospects. Runners tried to avoid contact with anyone who might be carrying infections, and they kept away from crowded places, buses and trains. They avoided being too close to children who might bring colds or flu from school. They were often so tired that they lacked the desire to be very close to their spouses or lovers, but they also kept at a distance to avoid picking up any winter infections. A few even moved out of their marital beds or bedrooms and slept in isolation.

May also brought the start of the cross-country season. Cross-country running was fairly popular, and league and other races were traditionally held on Saturday afternoons during winter. As the days grew shorter, and a certain sharp coolness came into the evening air, Tony's thoughts always turned to the cross-country season. He enjoyed the technical, physical and mental challenges of racing on different courses over varying natural terrain. He also loved the combination of competitive racing of a very high standard with the informal village green atmosphere that usually prevailed. He believed it to be one of the ultimate tests of running, and felt that it was no coincidence that so many great cross-country runners had also excelled on the track and on the road, from the middle distances to marathons and ultra-marathons.

Tony invited his Hadedas to accompany him to the opening cross-country event of the season, and some of them came. Naturally there were discussions as to the part these races would play in their Comrades preparations, as well as the role cross-country running played in their training.

"No, it's not just because I'm a cross-country runner myself," said Tony, "although I have discovered the benefits because I am one. We need to be able to run well on all surfaces at all times, not only on the road. In cross-country running there is less of that damaging endless repetition of very similar movements, and continual pounding on a hard surface, that we have on the road. The surfaces are often softer and so easier on the feet and legs. Our feet and ankles and legs are also protected and strengthened in a more general way than is possible on the road, because the running movements are infinitely varied, depending on what is underfoot, and more muscles and other parts are brought into play. Because we need to adapt all the time to the unevenness of the ground, we are forced to run more relaxed, and to develop our running techniques. Cross-country is often thought of as more dangerous than road running, but in fact it is very beneficial. So we have been doing a lot of cross-country running in our training, but not only because of the beautiful environment away from the roads. Obviously, as we've been coming closer to a major road race, we have been gradually running more and more on the road, and this has also happened naturally because it has become more difficult to train on the country as the available daylight has become less.

"However, cross-country can still add variety to our running and help us not to become bored, especially as we are now spending so many hours running. Also cross-country racing is fun, and it is relatively short (eight to twelve kilometres) and very fast, so it will help us to run faster. Some of the finest Comrades Marathon runners are also really good cross-country runners. Alan Robb is one of them, and so is Bruce Fordyce. In fact I first really believed that Fordyce would win Comrades, after he had already come close, when I saw him running beautifully in a cross-country race at Krugersdorp."

Tony was sorry that Sylvia was away, but the others who came enjoyed the afternoon. One or two of the slower runners felt a little awkward running at the back of the quality fields that were found even in the older age groups, but they managed well enough. Tony ran near the front of the veterans' race, despite the heavy training he was doing. However, Mandla, under instructions to run fluently and easily, was a real star as he ran effortlessly near the front of the field in the men's 12km race.

Mandla had fortunately suffered no serious ill effects from his effort in the Club's long training run. His Achilles tendon had been rather stiff on that critical first step on the following two or three mornings, but Mandla, now suitably chastened, took a day's rest and then continued with the sensible progression of his training. His confidence was high, for he had run very well in the long run before he had been stopped. However, he was also learning the importance of not overdoing things, and of running his best when it really mattered. He joined the Hadedas occasionally for an easy session, but because he was training at essentially another level, he did most of his running away from the group. He kept in close touch with Tony, and often joined him and the others for a drink in the Hadeda bar in the evening.

Fred was running steadily and well enough for him to be reasonably satisfied with his progress. When tired he did not feel as well balanced as he should have been, and his left heel was a little sore. Perhaps it did not have the flexibility of the other after his foot operation. However, he was nursing himself along reasonably well.

He had come to enjoy being with the Hadedas and ran with them quite frequently. He often helped them with advice, born of his long experience, and was now being asked more and more questions about the Comrades Marathon, and the course over which it was run, as the race came closer. In many ways he was also a good example to the less experienced runners, and used as such by Tony in his coaching. For example, there was a tendency for many to start training runs and races too quickly as they felt fresh and full of energy.

"Don't start out too fast," warned Tony, "and don't run the first half of your races too fast. Just watch Fred. He always starts slowly, in training and in racing. His pace seems ridiculously slow early on, but he sticks to that same pace, and it seems lightning fast when you are dying in the second half of a race and he comes flying past you."

Fred's flow of stories and snippets of information continued, some long enough to make long weary kilometres seem less long, and some quite short.

"Many Comrades runners are very proud of their race numbers, especially those who have earned green numbers, reserved for them in perpetuity. One can earn a green number by winning the race three times, or by getting five gold medals for finishing in the top ten. However, most earn their green numbers the long way by completing ten Comrades in under the cut-off time of eleven hours. The most medals won by anyone so far is thirty-nine by Liege Boulle, number 141. That is far ahead of anyone else. Race number 1 belongs to Clive Crawley, who won the novices trophy in 1957 and is still going strong. He should have over thirty medals quite soon, unless something goes wrong.

"One of the best known numbers these days is 2403, which is worn by Bruce Fordyce. It had been used by another runner, who had not been able to finish the race. He concluded that the number was unlucky, and asked to be allocated another one. He did win his first medal in his new number, but Fordyce was given 2403 and has certainly proved that there is nothing unlucky about it."

After the Two Oceans Marathon, Melanie had progressed from walking to jogging and was now training quite well, even though her knee still troubled her a little at times. She was taking a more cautious approach than before, and was listening to Tony, and to Bill who often reminded her of Tony's advice, most of the time. In truth, Melanie had been shocked after Two Oceans into confronting the very real possibility of not actually starting the Comrades Marathon. She realised that it really was possible to do too much training and racing. She simply had to run Comrades, and could not afford to be stopped by injuries, especially self-inflicted ones.

She was still very busy at work. The volatility of the stock markets had not yet lessened the flow of investors who wanted their money to be placed in shares. So far the Stock Exchange had recovered from every recent setback, and it seemed sensible to take the advice of the experts who advocated buying shares on any weakness in order to benefit from the recovery and the further advance in prices which was expected to follow. That was also the view of the Bank's investment analysts whom Melanie was supposed to follow in giving advice to clients. However, she heard Tony's contrary, more cautious views on the stock markets, and began to wonder whether he might not be right there too. Only the future would tell, but she began to take more careful note of the degree of risk which her clients were able to absorb before advising them to invest in the stock market. She also quietly began to advise certain clients to sell some of their share investments and to preserve their profits in cash.

The end of April had been sad for Melanie, for it had brought the second anniversary of David's death. She was coping well now on her own, and new horizons were gradually opening up before her, but she could not mark the anniversary of the death of her beloved husband without a deep feeling of loss and sadness. Moreover, she still had her promise, to run their tenth Comrades, to keep. It therefore helped and soothed her, after a busy day at work, to put on her running shoes and do a really good training run. Surely David would have approved could he have been there. How proud he would have been of his once sedentary wife!

Melanie had written to the Comrades Marathon Association to request that she be allowed to run in David's race number. She knew that race numbers were reserved for competitors for a period of two years before they were reallocated. David's number would not yet have been allocated to anyone else, and if possible she wished to run their tenth Comrades Marathon in the same number that David had worn. She explained the circumstances in her letter and then waited for a reply.

Early in May she received a very kind letter from the Comrades Marathon Association. They sympathised with her about David's death and sent their condolences. They confirmed that David's race number was still being held for his use, but that in the circumstances they would allocate it to her to wear in the coming race. As she was a novice, who had not run a Comrades Marathon, she would naturally have to wear a standard race number, and not a yellow one that David would have worn in attempting his own tenth finish. They wished her well in her race.

Melanie was overjoyed.

"I must phone Bill and tell him the wonderful news," she thought as she reached for the telephone.

It was a sign of the importance he was increasingly assuming in her life.

Bill was of course delighted. He and Melanie were indeed growing closer and closer together. They were coming to depend on each other for support, and for sharing their hopes and fears and activities. Bill's divorce had become final at the end of April, so he now felt that there were no legal impediments to the progress of his relationship with Melanie. He realised, of course, the importance of the forthcoming Comrades Marathon for Melanie, and that she would not finally be able to leave her marriage behind her, and look ahead to a new life, until after the race. Bill fervently hoped that she would succeed.

The Comrades was also looming as a test for Bill himself. He had run and failed before. His health had failed him, and he had failed in his marriage and lost his job. Whatever the extenuating circumstances, he had been a failure. Now he felt that he was well on the way to recovery. His health had improved, he was running consistently and better than ever before, he had a close friendship with a lovely Melanie, and he had hopes of soon having a permanent job. His employer had taken a strong interest in his progress and determination in pursuing his Comrades goal, and had almost undertaken to offer Bill a permanent position if he could prove his physical and emotional recovery by winning a Comrades medal. The race had become a symbolic test, the passing of which would enable him to leave all his past failures behind him. Would it not be wonderful if he could present himself to Melanie, not only as one who loved her, but as a person made whole again, recovered from his past, and with a good job?

Josh and Sipho were continuing to follow Tony's advice closely and were generally making good progress. Both in turn had had early winter colds, and each had had to stop training for two or three days and then gradually work back to full volumes over the following few days. Tony had told them not to be too anxious about this temporary loss of training, but to be careful to allow the body the chance to recover, so the loss was minimized by a quick recovery. They continued to share all their long training runs and also ran together occasionally in the mornings. Josh still found it most convenient to run very early, before his day became busy, but he always tried to be at the Club on Tuesday evenings. Sipho enjoyed training with the Hadedas and still ran to the Club on most evenings in order to join them. He was now quite at home both there and at the Church, where he was also content to sit quietly in a corner in the back row during services.

As expected, fund-raising had picked up speed since Josh and Sipho had qualified for Comrades. Sponsorships, at so much per kilometre completed by each of them, were now being actively sought and obtained. Competition tickets had been printed and were being sold to those who would buy them for a chance to win a car if they were closest to predicting Josh's finishing time. Sister congregations were participating and sales were going well. However, the question had been asked as to what would happen if Josh did not finish. It had therefore been written into the rules of the motor car competition that all moneys would be refunded if Josh could not run or did not finish the race for some reason.

The mother church in the United States had been so impressed by the growth of Josh's congregation, the enthusiasm of its minister, and the concerted fund-raising efforts of the worshippers, that they had undertaken to make certain funds available to assist in the building of the new church. Even with all that activity it still seemed that there might be too large a gap in available funds to start building operations. However, certain wealthier members of the congregation then undertook to provide personal guarantees, which would allow the Church's bankers to advance sufficient money to enable the building project to be completed, provided the shortfall was within specified limits. It was a joyful moment when Josh and the fund-raising committee calculated that, provided the money from the Comrades Project came in as hoped, the shortfall would be within those limits and they would actually be able to start building their new place of worship. It really was now a case that if Josh and Sipho, and particularly Josh, could finish the Comrades Marathon at the end of the month, the new church building would become a reality.

"The prices of our shares have also gone up well," said the Chairman of the fund-raising committee. "Perhaps the shortfall will be even less if they rise further."

46

It was a cold, clear Monday morning. As Josh stepped out of the front door into the Church grounds and looked around him, his breath smoked in the cold air. Stars glittered in a dark, cloudless sky. Only in the east a faint luminescence on the horizon gave promise of the coming dawn. Josh shivered as he walked to the road to begin his early morning training run. He had put on a warm white top, and he knew that his bare legs would warm up once he was into his running and his body was generating heat. His beard and long hair would keep his face and head reasonably warm, but he wondered whether he should go back and find a pair of gloves to put on his hands.

"No, better not disturb Maria," he thought as he began to jog. He moved slowly at first, partly because he needed to warm up, and partly because the lighting was poor in this relatively new suburb. There were no street lights, but most of the houses had outside lights and they helped him on his cautious way towards the main road about a kilometre away. There the better lighting made for safer running, so he was able to pick up his pace and settle into his desired rhythm. Then he could let his thoughts go into free flow. He was aware of a hint of colour in the east, and the first bird calls. How did they sense the dawn so early? Once he had made the effort to leave his cosy home, and once he had warmed up and could feel the familiar rhythm of his running, he found that he could enjoy the early mornings. He loved the dawns, for they always reminded him of regeneration, renewal and the Resurrection. Today, however, his mind turned towards other matters.

The weekend newspapers had been full of news and opinions about the stock markets, here and abroad. The majority view still appeared to be that share prices would rise further. However, the papers had also quoted one or two more cautious opinions, which suggested that shares in general were overvalued and that the markets were overdue for a reversal. Wall Street, and the Johannesburg Stock Exchange, were both showing a degree of volatility which suggested to some that the various market players were uncertain as to which way prices would go. Josh had been monitoring the shares in which part of their Church building project funds had been invested. They had done well and on balance were holding onto their gains, but Josh had noticed that recently prices were rising and falling by increasing amounts, even on a daily basis. He was becoming a little anxious. What if prices fell just before they needed the money? The fund-raising committee, and particularly the Chairman who had suggested the share investments on the advice of his broker, were still optimistic about them. Josh was no longer so sure. He turned these things over and over in his mind as he ran. He had heard Tony speak of the share markets, and understood vaguely that he had lost his job because he had been too cautious. Josh thought of the funds they had collected and what they still needed. It would be disastrous if they lost money on the stock exchange. It would seriously delay their project.

He stopped running as he reached the gates of the Church property and stepped onto the lawn in front of the hall, scarcely aware of where and how he had run. He looked around him. The sun had just risen and the sky was bright in the east. The church grounds were neat and still pretty, despite the fact that the early frosts were slowly turning the grass to a yellow-brown. Josh looked at the open area reserved for the new building, and in his mind saw it soaring heavenwards. He decided to talk to Tony.

Tony was, indeed, still very cautious about share prices, which he was convinced were grossly overvalued. The risk of a fall was increasing all the time, although it was not possible to predict precisely when that might happen. It could be in days, or even months, if it happened at all.

"Tony, would you be prepared to come and give your views to our fund-raising committee?" asked Josh. "I fear that they are only hearing positive opinions, but I think we should look at a different view and assess the risks we are taking. We have a meeting arranged for tomorrow evening at seven o'clock. I would be very glad if you could come."

"That would be a pleasure," said Tony. "I'll come after running. I'll probably have to go your way in any case, in order to take Sipho home."

So Tony met with Josh and the fund-raising committee. He presented them with his analysis of the current international and local economic environment, and the position of share markets, particularly the local stock exchange. He understood their optimism, but was unable to share it. Most importantly, the funds they had invested in shares would probably be needed quite soon. Ideally such moneys should not be invested in the stock exchange, which should be for long-term funds, which would hopefully grow over time, but where short-term market fluctuations could be viewed as less important. He felt that the risks they were taking were too high, especially in view of their imminent need for the funds which they had worked so hard to gather. He advised them to sell their shares at once, or at least to start a selling programme, and keep the proceeds, including the profits they would realise, in cash so that the money would be there when it was needed.

There was much doubt and discussion, but the meeting felt that Tony's views could not entirely be ignored. They would have further discussions amongst themselves.

"Thank you very much for meeting with us and giving us your advice," said the Chairman, as Tony was about to leave.

"Thank you, Tony," said Josh. "We will pray about these things."

47

Sylvia had been away for a little over a week. She had managed to spend some time with her sons, despite the fact that they were well into the school term, and had then drifted towards the Drakensberg Mountains in northern Natal. By phoning ahead, she had been fortunate to obtain a reservation at the hotel at Cathedral Peak, a mountain resort in what Sylvia believed to be one of the most beautiful parts of the world. Set in pretty gardens on a natural shelf above the scurrying Umlambonja River, it was surrounded on all sides by mountains. Lower down were the green foothills, or 'Little Berg', with their eroded sandstone cliffs, protea tree savannah and open grassland. Towering above them were the spectacular rocky heights and peaks of the Cathedral Peak ridge and the main escarpment, rising to more than three thousand metres above sea level.

At this time of the year the weather was usually excellent, with cool mornings and evenings and mild clear days. Each morning, Sylvia took a daypack with food, drink and warm clothing and set out on one of the many paths leading from the hotel. She wandered amongst the mountains, beside streams, in friendly valleys and wild gorges, and through the subdued lighting of the yellowwood forests in the damp, sheltered folds of the upper valleys of the Little Berg. She covered great distances, but took her time, and paused to absorb the beauty all around her. When she was high up, there were the wide views, of the wild high mountains with their varied peaks, of steep cliffs and serrated ridges descending to the friendly grassy heights and watered valleys of the Little Berg, and the rolling Natal midlands extending far into the hazy distance. When the land closed in around her, there were always the smaller things to attract and delight. There were cool streams from which she could drink, and waterfalls, plunging into inviting pools surrounded by tall green yellowwoods, or with sunlit rainbows suggesting the hope of happier times. There was the varied vegetation, with different grasses now in seed, ferns on the forest floor beneath the high canopy, and tree ferns standing in little valleys. There were aged looking oudehout trees, the twisted candelabra shapes of the proteas, and, despite the season, many flowers, including the bright orange of some tall late-flowering leonotis, and both pink and white helichrysum, or everlastings. There were also many birds, from the little ones that Sylvia always found so difficult to identify, to the soaring black eagles and jackal buzzards.

Like Tony, Sylvia always felt closer to God when in the mountains. She prayed for direction. Absorbed in the loveliness around her, she gradually began to relax and somehow feel whole again. She often thought about Tony, how he would love to be in this beautiful place, and wondered what their future might be. As she walked, and as she ran in the evenings to keep in touch with her training, her mind was often in free flow, but somewhere below the surface of her immediate thoughts it was analysing her problems and evaluating alternatives.

On the Thursday evening before she had to return to work, Sylvia was jogging on an easy circular route she always enjoyed. It was mainly on a broad gentle slope, which was really an extension of the shelf on which the hotel had been built. She seemed to be in a deep hollow completely surrounded by mountains. As they were so high the sun went behind them quite early, so she was running in shade and the evening light was soft. She marvelled as she always did when she saw the wonderful shape of the Cathedral Peak ridge to the west in silhouette against a translucent sky, but it disappeared from view as the path took her close under One Tree Hill just across the river which it then followed.

Sylvia was running slowly, even though the path was relatively safe, for she had already walked about eighteen kilometres that morning. She was also trying to summarise her thoughts and decide whether she had reached a point of decision. She was now fairly sure that Tony's relationship with Nora would probably have ended sooner or later, and that she had played little or no part in its break-up. It was clear too that the marriage could not be repaired after recent events. She also now realised that her relationship with Tony was not something that had grown simply on the rebound, out of his shock at the suddenness and manner of Nora's departure. Certainly that had brought them closer than they had ever dared allow themselves to be before, but it was a closeness born of several years of friendship and trust, and so was firmly based. On that dreadful night his first call had been to her. Surely that was significant? Also, she should have remembered that Tony was not naive. He was a mature man, who was quite capable of evaluating even his most intimate relationships and deciding whether or not he wanted to continue with them. If he said he wanted her, why should she not accept that? She was still concerned that Nora really would cause trouble if she went back to Tony, and she did not want to be the cause of hurt to him. But if he really wanted her, was she not hurting him more by staying away, and harming herself at the same time? If she were close to him to support him, surely any vindictiveness on Nora's part would not have any great effect? And why should Nora be allowed to keep Tony and her apart, as they now were, simply by making threats? Indeed, Nora was winning, while she and Tony were the ones to suffer. Had she damaged her relationship with Tony by coming away? How would he react if he phoned her? Should she contact him and say that she now wanted to take up their relationship again? Her longing was there. Should she now act?

As her thoughts reached that point, she was coming to the end of One Tree Hill on her left. The next valley was opening out to reveal high above it a wonderful silhouette of the lofty western ridge. The high points of the Outer Horn and Cathedral Peak on each side were linked by what seemed a long saddle with the Bell peak rising from it. Sylvia stopped, as she always did at that point, to wonder, and to absorb the beauty. Then she saw the clear pale curve of a new moon hung above the dark rim of the mountains in the blue-white radiance of the sky. She caught her breath. It was so beautiful. It was the sign she had prayed for. It spoke of hope and a new beginning. She knew what to do.

Sylvia telephoned Tony as soon as she was back in her room at the hotel. The voice that answered the phone was cautious.

"Hello."

"Oh, Tony, it's wonderful to hear you. I've missed you and I want you. Please come. Come at once. I'm sorry to have been so stupid. I see that now. You do still want me, don't you?" She ended a little less confidently.

"Where are you? I have a meeting with a potential client tomorrow morning, but I'll leave as soon as I can."

It was dusk by the time Tony had driven down into Natal, and wound his way over the narrow snaking roads that led to Cathedral Peak. Sylvia had been looking out for him long before he could possibly be there, and their reunion was joyous. As soon as Tony had put his things in their room, they walked to the edge of the hotel grounds and held each other closely as they looked at the new moon, and the silhouette of the Cathedral ridge against the last lingering light.

Over a relaxed and sumptuous dinner, and later in the comfortable lounge before a warm fire, they caught up with the events of the past few days. Tony told her of the progress he was making in setting up his new business, of the fallout from the Club long run, of how his training was progressing, and most of all, how he had missed her and had been longing for her to call. He had not heard from Nora. Sylvia told him of her walks in the mountains and of her evening runs. She had covered long distances and was feeling much stronger, but a little slow in her running. She told him more of her thoughts and doubts and longings during those past few days, and of her final decision to phone him and ask him to come to her. At last they went happily to bed.

Saturday morning dawned clear and sunny, and they decided to celebrate their reunion by taking a long hike in the mountains they loved so much. They were due to complete the last of their very long training runs that weekend, but Tony felt that a major hike would do very well, and they could appropriately adjust their training in the coming week.

They set out on the narrow winding path which was ironically one of the main routes in that area to the mountain kingdom of Lesotho. They walked up through the Little Berg to Ribbon Falls, where they paused to drink from the stream, then crossed the grassy plateau and climbed steeply as they entered and wound their way through the narrow Camel ridge. They climbed for hours, and their surroundings grew ever more wild and rocky. They helped each other through the awkward Windy Gap, and went up through Organ Pipes Pass to the top of the escarpment. A turn to the right brought them onto the spur called Castle Buttress, where they decided to rest and eat and drink before the return journey. The views were breathtaking and utterly spectacular. They were on the edge of the escarpment, with the rugged bulk of Cleft Peak next to them on the left, and cliffs falling precipitously from their feet for hundreds of metres. Away to the left was the Cathedral Peak ridge, and far to the right that of Cathkin Peak. Ahead of them the land stretched out into KwaZulu and Natal to the far horizon. In this place wars and politics, the disputes and jealousies and worries of man, the rise and fall of investment markets and economies, all seemed of little importance. It brought a proper perspective to things. They silently thanked God for the beauty and the loveliness, for the opportunity and strength to be able to share it, and for this healing transition from their recent trials to a new time together. When they reached their hotel after the long descent, they were weary but happy, and very much at one with each other.

48

By the middle of May the long hard weeks of peak training were ending, or had ended, for the Hadedas. Those who had not experienced significant interruptions in their training, either for illness or injury, had already commenced their planned three-week taper. For those who had lost important training time, and for Sylvia who had to adapt to her late decision to attempt the Comrades Marathon, Tony had extended their peak training by a few days, and they were now entering a slightly shortened tapering period. Training had not stopped, and some sessions were still quite taxing. However, they were now gradually taking off the pressure, and allowing their bodies to recover from the heavy work, to realise the strength they had been training for, and to move towards a physical and mental freshness that would enable them to perform at their best on 31st May.

The Comrades Marathon now increasingly occupied all their thoughts, including final training and resting, race strategies, diets, drinks, what to take with them to Natal and on the run itself, as well as arrangements for transport and accommodation. Long ago Tony (or more correctly Mary at his request) had reserved a number of rooms for himself and his Comrades hopefuls at a hotel in Durban. It was not at the Comrades start in the centre of the city, but was reasonably priced and well situated on the Snell Parade, which ran close to the waterfront. The rooms had splendid views of the sea, and it was a short step across the road and onto the relatively quiet and beautiful Battery Beach.

Mary worked her last day at Nigroup on 15th May, and began to work for Tony the day after. Apart from her duties in the new investment business, she was soon caught up in Comrades fever and efficiently took charge of their organisational needs.

Mandla had not been selected for the White Waters elite squad for the Comrades Marathon, so he was included in her arrangements. When the hotel reservations had been made, Tony had expected that Nora would go down to Durban with them for the weekend. Now it was arranged that Sylvia would share a room with him in order to make hers available for Mandla and Sipho. Melanie and Bill had separate rooms, while others in their party included Josh and Maria, Fred and his wife Linda, and Mary and her husband John who had agreed to join in the excitement of the Comrades.

Between them they had enough transport to take them all to Durban. Mary also organised the non-runners amongst them to ferry the runners to the start on the morning of the race, and to bring them back from Pietermaritzburg at the end of the day. She also decided to organise a refreshment and encouragement point for the Hadedas just before the dreaded Polly Shorts Hill towards the end of the race. John and Maria readily agreed to watch the race from there and to help with the table. Later they were joined by three or four other Hadedas who were not running but who decided to go down to watch and be part of the Comrades Marathon. Linda agreed to take the Hadedas' tog-bags through to the finish, so they would have dry clothes and other essentials waiting for them at the end of the race.

49

Naturally Mary brought with her news of the latest happenings at Nigroup. The most important of these concerned the Stella transaction and the Nigroup share price. After trading for some time between 510 and 515 cents per share, the price had gradually declined to a narrow range just above the critical 500 cents level. Andy grew more and more anxious. He spent a lot of time watching the share price on the computer screen in his office, and made a continual nuisance of himself by bombarding the investment staff, and especially Rita, the senior equity dealer, with questions about the market for the share. Who was selling? Who was buying? What were the prospects for the share price? What could be done to keep it above 500? Andy had discretely called in some favours due to him, and had so encouraged the purchase of quantities of Nigroup shares on the market. The price had so far been held above 500c, but selling had continued, and Andy was running out of potential support.

On Monday, 13th May, just after the Johannesburg Stock Exchange closed for the day, it was announced that regulatory approval had been given for the Stella transaction, which had thereby become unconditional and final. The sellers, Growth Financial Holdings, now had five business days in which to inform Nigroup whether it would receive payment in Nigroup shares or whether it elected to receive the cash alternative of 500c per share. Nigroup now owned a controlling interest in

Stella Insurance, and, as control of Stella had changed, was now obliged to make an offer to buy the shares of all the other shareholders of Stella at the same price at which it acquired its controlling interest. Andy's joy at having secured control of Stella was mitigated by his worry about the Nigroup share price.

Overseas stock markets were soft overnight, and the Johannesburg Stock Exchange opened weaker in sympathy on Tuesday morning. At the opening, the Nigroup share price dipped below 500c. Andy had been anxiously watching the screen in his office, and was immediately on the telephone. He summoned George Jones, Head of Portfolio Management and acting Head of Investments until a successor to Tony was appointed, to his office. He also instructed Rita to come to him urgently with details of the position of the market in Nigroup shares.

"We have to get that price above 500 cents," said Andy, without preliminaries, as George entered his office. "What can you do?"

Rita arrived before George could reply.

"There are a lot of sellers at 495 and 497," she said. "There was some initial small buying from Merchant at the opening, but they have withdrawn. Buyers have retreated to 490, and they are small. A few thousand shares only."

"I want that share price above 500," demanded Andy. "I want you two to do something, at once. Surely we have unit trusts and independent portfolios which could take Nigroup shares at these cheap prices?"

"I'm not sure that we can legally deal in our own shares yet," said George. "I'll have to check. But in any event those portfolios where Nigroup shares are appropriate are already full up. I would not want to increase their holdings now. The market is weak and it would not be fair to the clients."

"I know the market is weak," screamed Andy. "I want you to do something about it."

"I can ask the portfolio managers to have another look at their portfolios," said George diplomatically, "but I'll be surprised if we come up with more than a few thousand shares, if anything."

"That will not be enough to take out the sellers," said Rita, "let alone get the share price up, and I'm sure we are not allowed to manipulate it like that. You must understand that there has been persistent selling for days. You can't stand up against the tide the way it's now running."

"Don't tell me what I can or can't do. I want that share price up. Do you realise that we will have to borrow billions if we have to pay cash for Stella? We don't have that kind of cash. I want action not objections. If you can't help then maybe you shouldn't be here. Do you want to be fired?"

"I'm resigning," said Rita quietly. "I have now had enough. Perhaps Tony Drummond will need a dealer. Somebody will."

"Don't mention that man to me. Get out!"

50

More than ten thousand entries had been received for this year's Comrades Marathon. In thousands of homes around the country runners were opening envelopes, from the Comrades Marathon Association, containing their race numbers, general race instructions and other information. Melanie's was waiting for her in her letterbox when she arrived home on Friday evening. She tore it open and immediately checked her race numbers. There they were, to be worn on the front and back of her running vest, and most important of all, there was David's number. The organisers had been true to their promise. She felt a rush emotion, joy and relief mingled with sorrow. She hastily looked through the accompanying documents, which she would read thoroughly later on. There were detailed instructions, covering matters such as how and where to register as a starter of the race, how to wear the numbers, seconding, refreshment stations, sponges and so on. There were also details about the Comrades Shop, where souvenirs could be purchased, of how to ensure that photographs would be taken of one if one wished, and of matters such as road closures and parking areas on the route and at the finish. Final instructions, together with a souvenir programme and a map of the course, would be received later. It all made the race seem suddenly very near and very real.

Melanie went back to the two numbers. She looked at the strips at the bottom where her details were printed, her name, race number, club, age, and the fact that she had not yet earned a Comrades medal. In other circumstances, David's details might have been there. She retrieved David's yellow numbers of two years ago, and laid them next to hers. Her eyes filled with tears and she sobbed uncontrollably. She knew she could not wear his yellow numbers, but she would carry them with her, next to her heart, all the way from Durban to Pietermaritzburg.

After she had calmed down, and made herself a cup of tea, she phoned Bill.

"I received my Comrades numbers this evening. They were waiting for me when I got home. They gave me David's number as they said they would."

"Are you all right?" asked Bill, concern in his voice. "You sound strange."

"Yes, I'm fine now. It was just the emotion of receiving David's numbers with my details on. It reminded me of him and that terrible time two years ago. I must just make sure I keep my promise to run his tenth Comrades for him."

They chatted and he could sense that she was gradually relaxing and returning to normal. Somehow they always had something to say to each other, and now it was no different, even though they had been running together a little earlier.

"Shall I come round?" he asked.

"No, thank you. I'm fine, but I'm tired and I would rather be alone for now. But let's do something nice tomorrow. What about a late, easy run along the Spruit? We could meet at the Field and Study Centre. It's so beautiful there. Then we could have a picnic after our run."

"That's a good idea."

"I'll get some nice bread, and cheese and fruit."

"I'll bring some wine."

Tony and Sylvia also decided to run along the Braamfontein Spruit that Saturday morning. There was no cross-country race that afternoon, and they would be running a half-marathon the following morning, so they met at the Club, after sleeping late, and ran easily downstream for a few kilometres before turning back. A cold early morning turned into a lovely mild sunny day. They chatted happily as they took pleasure in the easy fluency and rhythm of their own movements. They enjoyed the changing aspects of the river, from rocky rapids and sandbanks to still, clear pools, as it wound through open grassy areas, banks of reeds and shady woods. They saw many birds: hadedas with white-lined cheeks and sides shining mauve and green in the bright light, noisy crown and blacksmith plovers, calm and silent white egrets, a chattering gang of red-billed woodhoopoes, and a pair of black ducks floating serenely on the mirror-like surface of a shady pool.

On their way back they stopped at one of their favourite places, beside a large placid pool, above a small weir near the Sandton Field and Study Centre. Early farmers had left ruins and graves behind them, but also eucalyptus trees, which had grown to great heights and whose branches met to form arches across the river. Tony and Sylvia stood on the riverbank and watched the effect of the dappled light and shade on the slow-moving water. It was quiet save for the whisper of water running over the weir some way to their left, and the repeated clear call of a honeyguide, which always helped give a special character to that place.

"*Wheat*-purr, *wheat*-purr, *wheat*-purr…."

There were three sacred ibises standing on a sandy area below the far bank. Sylvia's gaze passed from them to a picnic table on the grass on the other side of the river.

"Look," she whispered, catching hold of Tony's arm.

Melanie and Bill were sitting at the table, quietly enjoying a picnic together. Melanie had placed a white tablecloth over the wooden railway sleepers from which the table had been made. On it had been laid plates and paper serviettes, a salad, cheese, fruit and a crispy loaf of white bread. Two gleaming crystal glasses held red wine.

"What communion they share!" said Sylvia. "I hope something comes of it, for both their sakes."

51

The weather changed on Sunday night, so Monday was cold and wet with a strong wind blowing from the south. It was one of those miserable days when no one wanted to go out of doors, let alone go running. Tony's Monday group was very much diminished that evening, but he was pleased to see that most of the Comrades entrants were there.

"It's good to see all you here," he said approvingly. "It's miserable, but we need to be able to handle any conditions. Who knows what the weather will be like on race day?"

They were huddled together, shoulders hunched, and jogging on the spot to try and keep warm in the light rain and gusting wind as they waited to set off. They were warmly dressed, some with waterproof tops, some with gloves and woolly caps. Sipho wore for the first time the new blue and white cap that Maria had knitted for him. He pulled it down over his ears as the group started slowly on their training run. That kept his head and ears warm, but his cheekbones ached and his eyes watered in the wind. His hands were soon frozen and stiff and sore.

"What on earth am I doing here?" asked Melanie, shuddering as they negotiated the slippery wet road, trying to see their footing while blinded by the lights of oncoming vehicles.

"Because you want to run Comrades," said Bill.

"Thank goodness I only want to do it once."

"Famous last words," said Tony. "There are three sets of them in Comrades. 'I only want to do it once', 'I have run a down (or up) and now I just want to run an up (or down) run', and the other is at the end of the race when people say 'Never again!' But somehow they keep being drawn back again and again. It can get into your blood."

They kept each other going with chat and banter, or lost themselves in their own thoughts.

Mandla had joined them this evening, opting for company and an easy run in the foul weather conditions. One of the training techniques Tony had suggested was to visualise aspects of the big race to come, to rehearse strategy and tactics, and to prepare the mind for what lay ahead. The imagining of good results also provided positive reinforcement for the athlete's mental state and motivation for the race. Mandla imagined himself running from rain and cold into sunshine outside Pietermaritzburg. Many people lined the roads and cheered as he passed one competitor after another. Eventually he ran alone onto the grass at the finish at Jan Smuts Stadium. He circled the field, still moving at a good pace and keeping his form, and then threw up his arms in triumph as he crossed the line. If he did well and became well known, then perhaps Terry might give him a good job and teach him about running shoes and equipment and how to sell them.

Tony waited for the runners to regroup at the roadside towards the end of their run. Ahead was a long, quiet, safe and well-lit stretch of road.

"OK," he said, "let's do our last fast effort from here to the stop street. No sprinting, no slipping, but going fast and smooth. Let's go!"

Led by Mandla they were soon strung out along the side of the road, but there were smiles and cheerful exclamations as they stopped, panting at the end of their fast effort. Except perhaps for some hands, they were now thoroughly warm and were enjoying themselves, despite the weather and the darkness. They were starting to feel the stamina and strength and speed that they had been training for.

After the run they met in the Hadeda bar for a drink. It was good to be warm and dry in that cosy place. Their heads were clear and their drinks somehow tasted better than usual. They had that glow of virtue and self-belief that comes from having achieved something against the odds, while lesser runners and ordinary mortals had merely stayed indoors.

Their talk was about tomorrow's time trial, pace judgement, race strategy and other matters related to the big race. Tony wanted them to use the last two Tuesday time trials before the Comrades Marathon to practise running at Comrades race pace, and falling as soon as possible into that pace even with the distraction of many other runners around them. As hundreds took part in the time trials each Tuesday, and especially before Comrades, it made for a very good exercise.

"We should all have our basic Comrades racing pace ingrained into our minds and bodies by now," said Tony. "Most of you did well in the half-marathon yesterday, but, as you saw, it can be quite tricky to settle into the right pace and rhythm, especially when it feels so very easy and there are others around you all wanting to run much faster. It will certainly be like that early in Comrades, as everyone will be hyped up and most will go too fast once the crowd at the start stretches out and they have the space in which to run. Tomorrow and the next Tuesday will be good practice. See if you can mentally isolate yourselves from those around you, and get immediately into your own Comrades race rhythm. Then hold it for the first six kilometres. Over the last two you can gradually speed up and finish running fast and fluently.

"Mandla, please remember, no dicing tomorrow with the guys you normally race with. You must go out at four minutes per kilometre. It will not only seem easy, it will feel ridiculously easy, and that is what we must all feel for the first part of Comrades if we are not to begin too fast. It's possible that hundreds of runners at Comrades will start faster than four minutes per K, but they'll pay the price. I promise you, Mandla, that you'll see them later on, so you must not panic about being left behind. The arithmetic is simple. Four minutes per kilometre for ninety K's will give you six hours, and very few achieve that. Our route is only 88.5 K's, so four-minute kilometres will, in fact, give you well under six hours. Those that attack the course at Comrades will suffer in the second half of the race. We will not attack the course, we will treat it with respect, we will seduce it gently, and it will be kind to us.

"Remember, it's all about control. We need to use what we have to the best of our abilities in the race, so we must keep control of ourselves. We must conserve and use our energies like misers. We will have plenty of need for it all before the end of the race. We must avoid being swept away in the excitement of the start, and we must keep to our own planned pace and strategies, until we have good reason to depart from them. We must concentrate. People so often say, 'What do you think about when you are running?' You think about what you are doing. Your mind is a computer, constantly monitoring where you are in the race, what you still have to do, how your body is performing, how your pace is, what needs to be adjusted, and so on. Sure, you must relax and enjoy the race. It will be a wonderful experience, but while you are taking in the atmosphere and all that is going on around you, you must not stop thinking about what you are doing and what you are supposed to be doing. The further we go the more we will have to concentrate.

"Mandla, you'll be at the serious racing part of the field. You'll find that you will probably have to concentrate really hard for at least the last two hours. That is much longer than in any more normal race. You must also not get carried away. Don't get too excited. For example, be careful about surging the way you might do if you want to pick up speed on the track or cross-country or in a short road race. If you want to speed up, do it gradually, remembering how long the race is. It may be best to spread your effort over quite a long distance. Remember, it's all about control."

"What painkillers are we going to use?"

"No painkillers at all!" answered Tony.

"But many people I know take them in Comrades."

"We will not use them at all," Tony emphasised. "The medical people will tell us how such drugs can cause damage to kidneys or stomachs. But if you take painkillers you are masking pain, which should be a warning sign. You do not know then how much you are really hurting. You do not know how much damage you are doing to yourself, so you cannot make a rational decision about whether you should stop running or not. Besides which, it's cheating. We will not do that.

"If you do run into problems still try to finish, unless it's totally stupid and dangerous to your health to do so. Always keep moving towards Pietermaritzburg. The clock does not stop, even if you do. Remember the words of the poet, Rudyard Kipling: '…fill the unforgiving minute with sixty seconds' worth of distance run'."

52

Old Fred was having a very difficult time in the last two or three weeks leading up to what he hoped would be his twenty-sixth successful Comrades Marathon. On Sunday, 12th May, he had completed his last very long training run reasonably well. He was tired, but his left heel, which had been niggling at times, had not been much of a problem once he had warmed up thoroughly. With all the hardest of his training now completed, he was looking forward to a relatively comfortable period of tapering towards the race itself.

On Monday he had joined the Hadedas for an easy training session, which he had enjoyed. Tony had just returned from the Drakensberg with Sylvia. It was good to have her back after a few days away. He remembered telling her, and those nearby, how exciting it was to be at the start of a Comrades Marathon, even for him after all his years as a competitor. That had, of course, led to the subject of Max Trimborn.

"Max Trimborn is one of the great characters of the Comrades," he had told them, as they ran along a quiet, dark road, "and not because he was one of the greatest runners of the race. His best position was in fact fourth, in a small field, but he earned 'only' eight medals between 1933 and 1948, when he had his last finish. Of course, the world war intervened, so the race was not run for five years. Max could produce a very realistic imitation of a cock's crow, and, sometime in the thirties he began to produce it at the early morning start of each race. It became a traditional part of the start, so even when he had stopped competing, he would still be there each year to watch the start and produce his famous cockcrow. As he grew old his voice gradually became hoarse, but fortunately his cockcrow has been recorded and is now played each year at the start. Make sure you listen out for it on the thirty-first."

That evening he and his wife, Linda, had gone out for dinner. He had woken up in the early hours of the next morning feeling very ill and with bad diarrhoea. He had been unable to go to work, and had spent most of the day on his bed, aching and ill, with a 'running tummy'. The next day he was not much better and stayed at home. On Thursday he only worked part of the morning, but felt so ill that he went to the doctor, who said the cause was something he had eaten and prescribed medicine. By Friday morning the diarrhoea had stopped and he was able to start eating a little. He managed to get through the day at work, but felt too weak when he reached home to be able to train. He was now seriously worried about his prospects of running Comrades.

He slept late on Saturday and then tried to train. He found he was too weak to run so he had to walk. Even then he could only move very slowly. He dragged himself for about two kilometres, but felt totally exhausted at the end of it. Sunday was a little better, and he managed to walk about three kilometres in the morning, and another two in evening. On Monday, he was able to jog three kilometres very, very slowly in rain and a bitterly cold wind. The next day he forced himself to shuffle seven kilometres in an agonizingly slow 47 minutes. On Wednesday he did better, completing ten kilometres in an hour, but his left heel was sore towards the end. He tried to repeat that run the next day, but had to start walking after a while, as his heel was hurting too much. He limped home in about 95 minutes, tired, sore and dispirited. In total he had not covered much distance in the past few days, but it was now clear that even that had been too much too soon in the circumstances. After being immobilised for a few days, he had aggravated his latent injury by trying to get back into reasonable training too quickly. His progression had been too steep.

Now all he could do was to try to recover as best he could, and then decide whether it would still be worthwhile to go down to Comrades. He rested a day, then covered a lonely four kilometres, alternately walking and jogging very slowly, on a grass sports field near his home. The next day was Sunday, so he went again to the field, when the weather had warmed up a little, and coaxed himself to jog. It seemed once again his lonely struggle of the past year. With several stops, he managed to cover six kilometres. The pace was far too slow to allow him to complete a Comrades Marathon, even if he could maintain it all the way, which now he could not. However, he was making progress, and was recovering from his injury. On Monday he again trained on the grass, too scared to risk his heel on the hard road. It was cold and dark and he had to dress warmly, as his body seemed to generate very little heat at the slow pace he was going. This time he managed to complete about eight kilometres, again very cautiously. The Comrades was now in four days' time. He could have one more easy run, and then rest for two days before the race. If his heel continued to improve, he might just be able to get himself into the race by starting very slowly. If he could get going, he might be able to hold on for a finish.

He decided to go to Durban for the race. It was not what he would advise anyone else to do in the circumstances. However, Comrades came only once a year, so he would have to try it or wait another year, when yet other problems might be there to keep him away. He would go and do his best on the day. He hoped his best would be good enough.

53

However the decision was taken, Tony was pleased to hear from Josh that the Church had sold its shares, and had deposited the money to earn interest at the bank. There were now growing numbers of voices in and around the investment markets saying that share prices, locally and abroad, had run much too far and were way too expensive. Most said the markets were due for a correction, some said they were headed for a fall, and a few were even speaking of a crash. As the consensus regarding lower prices grew, many professionals began to lighten their portfolios. That selling pressure did, indeed, cause prices to move lower.

The price of the shares of Enduring Bank, and of other financial services companies, began to slide quite rapidly. The market knew that if equity prices did fall substantially then the volume of merchant banking and other related types of business would decline. At least for a time, there would be fewer new listings on the Stock Exchange, fewer companies would be raising capital by new share issues, and there would be fewer takeovers and mergers. Nigroup was the largest shareholder in Enduring, so the Nigroup share price fell in sympathy. It had fallen to 450 cents when Growth Financial Holdings formally exercised its option to receive payment for the Stella Insurance shares in cash at 500 cents per share. There was little doubt that in due course the other, minority, shareholders in Stella would also choose the cash offer. Tony knew that Nigroup and Nilife did not have the cash, so their executive directors and managers were no doubt now frantically seeking ways to finance the purchase of Stella.

Tony also knew the relationship between Nilife's assets and liabilities. Shares in Enduring Bank, and in other financial services companies, formed far too high a proportion of the assets. Their market values were falling, and Tony knew that soon the value of the assets would be insufficient to cover the liabilities. Nilife would be borrowing very large amounts of money on top of a faulty structure that was weakening as the markets fell.

By Friday, 24th May, the voices predicting declines in the stock markets had swelled to a chorus. There had been persistent selling all that week. Wall Street was nervous, and by the close of business on Friday, the New York Stock Exchange had fallen by around nine percent that week. The Johannesburg Stock Exchange had fallen by eleven percent, with four percent on Friday alone. The market closed very nervous.

The weekend newspapers were full of the falling stock markets. Fund managers, and many individuals, had the whole weekend to contemplate falling share prices, and the possible further evaporation of gains they thought they had made. Also, thousands who had borrowed money to buy shares were now worried about how they would repay their loans if share prices fell. Suddenly everyone wanted out before prices went even lower.

On Monday the markets crashed.

54

Tony would never forget that last Monday before the Comrades Marathon. First of all, share prices on the Johannesburg Stock Exchange plunged from the opening bell. The market was in a state of near chaos all day as speculators and investors panicked, and tried to dump shares on elusive and unwilling buyers. Share prices fell by nearly twenty-five percent in the first two hours of trade. They recovered somewhat through the middle of the day, though the London market was also weak. However, before the close, Wall Street opened to a wave of selling and the Johannesburg market saw renewed frenzied selling pressure in the final half-hour of trade. It finished down nearly twenty-three percent on the day. Some individual counters were even more badly hit. One of them was Nigroup, which fell to 315 cents by the close.

For Tony it was a hectic day, keeping up with the progress of events and answering his telephone, which never stopped ringing. One call was from Josh who heard of the crash on the radio news.

"Tony, I just want to say 'thank you', from the bottom of my heart. The Lord has blessed us by bringing you to us as He did. Thank you for coming, and for your advice. Thankfully we can still sleep tonight."

It was with relief that Tony left his home office and drove to the Club to lead his group on an easy, relaxed run, which would be their penultimate training run before the Comrades Marathon on Friday. He was a little early, so, to relax after his hectic day, he took a stroll across the main field to the edge of the river. It was calm there, above the weir and rapids, as it flowed quietly through its grassy banks. The sun had already set, but the scene in the gloaming was a peaceful contrast to the frantic doings of men and women.

After a while Tony turned and walked round the edge of the field towards the meeting place with his running group. In the light from the main terrace of the Clubhouse he saw a patch of green clover to his right. As he glanced at it, his eyes caught sight of one stem that appeared to have four leaves, instead of three. He stopped and looked at it more closely. It was the first four-leafed clover he had ever seen. He searched the area for more, but there were none. He picked it carefully and placed it safely in his car before joining the group.

After their training run and a drink in the Hadeda bar, Tony and Sylvia eventually found themselves alone.

"I've got something to give you, to bring you luck at Comrades," said Tony, giving her the four-leafed clover.

Sylvia had also never seen one before and she accepted and examined it with delight.

"Thank you! I'll press it in a book, which I'll take with me to Comrades. I'm sure it will bring us good luck."

As they were finishing their drinks, they heard a shuffling sound and Melanie appeared. She was panting, perspiring, and still in her running clothes.

"I need a quick Coke, then I must go out and run some more," she said.

"Melanie, what on earth are you doing?" asked Tony in surprise. "We've finished training. We only have an easy time trial to do tomorrow. What are you doing?"

"My knee was hurting again last week," said Melanie, "so I went to see a specialist today. He said he would give me an injection to stop it hurting, but he needs to know where to inject. He said I must run until my knee hurts, so when I see him again tomorrow he'll be able to tell where to put the needle. I can't make it hurt, so I must go and run some more."

"Melanie, Melanie, give it up. You're not supposed to be running hard today. Just be grateful that your knee is not hurting any more."

55

At the White Waters Running Club, the last Tuesday evening club night before a Comrades Marathon was always a special occasion. For most of the members the running year revolved around the Comrades. All their hard work, fears and hopes, setbacks and progress were reaching a culmination with the race in three days' time. Most of them came to the Club to give and receive best wishes, to exchange last minute news and views, to soak up the atmosphere and share the excitement of the occasion. There was a general feeling of anticipation mingled with apprehension.

Tony arrived to a busy and colourful scene. Last minute arrivals were hurrying to the change rooms to change from working clothes into running gear. Others, in a motley array of mainly light-coloured running shorts, T-shirts or warm tops, and reflective belts, milled around the front terrace and adjacent lounge, where Trixie set up her helpers' tables in winter, and spilled onto the floodlit main sports field towards the start of the time trials. Sylvia joined Tony as they moved to the start for their final training session before the great race. They would do only five kilometres, at their respective planned Comrades Marathon paces. All around them was animation as people exchanged greetings and good wishes for the race on Friday, as well as news about themselves, their state of fitness and plans for Comrades. To Tony the conversation seemed to continue all around him, not only before the time trial, but also during it and afterwards when everyone dressed warmly against the winter chill and pressed into the bars, the lounge and the warmer fringes of the front terrace.

Trixie sat at her table, pink-cheeked, bright-eyed and animated, excitedly greeting people and wishing them well for Friday, answering questions, and giving final instructions to the Club's elite squad which would be travelling to Durban in a specially hired bus. Victor ran in the time trial, and would be racing on Friday, but he still managed to wander around, shaking hands, wishing people good luck, and motivating particularly those whom he expected to run into scoring positions in the various inter-club competitions within the race.

"Hello, Beth," greeted Victor. "How are you? You're tired and sore? Never mind. You should be all right by Friday. Get some sleep. We want that ladies' team trophy. Hello, Mandla! Are you getting fit again? A pity you're not taking things seriously this year, but I hope you have a reasonable finish. Hi, Richard! Ready for a good run on Friday? We need you…"

"Just ignore that, Mandla," said Tony quietly as Victor moved on. "You are ready to have a good run. I'm sure that on Friday you'll show them what you can do. Then we'll hear what they have to say."

"Ken, my mate, we've finally got here. That was a good, long run on Sunday, and I'm ready for my silver on Friday."

"I'm still with you, Kobus. The time has come for silver. I'm going to go out hard to make sure I get to half way at Drummond in three and a half hours. That will give me a chance for seven hours, and will give me half an hour in reserve in case I slow down in the second half."

"I agree, but we shouldn't slow down, because the second half is easier."

Johan and Simon were also full of confidence. They had trained hard for months and felt they could only do well.

"We'll see how things go on Friday," said Johan, "but we should be feeling strong, so we'll set out at a good pace and aim for a decent time. If we do slow down for some reason we'll have plenty of time in reserve."

"Hi, Tony! How are you? How's your group doing? Do you think they'll finish?"

"We should be OK, barring unforeseen circumstances," said Tony. "We've prepared well, had a good taper and will start slowly."

"No, I won't be running Comrades this year. My wife is having a baby. It's due any day now. If I can I'll be watching you all on TV, though."

"Hi, Tony! I saw your former boss, Andy, this afternoon. He can't wait to nail us at Comrades. He's full of confidence."

"I thought he'd be worrying about the stock markets," said Tony.

"Oh, I'm sure he is really, but he says that this is a temporary blip and that they'll recover soon. He says they always do."

Tony was of course mainly concerned about his own little band of Comrades aspirants. As far as he could tell they were all being disciplined, running easily at their planned basic Comrades paces. Mandla was ahead of him in the time trial, running easily and fluently in the dim light of the street lamps, and studiously avoiding the temptation to race.

Bill and Melanie were running together, as they planned to do on Friday for as long as it made sense for them to do so. Melanie was tired after a very demanding day at work as a result of the fall in share prices. She had cancelled her medical appointment, and thankfully her knee was not at all painful. She ran silently, concentrating on her pace and thinking about David and the enormity of the task she had taken on for him, for his memory, and, she now realised, for herself as well. Bill ran next to her in companionable silence, perhaps understanding her thoughts, but also asking himself whether he would finish the race this time, and trying to think positively.

Josh ran with his mind full of the church he would build for the Lord. The plans had been finalized, and approval from the municipal authorities had just been received. Sipho ran as in a dream, wondering at the change in his circumstances over the past few months. Six months ago he could not have imagined that he would be going to Durban to stay in a hotel on the beachfront and to try to run the Comrades Marathon.

Sylvia ran in a state of controlled excitement, taking in the banter and laughter, the anticipation and anxiety, all around her. She was glad that she had made her late decision to enter Comrades. It was good to be part of it all, rather than an outsider looking on.

Fred was right at the back of the field, cautiously testing his injured heel on the road for the first time.

PART FOUR

56

Sylvia's long-suffering headmaster granted her two days' leave so she could travel to Durban on the Wednesday before Comrades. Tony called for her at her home about nine o'clock when the heavy morning rush hour traffic had subsided somewhat. Tony then drove to the Club, where they picked up Mandla, who had also been given leave. After briefly conferring to ensure that they had not left anything essential behind, they set out for Durban. It was a cool highveld morning, but warm inside the car. They chatted happily as Tony picked his way through the traffic onto the ever-busy main highway to Durban. They were excited, for they were on their way at last, but also a little nervous because the great test was rapidly approaching. After a while they settled into near silence, wrapped in their own thoughts.

Sylvia tried not to think too much about the coming race as it made her feel weak and nervous and sent adrenalin rushing through her system. She tried to relax and keep her thoughts neutral, concentrating on the journey and the places they were passing. They left the smoggy urban sprawl behind them and found themselves in the browning highveld winter countryside. They passed hilly Heidelberg with its ever-vigilant traffic police, crossed the murky Vaal River into the Orange Free State, and followed the road through miles of undulating grassland and cultivated fields. Then in the distance they could see Platberg, the flat-topped mountain at

Harrismith. They drove down into the pleasant little town, situated in a hollow below the mountain, and stopped for a short break. They admired the splendid heights of Platberg, and talked of the famous, gruelling mountain race, in which every October hundreds of runners raced from the town to the top of the mountain, across part of the broad summit, and then down again.

Refreshed, they continued through hilly countryside, characterized by unusually shaped koppies with rocky krantzes near their tops, and golden light from the winter grasses. They crossed the Drakensberg Mountains into Natal as they wound their way down the spectacular Van Reenen's Pass, with wonderful views of the mountains and the broad sweep of Natal and KwaZulu below. Soon it grew warmer and they passed through miles of hilly thorn tree savannah, many of the trees being broad and flat-topped. The scene changed once more, to large forests and rolling hills, as the road descended through long green valleys on its winding way towards Pietermaritzburg. At last they were on the steep and pretty descent into the provincial capital, lying in a sleepy hollow below darkly wooded hills.

Tony drove into Pietermaritzburg and made his way to the lovely Alexandra Park on the Durban side of town. There they stopped for a rest, and for Coke and chocolate cake which Sylvia had brought for them, under now sparsely covered plane trees beside the lazy Msunduze River. Then Tony drove to the nearby Jan Smuts Stadium, where the Comrades Marathon would finish on Friday, and began to follow, in reverse, the route that the race would take. They planned to drive over the course on Thursday, but it would be a wasted opportunity to help familiarise themselves with the route if they did not take that way to the coast now. It was, moreover, a very pretty and interesting drive.

Tony had recommended that all his Comrades Hadedas drive over the course if at all possible. It would help them in the race if they knew what lay ahead. Almost more important, seeing the course in advance instilled in one's mind an awe and respect for the sheer magnitude of the distance, and of the hills along the way. One would then be unlikely to treat the course lightly, and would understand the imperative to use one's physical reserves wisely in the race. Josh and Maria, with Sipho, were also travelling to Durban that day, and they would follow the course in reverse as Tony was now doing. Josh had Church business to attend to on Thursday, so would not be able to drive over the course then. The others, who for work reasons could only travel on Thursday, would also see the course in reverse on their way, with the exception of Fred who felt that he already knew it well enough.

For Tony and Mandla, who had both previously run the Comrades, it was indeed a sobering reminder to see the course again, but Sylvia was appalled.

"How on earth am I going to do this?" she cried. "Is this really what I've let myself in for? I must be mad."

"Don't worry," said Tony. "For now just familiarise yourself with the course. Remember you've trained for it, and you'll have all day on Friday if necessary. Also, we don't have to do it all at once. Remember that we're going to the start, and will then run eight and a half kilometres. Then we'll run ten, and then another ten, and so on. We'll break the race down into small sections and achieve them one at a time."

It was almost dark by the time they reached their hotel. They settled into their rooms and discovered that Josh, Maria and Sipho had already arrived. They all had a quiet evening, relaxing after the day's journey. It was lovely to step out of their rooms onto their balconies and breathe the mild, moist, salty, sea air. They had come down about a mile in altitude during the day. The coloured lights of the Durban beachfront stretched out to their right, the lights of ships gleamed out at sea, and they could hear the restless sound of the surf rolling onto the beach across the road. Before they retired for the night, they all went down onto the beach and wet their feet in the shallow, foaming edge of the Indian Ocean, watching the reflections of moonlight on the restless water further out.

As they walked back to the hotel, Tony was reminded that running, and the Comrades Marathon in particular, were helping to move the country towards a normal society. There the colour of one's skin was not important, and all people could live and work and play and be comrades together. That there was a long road still to be travelled in that direction was drawn to his attention by a sign, indicating that that beach was reserved for white persons only.

57

The Comrades Marathon is one event that draws almost the whole country together each year, thought Tony as he queued at the Comrades exhibition to register himself as a starter for the race.

It was Thursday morning, and Sylvia, Mandla and Sipho were all with him. After a lazy morning lie-in and a late breakfast at the hotel, they had strolled along the beachfront to the Pavillion, on the corner of Old Fort Road, where registration was taking place. Apart from the race registration facilities, there was a popular Comrades Shop, selling a wide variety of clothing and numerous other souvenir items, as well as a number of separate stalls where manufacturers and marketers of running shoes, clothing, sports drinks and other products were promoting their wares. It was a noisy, colourful scene, where male and female runners and their families and friends of all races jostled and mingled, sharing smiles and greetings and pleasantries as they queued to register or wandered around to see the exhibits. Tomorrow they would all be involved in the race in one way or another, as competitors, helpers or supporters. They would be joined by perhaps a hundred thousand spectators along the route and at the start and finish, and by millions following the progress of the race on radio and television. It was truly a national event, and a unifying influence.

Everywhere there was talk and speculation about Friday's race. Would Bruce Fordyce, 'the Comrades king', win again? Would a black runner win for the first time? Would Lindsay Weight be able to win the ladies' race once more? Only tomorrow would tell.

Meanwhile the thousands of runners could only compose their minds and control their anxiety as best they could, trying to keep occupied without staying too much on their feet and utilizing too much energy, so the long day of waiting could pass as quickly as possible.

While the runners waited for Friday to come, the efforts of the race organisers were reaching a crescendo. The Comrades Marathon Association had begun to plan for this year's Comrades almost as soon as the last had been run. The results of all their plans were now falling into place, but it took a massive organisation of mainly volunteers to ensure a smoothly run race. The course had had to be finalised, taking things like safety and road works into account, and approved by all the municipalities and other local authorities through whose areas the race would pass. The finish, with its related structures and including computers and medical facilities, had been built over the past week, and the start was now also in place. Countless tasks had been undertaken. These included the sending out of entry forms, the processing of entries, communication with entrants including answering endless questions, liaison with traffic police and the organisation of marshals along the route, the organisation of refreshment stations for the runners, the volunteers to man them and the logistics of supplying them. About 4 000 officials and helpers would be on duty on race day, including nearly 3 500 people at the 58 refreshment stations along the route. Overnight, some 350 000 drinking bottles, 100 000 sponges, 70 000 litres of Coke, 25 tons of ice, as well as many other items, would be delivered to those stations. For many there would be little or no sleep that night.

After registering, and having looked at the exhibits and bought souvenirs at the Comrades Shop, Tony and his three companions returned to the hotel. The day was uncomfortably warm, which was something of a worry for the race tomorrow. The newspapers were already writing about the possibility of a 'warm race', and were quoting authorities who were urging runners to keep themselves properly hydrated. The four had an early lunch, and then set out to drive over the course again, in the direction they would run it on the morrow.

They took a leisurely drive, taking in the main features of the route, and discussing tactics from time to time. The big hills made the greatest impression on them, particularly on novices Sylvia and Sipho. Cowies, Fields and Botha's Hills were all in the first half of the race, while Inchanga was just past halfway. All were more than two kilometres in length and all climbed for more than a hundred metres. It was clear that the first part of the race was more demanding, in terms of climb at least, than the latter half, and that emphasised the need for early caution. Polly Shorts was 'only' 1,8km long, and climbed for about 120m, but was feared because it was placed about 80km from the start, when the runners would be very tired.

As they spent time on the course, Sylvia found that familiarity began to soothe her worst fears. She gradually came to terms with the fact that she would spend the best part of her Friday there, but she retained a very healthy respect for the length and difficulties of the course.

On the way back they stopped at Drummond, halfway and at about the same altitude (650m) as Pietermaritzburg, and made a picnic of Coke and cake and fruit at a pleasant spot overlooking the lovely Valley of a Thousand Hills. They returned to their hotel in Durban in time to meet and welcome the remainder of their group as they arrived after their long journey to the coast. Melanie and Bill had registered at Jan Smuts Stadium in Pietermaritzburg, and had then followed the race route, in reverse, from there. They were thus able to relax, without having to worry about registering in Durban.

They all had a quiet evening, including a comfortable and pleasant mainly carbohydrate dinner at the hotel. Afterwards they made arrangements for the following morning. The hotel dining room would be open from 4 a.m. for the benefit of their Comrades guests. Mary, John, Maria and Linda would act as chauffeurs and would transport the runners of their group to the start at the City Hall. They would watch the start if they could find parking nearby, or would return to the hotel to watch it on television, after which they would leave to set up their Hadeda support table near Ashburton before the access roads were closed. As the race was due to start at 6 a.m. it was agreed that they should meet on the front steps of the hotel at ten past five, ready for the race.

58

"Are you awake?" whispered Sylvia.

"Yes. Are you?" asked Tony unnecessarily.

"I can't go to sleep. Things keep racing around in my mind. The race, the hills, will I make it?"

Tony sat up in bed. The room was softly lit by light from outside which filtered through the drawn curtains. All was quiet, save for an occasional passing car, and the breaking, rushing, retreating sounds of the ever-restless surf outside. Sylvia lay uncomfortably amid crumpled sheets. She stretched out an arm and turned her alarm clock so she could read the time.

"It's only just after one o'clock," she groaned. "How are we going to get through the night?"

"Don't worry. It's normal to be wakeful before a big race. If you can't sleep, at least try to rest. Try to relax."

"I can't. I've tried."

"Let me help you."

Tony got up and sat on the edge of Sylvia's bed.

"Now get comfortable, close your eyes, and relax."

He kissed her eyes lovingly, and then began to stroke her gently, caressing and soothing her. Gradually she relaxed and her breathing grew more regular. She turned onto one side, away from him. He stopped his caresses, believing her to be asleep, but she protested sleepily. He lay down alongside her, and continued to stroke her.

They were startled by the sound of the alarm clock at 4:15 a.m.

They laughed as they remembered how Tony had beguiled her to sleep, and as they realised that they were still lying together on one bed. They hugged each other tightly, and then got up to commence their race preparations.

The adrenalin began to rush through their bodies as they began to think of the race ahead, and Sylvia had a moment of panic. However, by quietly and methodically following their usual pre-race routines, they kept their nervousness under reasonable control. They concentrated on what they were doing: washing, shaving (Tony), using the toilet, mixing and drinking their pre-race liquid meal of Sustagen, putting Vaseline on their nipples, dressing in the running gear that had carefully been laid out the night before, and so on. The familiarity of the routine, even though in strange surroundings and in one another's company, eased them into racing mode and made them focus on the race itself.

They met the others on the front steps as arranged. Everyone was on time and the greetings were both cheerful and a little nervous. The early morning carried just a touch of coolness in the air, so the runners amongst them wore old T-shirts (which could be disposed of later) over their running vests. They were about to move towards the cars when Josh called for their attention.

"I think we should pray," he said.

They closed their eyes, and stood together in a close group, while Josh led them in prayer.

"O Lord, our heavenly Father, thank you for bringing us to the beginning of this day. You know the challenges that we will meet today. Please help us to face them bravely, and in a true spirit of comradeship. We know that anything we do in your name we must do to the best of our abilities. However, we have learnt, in these past few months, that it is difficult to run and not be weary, to keep going when all our strength is gone. Please go with us today, and, even if we cannot mount up with wings as eagles, help us on our way, and bring us safely to the end of our journey before the darkness of night overtakes us. Amen."

59

Fred was right, thought Sylvia. *To be involved in the start of a Comrades Marathon is really special, and never to be forgotten.*

She was standing in Smith Street, amongst nearly ten thousand other runners, waiting for the race to begin. There was a system of voluntary seeding in force, with runners requested to start in areas, demarcated by signs on the lamp posts on the City Hall side of the road, based on their expected finishing times. Sylvia, with Josh and Sipho, was quite far back in the crowd, in the large area for estimated finishing times of between nine and eleven hours. Fred had positioned himself even further back, almost at the end of the field, as he anticipated starting very slowly. Sylvia was not sure where Melanie and Bill were, as she had been separated from them in the crowd soon after their arrival at the start. Mandla and Tony were of course nearer the front, and Sylvia could not see them.

The sky was still dark, but the whole start area was brightly lit for the television cameras, reducing the still-shining street lamps to glowing points of light at the ends of their tall, elegant, stooping lamp posts. On the runners' right was the grandly ornate and floodlit City Hall, completed in 1910, beside which a sponsor was serving free coffee and tea. On the left, an assortment of buildings included the pseudo-Tudor Playhouse theatre and, adjacent to the starting line, the grand Royal Hotel. Sylvia could just see, in front of the City Hall, some of the tall palm trees on the edge of the Francis Farewell Square, or 'Town Gardens'. There, and in the Medwood Gardens on the other side of the City Hall across West Street, hundreds of Indian mynah birds had been wakened early, and their raucous noise competed with that made by the runners.

From the start banner, which spanned the wide road above the starting line, there stretched a sea of runners of all complexions, shapes and sizes. Some had been there since four o'clock that morning to secure a place, often regardless of the voluntary seeding, in or near the front row where they would be filmed by the television cameras. The runners were all dressed in their club colours, though many still wore T-shirts over them to keep warm, and the result was a kaleidoscope of colour, stretching far back along the road. Many had banners or posters raised on long poles, proclaiming the names of their clubs, or the towns or villages from which they had come, or carrying messages such as 'Here I am, Ma' and 'Will you marry me, Sue?'. Some of the runners were silent, but many were chatting and exchanging friendly smiles and greetings. For most there was an underlying nervousness, accompanied by an adrenalin-induced queasiness.

Sylvia was one of those, but her nervousness was under reasonable control as she absorbed the atmosphere. She took in the sights and sounds, and also the smells of people standing close to one another: the strong whiff of wintergreen, the scent of perfume and of deodorants, the odour of stale human sweat, and even of garlic.

Music was playing, and could be heard above the hubbub of the crowd. As the time crept on to six o'clock she recognised Vangelis's famous music from 'Chariots of Fire', which would forever stand for the nobility, excitement and grace of running. She felt goose pimples all over her body as she listened. She looked at the runners around her and at the sea of heads stretching away to the start banner. Today they would attempt to do their own noble deeds. Today they were facing their own Everests. The thought was daunting, but they had all earned the right to be there. Today they faced a searching examination. They would confront themselves and look into the depths of their own inner beings. Afterwards, some would be hurt and weakened by failure, some would be stronger for having tried valiantly and failed, while many would be strengthened and elated by success and be forever respected as members of the community of those who had completed the Comrades Marathon.

With the mild Durban weather and the press of people around her, Sylvia began to feel quite warm. She wriggled out of her T-shirt, trying not to poke an elbow into anyone next to her. She drank deeply from the water bottle she had brought to the start, and then passed it and her T-shirt along the row of runners to be placed safely out of the way. They would later be claimed and put to use by less fortunate individuals. She adjusted her clothing and checked for the hundredth time that her shoelaces were properly tied. She made sure that her little bank bag of items that she was carrying with her was securely pinned to her shorts, and she checked that the sponge she had been given the day before at race registration was comfortably tucked into the waist band of her shorts. It was almost time to start.

Next to Sylvia, Sipho was also fiddling with his clothing, and was trying to jog on the spot a little to loosen his muscles. He was also taking in everything around him, and was apparently very calm. It all still seemed to be a dream, from which he hoped he would not awake. He could not believe everything that had been happening. He kept close to Josh.

Josh stood tall and austere, but with eyes gleaming and all his senses alert. He had a rush of emotion as he recognised the strains of the 'Chariots of Fire' music. He remembered how he had been led to embark upon the project which had brought him to this moment. The challenge, for which they had prepared so long and so hard, was at hand. Internally he was praying for the control to keep calm and to set off at the right pace and rhythm.

Melanie was very emotional and very full of David. She almost saw things through his eyes, and she tried to feel how he had felt on those nine occasions when he had been at the start of a Comrades Marathon. She had made a pocket by sewing to her vest three sides of the race number she wore on the front of her vest. She had carefully folded David's yellow race numbers of two years before and placed them into that pocket, so she would carry them next to her bosom. Periodically she touched them and pressed them to her chest. When the 'Chariots of Fire' music was played the emotion was too much for her. She remembered the television broadcast when she had heard the same music, and had seen a graceful figure, in blue and gold with blonde hair flying, reaching the crest of the Polly Shorts hill. It was then she had realised what this race had meant to David, and then she had made the promise which she had come this long way to keep. The tears streamed down her cheeks. She clasped the hand of Bill, who stood close beside her, and rested her head for a moment on his shoulder.

Bill was trying to keep calm, but was full of apprehension. He had been there before and had failed. Although he was now well prepared and determined to succeed, he could not stop the fact of failure from gnawing away at his self-confidence. He was helped by the need to watch over Melanie, who was far too emotional and needed his support and a calming influence.

At the back of the field, Fred was calm and determined. He had faced many Comrades starts, and still found them exciting, but he had learnt to control his emotions. Today he was far from assured of success. He was worried about his foot. He was able to walk on it, but would it stand up to the abuse of this very long race? At least the weather was mild. He remembered the previous year in Pietermaritzburg when he had had to wash the ice off the windscreen of his car, and when many of the field had been dressed in black rubbish bags to keep themselves warm while they waited for the race to start.

Mandla had placed himself about five rows from the front of the field, in the elite category of those who aimed to finish in less than six-and-a-half hours. He wanted a clear start, with no delays, but he also wanted to avoid the 'TV' runners who would go out much too fast. He had been one of them before, and was determined not to make the same mistake again. He kept himself calm, even as he allowed himself to enjoy the build-up to the start. About ten minutes before six o'clock he saw, with mixed emotions, members of the White Waters 'elite squad' move down the front steps of the Royal Hotel, where they had been staying, to find places at or near the front of the field. He was greeted by two or three of them as they took up positions nearby. Mandla wondered whether all the special attention really would make a difference. Time would tell, but he was very happy about his own final preparations.

A little further back, in the six-and-half to seven-and-a-half hour category, Tony was also interested in the goings on at the Royal Hotel. As six o'clock approached he noticed Andy and Nora pushing to the front of the throng in the entrance. Andy was in the red, white and blue colours of the Sandown Runners Club. Despite the early morning, Nora was perfectly groomed, and cool and elegant in a smart beige suit. The couple stood for a moment and surveyed the scene, which no doubt they had watched from the luxury suite they had occupied since flying down to Durban the previous evening. Tony was only about twenty metres away from them, and Andy easily picked him out in the crowd. He offered no greeting, but tapped Nora on the arm and gestured in Tony's direction. Tony was sure that Nora also saw him. Then she turned her back to him and put her arms around Andy. They enfolded each other in a close, public embrace, and kissed tenderly. Then Andy walked down the steps and took up a position near Mandla at the front of the field. Tony doubted that Andy could do less than six-and-half hours. However, he was either making a statement of intent, or his personal arrogance would not allow him to take a more backward position.

Tony felt a moment of desolation as he saw his wife embracing his former boss. However, he banished negative thoughts from his mind. He thought of Sylvia further back in the field, and made himself feel for a moment their love for each other. As far as Andy was concerned, Tony had already been proved correct about Nigroup and the financial markets. The best way he could reckon with Andy now was to beat him in the race. He was determined to do that. He knew that Andy would be going out fast, for that was his aggressive way, so he would not be following closely. However, he would be looking out for those red, white and blue colours later in the race, and hoped to see them.

It was almost six o'clock. The general anticipation and excitement grew with each passing moment. The 'Chariots of Fire' music faded, the unmistakable sound of a cock-crow rang out, the old Post Office clock began to chime the hour, the Mayor of Durban fired the starting gun, and they were off.

There was a roar from thousands of voices and a general surge forward. The 'TV runners' took off at a sprinter's pace to secure their fleeting moment of glory as they led the field into the relative darkness beyond the brilliantly lit start area. As space opened up before him, Mandla was able to move off smoothly, relieved to settle at last into his easy racing rhythm. Tony was quite soon over the line and beginning to pick his way through the crowd around him. After the initial surge, Sylvia, Sipho and Josh were held back by the numbers in front of them. At first they could not move forward at all, then they found they could walk hesitantly, then shuffle-jog, until at last they could jog and then run properly and begin to find the pace at which they wanted to go. Sylvia carefully picked her way forward to avoid falling in the crush. She checked her watch as she passed under the starting banner. It had taken forty-six seconds for her to cross the line, and it was another thirty seconds or so before she was able to jog fairly comfortably.

Tony ran out of the brightness into the relative dimness of the normal street lighting in Smith Street. As his eyes adjusted to the change in light, he found the space to allow him to pick up speed and settle into his planned racing pace. He noticed that he was passing a few slower runners who had obviously started too close to the front of the field and were already falling back, obstructing the faster runners. Tony stepped to his right to avoid a slower couple, and was surprised to recognise them as Bill and Melanie. Melanie was racing for dear life, with fists clenched, arms pumping, jaw set and shoulders tensed. Bill was following, remonstrating and trying vainly to rein her in. Tony immediately slowed down and fell into place next to her.

"Melanie, slow down!" he commanded. "What the hell do you think you're doing? Do you want to ruin your chances right now? Follow my pace!"

Tony gradually reduced the pace to what the pair should have been running and ushered them gradually to the side of the road so the faster runners could overtake them more easily.

"Right, now get into this rhythm, and relax. Drop your shoulders. Wiggle your fingers to relax your hands. That's right. Why did you start so near the front?"

"We didn't see any signs," said Melanie. "Sorry, Tony. I've been too wound up to think straight. I should've listened to Bill too, but I just forgot my training and everything for a moment. I'm all right now."

"OK. Are you both sure you have this rhythm and this degree of effort in mind? Remember to relax; and you're also allowed to enjoy yourselves."

They turned right and soon found Berea Road, wide and brightly lit, ahead of them.

"Here comes our first hill. Keep the effort the same as this. It should feel easy. You will slow down, but remember that you'll pick up the time you lose on the downhill beyond Tollgate."

"Thanks, Tony. We're OK now. You're losing time. You must get back to your own race again."

Tony ran a few more paces with them, then picked up his speed and moved smoothly away from them.

Further back Fred had started even more slowly than usual, easing into a walk and graduating to a slow shuffle to allow himself, and his left heel in particular, to warm up gently. He was not last in the field as there were a number of stragglers behind him. He began to move more freely, but still cautiously, as he went along. He found that he was favouring his left foot and tried to balance himself better and run more evenly. As he hauled himself up Berea Road, he even began to pass a few slower runners. He noticed that the arched Tollgate Bridge, which spanned the road at the top of the hill, was crowded with early morning spectators. He passed under the bridge and commenced the downhill stretch to Mayville. He was brought to a halt by a stabbing pain in his left heel.

60

For most of the runners the first part of the race was relatively easy, and a joyful celebration. The long months of preparation and of waiting were over, and they had at last been released into the race. They were full of adrenalin, highly motivated and well enough trained for the early kilometres to seem to fly past. It grew lighter as they ran, and the coming dawn encouraged cheerfulness and optimism. Sylvia tried to ignore the huge numbers displayed on the distance-to-go signs every kilometre. It was simply too daunting to contemplate a further eighty-five or eighty kilometres still to be covered. She concentrated on what she was doing, while absorbing the changing scenes around her.

She noticed that the route was already very hilly, winding down to Mayville, up through Sherwood and over 45th Cutting into Westville. With the early light came lovely, leafy suburbs with vegetation that was still subtropical. Sylvia noticed frangipani, flamboyant trees and an avenue of tall palms. Through Westville, the morning was bright, and there was a first hint of crispness in the air as they began to climb out of the humid coastal belt. The road was wide, like a freeway, so the runners had a feeling of open space they had not felt in the city-centre streets and suburban roads. The combination seemed to renew the chat and banter, which had been all around Sylvia for much of the way so far. The support of helpers and of spectators beside the road also seemed to encourage the more vocal and ribald of the runners.

Marshall: “Well done! Keep it up!”

Runner: “That’s what my wife always says.”

Runners: “Thank you, Marshall. Thank you.”

Spectator: “Come on, ladies. Up the ladies!”

Runner: “Oh yes!”

Lady physiotherapist, standing in front of aid tent: “Come and let me show you my little place.”

Runner: “Wow! Yes, please.”

Runners: “Thank you! Thank you!”

So the stream of runners, now several kilometres long, climbed its steady way inland. Sylvia took in a wide view to her left as their route followed a long sweeping curve to the right and then crossed over the freeway. Soon she began the 2.1km climb of Cowies Hill, nearly fifteen kilometres from the start. The climb did not feel too onerous, as it was still relatively early and the air was cool. She climbed through a pleasant residential area, with pretty gardens, grassy verges, and trees leaning out over the road. Many of the residents and their friends had turned out to watch the race and several had set out tables and chairs on the grass beside the road. Many were cooking or eating leisurely breakfasts, and were drinking coffee or champagne and orange juice as the runners passed by. Some had radios and portable television sets so they could also follow the progress of the race near the front of the field.

The leaders had long since swept round the bend at the top of Cowies Hill, with a view across the valley through the trees to the left, and plunged down the long descent into Pinetown. Mandla was four or five minutes behind the leaders, and about three minutes behind the ‘Fordyce bus’ (the group of runners keeping close to the defending champion), as he eased his way down the hill. He was moving fast, but smoothly, conserving energy by letting gravity take him down the hill, and preserving his legs by avoiding heavy impact on the road as he flowed downwards. He was a little worried about the number of runners ahead of him, for the road seemed crowded when he was able to see some way forward. However, he was running more or less to schedule, and Tony had warned him that many would go out at speeds faster than they could sustain. It was too soon to panic.

The run through Pinetown was relatively flat. It was an urban area with shops and commercial properties on both sides of the road. The route was lined by thousands of spectators, many of whom would stay there until the last runners had passed by, and the support for the runners was electric. Mandla enjoyed the encouragement, but also kept control of his pace, for it was all too easy to be carried away by the excitement of the crowd, as they willed the runners forward, and speed up injudiciously. As it was, it did not seem long before the long straight and the crowds were behind him and he had turned to the bottom of Fields Hill.

61

This is where things start to get tough, thought Tony as he arrived at the foot of Fields Hill a few minutes after Mandla.

Fields Hill is the biggest of the major hills on the Comrades Marathon route. It is 3.2km in length and climbs 186m. At the top, the runners would have run almost 24km of the race, and would have gained 518m of altitude, although they would actually have climbed much more because of the hilly nature of the course. The runners follow the wide, dual-carriage-way main road which climbs out of Pinetown to Kloof. In parts it has a camber that is awkward for running, and, like other of the long Comrades hills, it bends several times so that it is difficult for the runner to see where the top is.

Tony settled into a rhythm suitable for the long climb. His strategy was to run as much as possible, and to walk only in the few places, like the exit from the highway at the top of Fields Hill, where the road was so steep that to walk would be as fast as running but with less expenditure of energy. The sun was bright upon the runners and reflected off the stone cliffs on the left-hand side of the road. As he climbed higher Tony was able to glimpse occasionally the view of Pinetown and beyond which gradually opened out on his right. The road was a busy one, and there was heavy traffic on the lanes not coned off for the runners. Tony appreciated the friendly hooting and shouts of encouragement from the cars as they went by.

The runners were now much quieter than early in the race. They had begun to feel the effort, and breath had to be spared for running. The hill began to take its toll, particularly of those who had raced too fast to that point. Tony found himself gaining places as he concentrated on his rhythm and climbed at a steady pace. Some of those around him were slowing down or walking. Near the top of the hill he closed in on a tired-looking, attractive lady runner in the blue colours of White Waters Running Club. It was Beth, rapidly falling off the pace of the ladies' race. Tony drew alongside her and ran with her for a while, offering encouragement.

"I'm tired, Tony," said Beth. "My legs are sore already, and there's still 65 K's to go. I've simply been doing too much running. Next year I want you to help me if you will."

"It would be a pleasure. But don't worry about that now. Even if you are tired, work at getting the best out of yourself today. Also learn everything you can to help you in the future. But keep on keeping on, whatever happens. You're still strong enough to finish well. Good luck! I may see you later."

He moved ahead of Beth. Despite his words of encouragement, he knew that it would be a very long day for her.

It was a relief to reach the top of Fields Hill and turn into the green suburbs beyond it. The next ten kilometres or so meandered through Kloof, Gillitts and Hillcrest, which was about 670m above sea level. Although the runners were still climbing, this part of the route was only gently undulating. The air was crisp and drier as they had now climbed fully out of the humidity belt, lower down and nearer the coast. Tony appreciated that, and also the shade under the trees, which were still green and leant over the road, sometimes touching in the middle to form arches of jacarandas and other trees which Tony could not identify as he kept moving forward. There were green banks and grassy verges beside the way, and in many places there were spectators, who clapped and shouted encouragement to the runners. There were numerous picnics, and many a braaivleis, which filled the air with smoke and the aroma of grilling meat. Many people had radios and television sets. There was an enormous crowd near the main Hillcrest shopping area. They were enthusiastically looking out for the brown and white striped vests of the local Hillcrest Villagers Club, and there was a crescendo in the volume of support as each of the local runners came by. On the way down the long hill after Hillcrest, Tony learnt from spectators that Bruce Fordyce had just passed through halfway at Drummond, about two minutes behind the leaders.

The road was very wide at the bottom of the hill, at the Assagay turnoff, where Tony began to climb the next of the big hills. Botha's Hill is 2.3km long, climbs 117m, and winds its way up to Botha's Hill Village and the turnoff to the Rob Roy Hotel. As Tony began to concentrate once again on a steady rhythm to help him grind out yet another climb, the road narrowed and grew steeper. Soon there were grassy banks and avenues of old trees arching over the road, at first dappled early winter planes, and then shady green jacarandas. There were spectators along the way, most notably a crowd of scholars from Kearsney College who stood near the entrance of their school, applauding and encouraging the long line of wearying competitors as they hauled themselves up the long hill, running slowly or walking even slower. There were still some fifty kilometres to go.

At the next drinking point there was the usual minor congestion, even this far up in the field. Tony slowed to take both Coke and water from the willing and cheerful helpers, drank hastily, dipped his sponge into a trough of cold water beyond the tables, and sponged his thighs and head to keep them cool as he moved on up the hill. Just ahead of him he saw Victor, walking and then breaking into a slow run. A few strides and Tony was up with him.

"How you doing, Victor?"

Victor uttered an expletive, from which Tony gathered that things were not going as well for the Club captain as he might wish.

"Keep going," said Tony. "We must be quite well up in the Vets' team race."

Victor grunted and concentrated on trying to keep pace with Tony.

At the top of the hill Tony was a few metres ahead of him, but as they began the pleasant, gently winding descent towards Alverstone, Victor closed the gap and the two ran together for a while. They had a glimpse of the Valley of a Thousand Hills to the right, and saw sugar cane fields beyond the railway line on their left. Tony noticed a line of tall eucalyptus trees, apparently bare of bark to show smooth, grey-white trunks and branches. The going was easy as they wound their way down to Drummond, with high, steep banks and eucalyptus forest on the right and sporadic views out across the wide valley below them on the left. Victor forced the pace and drew ahead, but Tony bided his time, keeping his rhythm, protecting his legs from pounding, and letting gravity take him down at what was still a good pace. That part of the road was quiet, with few spectators. As they neared Drummond, Tony saw again, for a moment, a view of the Valley of a Thousand Hills on his right, and to his left the niche in the cliff which had been a favourite resting place of the great Arthur Newton. The road turned right, wound left to cross a bridge over the railway line, and dropped the last few metres into Drummond. A short distance covered on a gentle down slope, and Tony crossed the halfway mark. He glanced at his watch. Race time was 3:31, about two minutes behind his original target.

The little village centre of Drummond was packed with a large crowd of noisy and excited spectators. It was a colourful scene, and the support for the runners was loud and genuine. The leaders had gone through forty-one minutes earlier, but it seemed to Tony that each runner was still greeted with as much enthusiasm as a race leader. He knew that the crowd support would continue for those many thousands behind him. As Tony made his way through the crowd lining both sides of the road, and passed the old hotel and the tall palm trees growing in front of it, the announcer on the public address system was informing spectators about the progress of the race up front. The two leaders were already more than ten kilometres away, and were racing hard, trying to open a large gap on the rest of the field. Fordyce was just over two minutes behind, looking determined, and apparently now setting out in earnest pursuit.

As Tony left the bulk of the crowd behind him, he noticed more palm trees, some dark Norfolk pines and bright flowering bougainvillea. The railway line ran along the left of the road for a while.

Just before the foot of Inchanga Hill, at the end of the village, White Waters R.C. volunteers had set up a table to provide information and assistance, such as special drinks, mainly for their selected elite squad. Because of the sheer size of the field, and the related logistical and traffic problems, the seconding rules for the Comrades Marathon had become very strict. So the days were gone when personal seconds could follow their runners along the route and give them sustenance at any time, and even give encouragement by running next to them. It was however permitted to stand still beside the road and hand a runner a drink, and give him or her information by voice or on a note attached to the drink bottle. The top runners often had teams of seconds, who tried to provide their preferred drinking requirements, and who gave them necessary information about the progress of the race and how near or far their rivals were ahead of or behind them.

Tony saw Victor, a few metres ahead of him, being given a drink bottle by one of the White Waters volunteers as he passed the table. They had no special drink for Tony, but they offered encouragement.

"Come on Tony. You're doing well. We're well up in the Vets' race."

"Where's Mandla?" asked Tony, slowing down and stopping briefly.

"Here he was twelve minutes behind the leaders and ten behind Fordyce."

"Did you see Andy Duke, of Sandown, go through?"

"Yes. They're also in the Vets' race"

"He went through about six minutes ago," said another.

"Thank you," said Tony as he set off again.

It all took less than ten seconds, but the information was worth it. Mandla seemed to be on schedule and doing well. Tony hoped he was feeling good. However, if Andy was indeed six minutes ahead, then that could be a problem. It was more than Tony had expected at this stage of the race. He, Tony, was a little behind schedule, having lost time with Melanie and Bill early on. Andy may have gone out too fast and could tire and slow down, but Tony realised that he had a long hard chase in front of him. He was absolutely determined to finish the race ahead of Andy. There were many scores to settle today. He would simply have to run Andy down, but little by little without any dramatic, exhausting surges. As he began the long, almost 3km, 140m climb up Inchanga, he had already run considerably more than a standard marathon. He had more than another full marathon to go.

It was past 9:30, there was no breeze, and the morning was beginning to feel warm. Inchanga is one of the great challenges of the Comrades Marathon, placed where it is on the course. It begins to find out those who have run too fast to halfway. It winds and winds and winds, so it is difficult to judge where the climb will end. Tony set himself again into a deliberate rhythm, which he felt he could maintain all the way to the top some 762m above sea level. There were views of green mountains, hills and wide valleys opening out to the left as he climbed higher. On the right side of the road there were bushy banks and cliff faces. However, Tony was now finding that the concentration, needed to keep going ever upward, left little time to appreciate the scenery.

About halfway up the hill, Victor began to walk. Tony soon caught him and slowly moved ahead. Tony found that he was picking up a number of places as many of those around him slowed down. Near the top of the hill he passed Ken and Kobus who were still together, but walking and looking distressed. Tony suspected that they would find the second half of the race to be very long indeed.

62

Fred managed to get going again, but with a struggle. The acute pain in his heel had brought him to a halt just past Tollgate. At first he was unable to put any weight at all on his left foot. Surely he could not give up so early in the race, after all the preparation and after coming all this way? He exercised his foot, stretched it, rubbed his heel, and gradually the spasm (if that was what it was) ended. He could put a little weight on the foot. Then he could limp slowly. He started again down the hill, walking with a limp, then walking a little better, and then shuffling into a tentative slow jog. The change of movement, and possibly of load bearing, that came as he moved into the next uphill seemed to help. Soon he was running again, slowly and cautiously in his characteristic, slightly stooping style.

Melanie and Bill did maintain a proper rhythm, and level of expenditure of effort, after Tony had left them on Berea Road. They settled down and began to enjoy themselves. They had each other for company, and there were all kinds of things going on around them, with a crowded field, plenty of chat and banter, and the encouragement of the spectators and of the many helpers at the refreshment stations. Many of these teams of volunteer helpers had dressed up in matching, brightly coloured clothes. There were many attractive women amongst them, and Bill pondered how it was that his drinks somehow seemed better when handed to him by a gorgeous young lady. Loud music was being played at some of the refreshment stations to add to a generally festive early morning atmosphere.

Melanie's mind was distracted from emotional thoughts about David, so she became a runner concentrating on her race and enjoying herself at the same time. She and Bill were both moving well, and their optimism grew with the daylight. They made good progress through 45th Cutting, Westville, over Cowies Hill and across the crowded flat road through Pinetown.

The first sign of possible trouble came on the long haul up Field's Hill. Bill began to feel nauseous. He could not think of a cause. He simply began to feel ill. Melanie was concerned when he told her, and encouraged him to concentrate on his running rhythm in order to keep his mind off how he was feeling. He tried, and he kept going with her, but doubts began to play dangerously in his mind.

Past the top of Fields Hill, Melanie began to feel the need for a toilet break. She knew that there were toilets along the way, including portable ones put out especially for the race, but she was unable to see one to use. As they were passing through residential areas, it was not possible to dive into bushes beside the road as in some country areas. At length she stopped to ask a friendly family, who were picnicking on the grass verge outside what Melanie hoped was their home, whether they would allow her to use their toilet. They were happy to do so, and the lady of the family showed her the way, while Bill waited for her in the road, chatting to the rest of the family. In the garden of the home was the family dog, which wagged its tail at Melanie as she was escorted into the house. However, when Melanie was returning to the front gate on her own, the dog decided that she was an unwelcome intruder and bit her painfully in the right buttock.

Melanie yelped in pain. The owners hastened to her aid, banished the dog, proffered profuse and embarrassed apologies, offered comfort, and aid in the form of ice and antiseptic cream. Melanie was anxious about the time she was losing in the race, and soon she and Bill were on their way again, followed by many good wishes for the remainder of the race. Melanie's bottom was very painful, and she was almost in tears. She stopped for a while, because of the pain and to regain her composure, once they had turned a bend in the road and were out of sight of the friendly family with the unfriendly dog. After rubbing herself to ease the pain, and watched over by her sympathetic partner, they started off again.

They had lost quite a lot of time by stopping, and they also ran a little slower until Melanie's pain eased and gradually merged into the general soreness of a body that ached more and more as it suffered the abuse of such a long and arduous run. Later she would be able to joke that she had sometimes found running to be "a pain in the butt."

As a result of these delays, Melanie and Bill were caught and overtaken by Sipho and Josh, who had so far been having a steady and enjoyable run together. The two couples exchanged greetings and news, and Josh and Sipho were concerned about Melanie when they heard her story. On the latter's assurance that she would be all right, they moved ahead slowly, leaving her in the care of Bill, who had forgotten his own problems for a while.

Josh was happy with the progress he and Sipho were making. However, he was fairly certain that Sipho was capable of doing much better than he, Josh, felt able to do. Josh was going through periods when, inexplicably, he did not feel well. Sipho, on the other hand, seemed to be cruising along totally untroubled and simply enjoying the occasion. Josh had frequently suggested that Sipho should go ahead and run his own race, but Sipho had refused, being content with the way things were going and anxious to watch over his benefactor.

At length they dropped down into Drummond and passed through halfway in 4:45, very much as they had planned. They made their way through the enthusiastic crowd lining the road and began the ascent of Inchanga. The time was now moving on towards 11 o'clock and the morning was warm. Josh felt ill again and began to walk. Sipho immediately stopped and walked beside him.

"You must go on, Sipho," said Josh. "I'll be all right. These spells when I feel sick come and go, but they will not stop me. You'll do much better if you run your own race."

"I think I should stay and help you, Mister Josh."

"No, Sipho. I will feel bad if you don't do as well as you should for my sake. Go on. Maybe we can help each other later on. Remember what Tony said about people having bad patches at different times, and not waiting for each other? Go ahead. Perhaps you'll have a bad patch and will need the time in order to finish. Maybe I'll see you later. I'll look out for you. Go, and God go with you."

Sipho hesitated, and then began to run as he realised that Josh was serious. He moved ahead of the walking Josh, who noticed that Sipho looked back several times before his blue-clad figure disappeared around the next bend in the road.

Further back, Fred was making steady if unspectacular progress. He was not moving fluently, as he was favouring his left leg, but he was managing to keep going. Ultimately, the latter part of his preparation for the race had not been ideal, and he felt that, and his unbalanced running motion, caused his legs, and indeed his whole body, to feel tired and sore much sooner than he would have expected. Eventually he was sore all over, and any discomfort in his left heel was simply submerged in a general aura of weariness and pain.

He would have to battle his way through to the end. He had to pass through Drummond before 11:30, or race time of 5:30. Anyone arriving at halfway after that time would have to retire and would be taken off the road. He had worked himself into a position where he had a few minutes in reserve towards beating the Drummond cut-off. However, there was still a very long way to go to the end of the race. He ran with an image in his mind of an official at the finish, holding a gun in his upraised right hand, ready to fire it at precisely five o'clock, to signal that the runners' eleven hours to finish the race had ended. He kept the image in his mind, telling himself that he needed to beat that gun.

Fred took a walk break near the top of Botha's Hill, as he drank the refreshments he had taken at the drinking station there. A younger, chubby competitor in green colours joined him and walked beside him.

"I hope I finish," said the one in green. "This is my third try, and I haven't made it yet."

"You keep going, son, and don't waste time," said Fred as he began to shuffle his way up the hill again.

Fred admired the youngster for qualifying and trying the Comrades three times, but was struck by the difference in their attitudes. Fred was not just hoping to finish. He was looking at the image of the finishing gun, and saying to himself: "I'm bloody well going to finish. I'm bloody well going to get there."

63

Bill's nausea returned. He had forgotten it for a while when caring for Melanie, but it soon compelled him to take note of it again. Partly buoyed and distracted by the large crowd, he and Melanie had settled into their stride again as they went through Hillcrest Village, and then down towards the bottom of Botha's Hill. However, Bill began to feel nauseous again as they hauled themselves up that long climb. At the next refreshment station, he gagged as he brought his drink to his lips. The very thought of swallowing anything made him feel ill. He knew he had to drink, so he forced himself to do so, but went on his way feeling unwell. Once they were over the hill, Bill felt a little better, and they made good progress down through Alverstone and on towards Drummond. However, Bill's mind dwelt on his problem, and he began to wonder how long he would be able to continue. Then, as they wound their way down the final descent into Drummond, he suddenly had another worry. Melanie complained that her left knee was hurting. It appeared to be the same injury she had had after Two Oceans, and leading up to the Comrades.

The pain in Melanie's knee eased off on the near-flat, gentle decline through Drummond. The support of the crowd also helped to distract them both from their woes for a few moments. They passed through halfway in 4:48, slower than they had hoped, but a reasonable effort in view of the delays they had experienced.

They both took drinks from the refreshment station at Drummond. Bill retched as he brought his drink to his mouth. He took it away, then brought it back to his lips, filled his mouth and forced himself to swallow. He abandoned the remainder of the drink and walked to the cold water trough into which he dipped his sponge. He covered his head and face with cold water, hoping it would make him feel better.

Bill felt very ill as he and Melanie began to jog up the mighty Inchanga Hill. The sun was bright and to Bill it felt very hot. He kept going for a while, but then began to walk. Melanie walked with him, now very worried. The next moment she saw Bill dive for the side of the road and vomit into the bushes there. He retched and retched alarmingly, as other competitors streamed past them, but eventually it was all over, and he turned despairingly towards Melanie.

"Go on, Melanie. You're wasting precious time. I'm finished."

"No!"

"I can't go on any more. If I can't drink I won't finish. Maybe I'm not meant to finish Comrades. Go on!"

"Come with me. Please, Bill! Remember all your reasons for doing this race. Come on! Try! You can't give up so easily! At least walk with me and see how it goes."

She took him by the arm and pulled him into motion. He followed passively, his mind full of thoughts of another failure. He found that he could walk slowly, and then gradually better as he eased his stiff and wretched body into forward motion again. Although he felt weak and had a nasty taste in his mouth, he did not feel as ill as he had before he had been sick. As they walked up the hill, his body slowly began to remember that it was supposed to be a walking and running machine. He became aware of Melanie reminding him why he had to finish this race: for his own good he could not afford another failure, and finishing held the prospect of a proper job. His thoughts became more positive. Perhaps he could keep going. Perhaps he would not feel so ill again.

Perhaps he could manage his drinking well enough to get to the finish. Meanwhile Melanie would not leave him and he was holding her up.

"Sorry, Melanie, and thank you! I'll try. But I don't want to hold you up. Let's see if we can jog at least part of this hill."

So they jogged and walked up Inchanga in stages. They were on their way again. It was with relief when they reached the top of the hill and began the long winding descent on the other side. Their speed improved on the downhill, and they both began to feel more optimistic. They noticed and commented on the valley view and the main road far down to their left. Later there were some spectacular brown cliffs and the Valley of a Thousand Hills on the right.

However, they began to worry again when Melanie's knees began to ache, and the left one became more and more painful.

Sylvia's progress had been steady and mercifully less dramatic. She had been following her race instructions, concentrating on what she was doing, but allowing herself to enjoy her race. She kept track of her progress, but also took in what was happening around her, and appreciated the surroundings. The green suburbs were pretty, and the scenery was sometimes spectacular. She found the big hills a strain, but kept running, even if slowly, as much as possible. She picked up her speed on the down hills, while 'resting' as she ran so as to make gravity do as much of the work as possible. As she grew more tired her legs began to stiffen and to ache, but she could cope with the discomfort as long as she was making good progress. As the day warmed up she found that her times were slipping a little, but she remembered Tony's advice not to push the pace in the first half, but rather to take a conservative approach. Her time at Drummond was 5:07, a little slower than planned. However, she was quite satisfied with it, and felt weary but well capable of continuing to make steady progress.

She found the atmosphere at Drummond exciting, and she enjoyed making her way through the vocal crowd, which had been there for hours and was still urging the runners on. She was also glad to learn from the public address announcer that Bruce Fordyce was nearing the top of Polly Shorts and was going away from his opposition, only having to remain on his feet to secure another fine victory. It seemed that the ladies' race was being fought out between Lindsay Weight and Helen Lucre.

Fred continued to struggle on. He passed the halfway mark just eight minutes behind Sylvia, in 5:15. He pressed on, satisfied that he had beaten the Drummond cut-off by a full fifteen minutes, and as determined as before that he would beat the gun at the finish.

64

The road no longer looked crowded ahead of Mandla. All the way through the long climbs, the downhills, the seemingly endless undulations and twists and turns of the course, he had been passing other runners. It would have been more surprising had he and Tony not discussed the matter and incorporated it into their race strategy. Allowing for the variations of pace dictated by the steep ups and downs, Mandla had been keeping a fairly constant average speed. He was running fractionally slower than his target of four minutes per kilometre, which he attributed to the heat, but was content with his progress. He had not slowed down, but those in front of him had come back to him, and fallen behind, one after another. To be running through the field was very motivating, and helped to buoy his spirits and to keep him thinking positively. It was all a most welcome change from the previous year. Then he had attacked the course, and had become more and more disconsolate and depressed as he had slowed down all the way to the finish and been overtaken by thousands of other runners.

At Drummond there had been no special drinks for him at the White Waters table, but his club mates there had urged him on. They had told him that there were more than thirty runners ahead of him at that stage, and that, if he kept going well, he could probably run into the Club's first four and score in the team competition. Mandla had tried to keep track of the number of runners he had passed since then, but it had proved difficult. He wished he had the benefit of seconds who could give him the information he needed. However, he kept on, knowing that he was moving up the field all the time. There were now large gaps between the runners, and for long periods he was running on his own.

The terrain had changed since he had flown down the long descent of Inchanga onto the Harrison Flats. The hills receded and the country opened into wide, more gently undulating slopes. Everything seemed drier than before, an impression heightened by the heat from the bright morning sun. The countryside displayed dry winter tones, russets and browns in the tall grasses, and, elsewhere, tired vestiges of green mixed with greys and winter brown. The vegetation varied from open grassland to dense bush, thorn tree savannah, and even some yellow-green sugar cane fields. There were occasional clumps of very tall, smooth-trunked, eucalyptus trees, usually near small settlements.

Many people believe that, on the up-run, the second half of the Comrades Marathon is flat. That is not so. Although most of the great hills were behind Mandla after Inchanga, there were still some significant climbs ahead. Even on the relatively flat sections there were undulations, which demanded that he concentrate on his running technique in order to achieve optimum performance, resting at speed even on the gentle downhills, and shortening his stride and using his arms to maintain rhythm on the ups.

In places there was still wonderful support from spectators beside the road. Mandla was especially thrilled by the large numbers of black supporters, cheering on the runners, near the bottom of Inchanga and on the Harrison Flats. Their excitement, and the volume of its expression, grew dramatically as they saw Mandla approaching. They were especially thrilled to see another black runner doing so well in the race.

"Phambili! Phambili", they cried, urging him to move up the field.

As Mandla passed by, children excitedly ran next to him on the dirt beside the road, shouting "Gijima! Gijima!" and surprised at his fast pace. He saw celebrating women in voluminous skirts with bright scarves tied around their heads, and men with smiling eyes watching more sedately.

In and near the small towns of Cato Ridge and Camperdown, there were very large crowds of spectators, and again the support for the runners was almost overwhelming. It was easy to be carried away by all the excitement, and to speed up too much, or want to show off, but Mandla managed to maintain his discipline, while enjoying being carried along almost effortlessly by the crowd.

However, in other areas, sometimes for long stretches of road, there were no spectators and it was very lonely. It was then easy to feel the heat and the weariness, the soreness in the legs, the stiffening in the knees, the tiredness in a body that had already had to hold itself upright in motion for seventy or however many punishing kilometres. It was easy for the mind to question why all this was happening, and to try to persuade the body to let up, if only a little. The further he went the more Mandla had to concentrate, simply to maintain the same speed. As a runner grows tired it is so easy to let the pace slip. The effort feels the same, but the speed imperceptibly falls off. One has to run harder and harder simply to maintain the same pace.

Mandla was concentrating for all he was worth. He kept thinking about his rhythm and his fluency, all the time adapting his technique to the terrain. He took note of his time over each kilometre, and here the markers telling him how far he had to go at the end of each kilometre were a blessing. His mind worked like a computer, calculating his rate of progress, where he was in the race, what he still had to do, and the performance, condition and needs of his tiring body. The fact that he was still moving well, and continually gaining places, helped him to keep motivated. Sometimes he could see no one in front of him, but as each new target came into view, Mandla imagined himself attached to the runner by a long rope that he was all the time pulling in to bring him gradually ever closer. Eventually he would go past and set off in pursuit of his next target.

At Umlaas Road, with less than twenty kilometres to go, Mandla passed the highest point on the course at 870m above sea level. Unfortunately that did not mean that there were no more hills to climb before he reached the finish in Pietermaritzburg. He continued on his way, soon passing under the freeway and following the old road that ran parallel to it. He entered Mpusheni, passed the chicken farm on his right, and then the Lion Park turnoff. The road swept left under the freeway and then curved downhill to the right and through a pleasant residential area with houses widely spaced on either side of the road. Soon they gave way to open grassland, and hills could be seen in the distance to the left.

As Mandla dropped down into a valley to cross the river at the Tumble Inn, on the left hand side of the road, he saw ahead of him a runner wearing the sky-blue colours of his own club. Mandla chased him up the long and testing Ashburton Hill, sometimes known to the runners as 'Little Pollys', and gradually closed the gap. As he drew closer he recognised Richard, whom he guessed correctly was the leading White Waters runner in the field. As they climbed, it became bushy on both sides of the road, but there were grass verges, and then houses on the right with palm trees and green lawns. Here Mandla found the Hadedas' table.

Mary and the others were delighted to see him. He felt good to see the friendly and familiar faces of his own support team. As he approached the table he listened for the information that he needed so dearly.

"Mandla, you're number fourteen!"

"You're now fourteenth."

"Well done! You could get a gold medal if you hurry."

"Here's your drink. Do you need anything else?"

"You're doing well."

"Go!"

Mandla took the special carbohydrate drink they had brought and kept cold for him, and set off with a wave and a 'Thank you'. He drank deeply from the bottle, before casting it aside to be retrieved by one of the team. Ah, it was good to drink something other than Coke and water for a change.

Mandla caught Richard in the next valley as the road turned left to approach the notorious Polly Shorts Hill. Polly Shorts is 1.8km long and climbs 120m. It is not the longest of the big climbs, but it is very, very taxing as it is placed just after the runners have completed 80km of hard running.

Mandla and Richard greeted each other as Mandla drew alongside, but their contest was fierce and determined. Often the racing against one's own team-mates is the hardest. As Mandla went ahead, Richard took up position just behind him, determined not to let Mandla get away from him. The road turned to the left and Mandla had a feeling of being closed in as the bush grew thickly on both sides. There were no spectators. He tried to push the pace as they climbed, but could not shake off his club mate. As they took the sweeping curve to the right, Mandla's legs were slowing. The two runners entered a long, steep straight, and somehow kept going, seemingly locked together. Briefly they glimpsed another competitor walking near the end of the straight. Mandla's muscles felt as though they were seizing up, it was difficult just to keep moving, and he desperately wanted to rest his legs. Could he stop for a moment? Just then he sensed that Richard was starting to fall back. Mandla urged himself to sustain the effort a little longer. The gap widened suddenly. He looked back, and saw that Richard was walking. Mandla slackened his pace just a little, but kept running until around the next bend. He looked back. Richard was out of sight. Mandla stopped running and walked for a count of just twenty paces. Tony had taught him that that was long enough for some of the local oxygen debt in the leg muscles to be repaid, but short enough to keep the runner disciplined and not waste time by resting for too long. By the time Richard rounded the bend, Mandla was on his way to the top of the hill with partially refreshed legs.

On the final straight to the top, Mandla saw that the competitor ahead of him was running again, but was much nearer to him than before. Mandla recognised the navy blue and white colours of the Germiston Callies Harriers club.

At the top of Polly Shorts, Mandla had 6.6km still to run, but the worst of the climbing was behind him. As he took drinks and sponged himself at the refreshment station, he learnt that Bruce Fordyce had only about a kilometre left to run and was well clear of the rest of the field. *I'll have to improve a lot before I'll be able to race with the Master of Comrades,* he thought as he concentrated again on his own race. He was now in thirteenth place. Could he get into the first ten for a gold medal?

He set off in pursuit of the Callies runner, who was clearly struggling. Mandla caught him quite easily, and surged past him very quickly, in the textbook way to discourage a runner from speeding up and trying to latch onto the one overtaking him. Mandla did not want another hard-fought struggle just yet.

They were now in the outskirts of Pietermaritzburg. The road took an undulating route into the residential suburbs. Gradually there were more and more spectators, and Mandla appreciated their encouragement. On a straight stretch of road he at last saw two runners together about two hundred metres ahead of him. He gradually managed to draw closer and was soon able to keep them in sight for most of the time. It was a struggle to close the gap, because the two were running side by side, and so helping each other to maintain a fast pace as they raced for tenth place and the last gold medal.

Mandla kept going at the fastest pace he could sustain. He was now desperately tired but he knew that the two in front were probably feeling as bad. He was enveloped in a cocoon of weariness, inside of which his mind and his whole being were focussed on the race and the need to keep going at all costs. He ran at the limits of his aerobic capacity, on the edge of serious oxygen debt. He was calling on everything he knew to help him close the gap. He tried to keep his quick steady rhythm, and to remain relaxed and fluent in his movements. He went into oxygen debt up the hills and then tried to repay it by relaxing at speed on even the most gentle of downhills.

As Mandla closed in on the pair, he found that he did not know them. However, he recognised the brown and white striped vest of Hillcrest Villagers, and the white vest with the diagonal burgundy stripe of Rand Athletic Club, or 'RAC'. Mandla caught them as they turned right into Oribi Road. They were warned of his approach by the shouting of the spectators, so they both responded immediately, and there was no chance for Mandla to sweep past them. Also the struggle to close the gap had told on him, so he simply slotted in behind them for a while, trying to recover a little from his recent chase. He was now glad of the time he had spent on the course before the race, for he knew what was ahead, and so was able to plan his tactics as he let the other two make the pace. In most places the people beside the way were now densely packed. They were very excited and very vocal. They had already watched the leaders go by, and they knew that they were now watching the battle for the last gold medal.

The trio turned left into Jesmond Road and went down a fairly steep hill. It was a wide road with grassy verges packed with people. It crossed a bridge at the bottom of a little valley, and then climbed steeply for about two hundred metres before levelling out. Mandla moved to the right and relaxed as much as possible as they went down the hill. He accelerated sharply as they crossed the bridge and began to climb. The Hillcrest runner dropped back almost immediately, tired out and taken by surprise. However, the RAC runner responded at once, and the two went together up the hill. Exhausted, they turned into Alexandra Road and ran shoulder to shoulder on the approach to the Jan Smuts Stadium and the finish.

Mandla moved into position on the left in order to be on the inside as they went round the left-hand bends into the stadium and onto the field. As they turned off the wide main road, Mandla was only aware of the runner in white at his side, the tapes now marking their way into the stadium, and the roar of the spectators. There was a steep ramp, up and then down, which took the runners over a big bank and onto the grass in the stadium for the last two hundred metres to the finish. Mandla somehow managed to surge again as they hit the up slope of the ramp. He gained two metres on the exhausting little climb, threw himself forward down the other side, led with his left shoulder into the bend onto the grass, and ran as fast as he could at a tangent to the final turn which swept around the field towards the finish. As a cross-country runner he adapted quickly to the different feel of the turf under his feet, and mustered the nearest thing he could to a sprint at that stage of the race. As he came out of the bend he had a lead of a few metres. He desperately worked his arms to try to maintain his pace. He was aware of brilliant light, the lush green of the soft grass, the public address announcer shouting in excitement, and the almost overwhelming roar of the crowd. He could not help looking back two or three times to be sure that he was not being caught in the final straight. He raised his arms as he crossed the finish, under the big clock which read 5:59:11. He had beaten six hours. A sponsor's towel was placed over his shoulders, and he knew that he had won the last gold medal. He stooped wearily, hands on his knees, but internally elated.

He looked round as the RAC runner came towards him. They embraced wearily but with great mutual respect. Mandla knew that the other runner had just finished in possibly the worst position in the race, just missing a gold medal, but was still sportingly recognising and acknowledging another's worthy performance.

65

Tony was chasing, chasing, chasing. He had six minutes to make up in order to catch Andy. He dropped quickly down the other side of Inchanga, then set out across the Harrison Flats, passed through Cato Ridge and then Camperdown. All the while he kept going at a quick but controlled pace, aware of his desire to catch Andy, but mindful of the need to spread his energy wisely over the remainder of the race. He kept himself concentrating on what he was doing, monitoring his pace, his running technique, his physical condition and his progress through the field. He had run well but conservatively for the first half of the race, so he was now able to maintain his speed. As a result he was continually passing other runners who had gone out too fast and were tiring. In this part of the field the runners were still well strung out, but Tony always had a few of them in sight. So it was never really lonely, except in the sense that every runner is always on his own, to run his own race and to use his capabilities to the best effect.

However, it is always possible to be despondent, especially in the third quarter of a race. The distance covered has been great, it is becoming more difficult to maintain one's desired pace as one tires, and it is still too far from the finish to obtain the mental boost which comes with knowing that the end is near. As it grew hot, and as he grew ever more weary, Tony's mind began to ask questions. First of all he began to worry about his charges elsewhere in the field. He hoped that

Mandla was still going well, but he was more worried about the slower runners, who would have to face the heat on the road for many more hours than those at the front. As it grew warmer, Tony was sure that there would be a larger than usual number of retirements that day. It was possible that even the last finisher would in effect have defeated as many as a thousand who would not reach the finish at all, or who would arrive there too late. Perhaps it would help that he and his little band had always done at least part of their training away from the cold early mornings, and so would have more tolerance to the heat.

In the quiet sections of the course, away from the support of spectators, Tony began to ask himself why he was there, and why he was subjecting himself to this arduous test of endurance. Then he had to pull himself together and remind himself why.

"I'm here to take part in this wonderful race," he told himself, "to do it justice by running it as well as I can in the spirit it holds and engenders. I'm here for the sake of my beloved Hadedas, who have worked so hard with me, to show them that I can do what I teach, and to be able to welcome them with pride at the finish. I'm here to find and to defeat Andrew Duke, to prove, even if only symbolically in this race, that sensible conservatism is better than arrogant and stupid fanaticism."

As he ran, Tony kept searching the road ahead for Andy in the red, white and blue of Sandown Runners. He overtook two or three of that club's athletes, but was past the highest point at Umlaas Road before he saw their colours being carried by Andy's familiar figure, some three or four hundred metres ahead of him. The chase was now easier as Tony knew that he was nearing his target, and could in fact now see him from time to time when the road straightened out sufficiently. The gap closed gradually, and then quite quickly as Andy lingered at one of the refreshment stations and walked for a while beyond it. Was he tiring?

Tony caught up with Andy in the dip at the Tumble Inn as they started to climb up to Ashburton. Tony was a very experienced runner and knew that he should have overtaken Andy very quickly. However, he felt that their race was almost won, and he could not resist a jibe as he drew alongside.

"Hi, Andy! I thought you'd be looking for a couple of billion today, instead of running. Or at least looking after some other men's wives."

"Drummond, you bastard, you don't deserve her. And the markets will recover."

Andy had indeed been tiring, but a rush of adrenalin at Tony's presence, and his remarks, kept him going. He fastened on to Tony and kept pace with him as the two pulled themselves up the long hill side by side. They were still close together when they reached the Hadedas' table near the top.

"Well that's Polly Shorts behind us," said Andy. *I have news for you,* thought Tony, but said nothing. He stopped at the table, and Andy went ahead.

"Can't you even run Comrades without your secretary to look after you?" he taunted as he saw Mary at the table.

Tony and his helpers rapidly exchanged greetings. He gratefully took the cold, carbohydrate drink Mary held out, and drank as he listened to the information they had for him. Mandla had gone past in fine style, looking good. The veterans' team race seemed to be between RAC and Celtic Harriers, after which it was anyone's guess. White Waters and Sandown were both doing well, with both Tony and Andy in scoring positions.

"You must at least beat Andy," said Mary.

"I have many reasons for that," said Tony as he resumed the race. "Thank you!"

Andy was now a few seconds ahead, trying to open as wide a gap as possible down the hill. Tony set off in pursuit, somewhat refreshed even if that were a strictly relative concept after some seventy-nine kilometres on the road. He took in the high, bush-clad hill looming across the valley ahead of them, and then concentrated on his race with Andy.

Andy made a big effort down the hill and held the gap he had opened up all the way to the bottom. Tony bided his time, knowing that Andy would be in for a shock when he came to Polly Shorts, which he thought he had already scaled. Andy slowed down as he began to climb the hill and Tony soon caught up with him. This time there were no jibes. Andy made another great effort to stay with Tony who was unable to go past. The two continued to climb, side by side as though attached to one another. *He's good*, thought Tony, *probably better than me, if he'd do things right.*

The hill became steeper and the contest continued. Tony felt they were running in slow motion, almost running on the spot. His legs were so tired he could hardly make them move. He had to keep going, and he willed himself not to give in to this man beside him. Surely all the excess training and racing that Andy had done would tell eventually?

They struggled for what seemed like an age, during which they only covered a few hundred metres. At last, when Tony felt he would soon have no option but to rest, he sensed that Andy faltered for a moment. Tony could not go any faster, but willed himself to hold the pace a little longer. He held on. Andy faltered again, and then was gone. Tony continued to run as best he could, not looking back. At the end of the long straight, just as the road was turning to the right, he glanced back. Andy was already well behind, walking painfully slowly and looking very dejected.

Tony decided that he could not afford to rest. He must open up a big gap, which Andy would not be able to close. He eased off his pace but continued to run. He tried to give some relief to his tortured legs by making changes to his running style, in order to change the way the muscles were stressed. It was still very hard, and he was grateful when he reached the top of the hill, to be greeted by the many spectators and the ever cheerful and encouraging helpers at the refreshment station there. Tony hastily drank and sponged and went on his way. He looked back once and could not see Andy at all.

With his race really now won, Tony tried to get into a pace and rhythm that he could maintain to the end. At first he struggled, for his fight with Andy had taken a lot out of him, and his legs in particular. However, he gradually picked up his former rhythm and set out to enjoy the remainder of his run. He won a brief skirmish with another of the Sandown Runners' veteran's team, hopefully helping to ensure White Waters a third place in that competition. While he enjoyed the support of the crowds, which still lined the road near the end of the race, he began to realise that he could finish in less than seven hours, which would be his best Comrades time. He kept his rhythm going, and eventually hauled himself over the ramp and onto the grass in the stadium. There were only a handful of runners on the last two hundred metres of the grass track as he ran in. He overtook one of them in the final straight, and passed under the big clock at the finish in 6:58 and some seconds. He was very tired but well satisfied with his run.

Tony was guided through one of the six funnels beyond the finishing line. The perforated strip containing his personal details was torn off the bottom of his front race number, he was given a card with his approximate finishing time stamped on it, and was then handed a small plastic bag containing his silver medal and some other items. As he left the finishing enclosure he encountered Trixie.

"Oh, Tony," she said as she saw him, "Mandla won the last gold medal. We're so proud. And now I think we might be third in the Vets' team competition."

It seems as though all is forgiven, thought Tony, as he moved on to find the White Waters club tent on the bank next to the finishing straight. Many clubs had been allocated places to erect such tents, where their members could meet each other, or obtain support, after the race. He spotted the sky blue of his White Waters club, and a banner with the flowing white WW on it. To reach the tent he had to go past that of the

Sandown Runners' Club, and there he found Nora, anxiously looking down the finishing straight for Andy.

"Where's Andy?" she asked as she saw Tony.

"I left him at Pollys. I'm sure he'll welcome your attention when he comes in."

There was an awkward pause. Nora seemed to struggle to speak.

"Well run. You were right about the markets too."

"Thank you."

"Andy says they'll recover soon… There he is!"

Nora rushed to the barrier to encourage Andy as he turned into the finishing straight. He was running, but very slowly, moving like broken man, despite coming in to obtain a good silver medal. He had lost ten minutes on Tony since Polly Shorts.

At the White Waters tent Tony found Linda who had his tog bag with dry clothes. He changed out of his wet vest and then sat by himself on the bank to one side of the tent, drinking a cold drink and watching the runners coming in.

Unaccountably, he found he was sobbing, crying quietly to himself. He had no reason to cry. He had simply let go of himself out of relief that all the past hours of intense concentration and self-control were over at last. It was not simply the race. It was also the months of preparation, the struggle at Nigroup, the break-up of his home, the effort to remain calm and focussed in the days and hours before the race. He felt a strange feeling of anti-climax, of let down, of hollowness. He had run well. He had beaten Andy as he intended. That had been a hard race, but in a way it had been too easy. He had proved his points. He had been right in so many ways, but he felt hollow inside. He knew the markets would not recover quickly after their recent shattering crash. They would take a long time to recover. He had fought hard and he had been right, but in the end he had failed to help those thousands of people who would now lose some part of their savings. He had failed to help those who would lose their jobs in the aftermath of the inevitable collapse of Nigroup.

Tony stood up and went to find himself another cold drink. He turned his thoughts to his little band of Hadedas still out on the road in the heat of the day. Their story was not yet finished.

66

For most Comrades runners the body is one big exhausted ache after several hours on the road. One simply has to manage it as best one can and keep going to the end. For the back-markers the test of endurance is no different in terms of distance, but is far longer in terms of time, compared with the leaders. The pain from Melanie's bite had merged into a general soreness, mainly of the legs, and an increasing weariness in the rest of the body. However, the pain in her left knee became worse and worse and began to dominate everything else. Something was clearly wrong, and by the time she and Bill reached Cato Ridge they still had nearly thirty kilometres to go.

As the pain worsened Melanie had to stop every now and again to allow it to ease. She experimented, trying to run in different ways to see how best she could keep going. She would hobble along for a while, and then had to stop. She could manage best on the level, not as well on the uphills, and very poorly on the steeper downhills. She could walk reasonably well, though with a slight limp as she almost involuntarily tried to protect her left knee. Bill stayed with her and urged her on, though very worried about her as he could see that her struggle was a hard one. At length, on the downhill before the climb into Camperdown, Melanie stopped, close to tears.

"I don't think I can do it, Bill," she said despairingly. "You carry on. You'll be able to finish the way you're going. I don't think I can."

"You must, Melanie! Think of your promise."

"Oh, David, I'm so sorry." Melanie held her hands against her chest to press David's Comrades numbers close to her as tears streamed down her cheeks.

"Come on," said Bill, taking her gently by the arm and leading her forward. "Let's walk while we think about things."

They started walking down the hill. Melanie made an effort to pull herself together and wiped the tears from her eyes, conscious again of the many runners overtaking them. She still held a hand to her breast. She looked ahead at the stream of competitors stretching out along the road ahead. Some were running slowly, many were walking, some obviously struggling. They were not alone.

Bill had been doing some mental arithmetic.

"We've still got nearly three hours and fifty minutes left to do about twenty-six kilometres. That's something like eight and three-quarter minutes per K. It's quite a bit slower than we've been doing since Drummond, even with our stops. If we can just keep going we still have a chance. But we'll have to run a good part of the way. We can't do it by walking alone."

Melanie was silent, but speeded up her walk, and then began to jog again as the downhill flattened out and they went through the bottom of the little valley and began to climb again.

"I think you should go on ahead," she said at last. "You'll be able to make it. You can at least run, even if you do feel sick."

"I'm staying with you, Melanie, just as you stayed with me. I wouldn't even have made it this far without your help. I think we can both get there. Let's see if we can find help at

Camperdown. There may be a physio there. You don't want to come back and do it all over again next year do you?"

"Not if I can help it," said Melanie, sounding more determined. "Bill, it's been such a struggle these last two years just to get here. Something could just as easily go wrong another year. I can't have this promise to David hanging over me forever, but I must keep it if I can."

They went on in silence for a while, even overtaking a few walkers as they managed to keep jogging.

"But you know, it's now not only for David," continued Melanie. "I've put so much into this that I must also prove to myself that I can do it. If I fail I'll come back for David's sake, but I'll also have to try again for myself, to prove that I really can complete a Comrade's Marathon."

"Like me," said Bill. "So let's try not to fail this time. We can still do it."

What Melanie did not say was that, if Bill insisted on staying with her, then she would also somehow have to make sure that he finished before eleven hours. It would be very bad for him not to finish again, even in a noble sacrifice for her sake.

Bill very much wanted them to finish. He had his own personal reasons, of course, and he now felt that he would be able to keep going to the end. He still did not feel well, and his legs were very tired and sore. However, by drinking only a little as frequently as possible, he was keeping his sickness at bay, and he felt sure that his weary legs could see him through to the finish. Worrying about Melanie, and trying to keep her going, also took his mind away from himself and thoughts of his own vulnerability. He desperately wanted Melanie to finish. He loved her deeply and did not want her to taste the bitterness of failure. He wanted her to keep her promise to David, and he wanted her to succeed for her own sake, but he also had selfish reasons for wanting her to finish this race. He knew that Melanie would not allow her relationship with him to develop beyond its present level until she had kept that promise to her former husband.

At Camperdown they found an aid station. A kindly and efficient physiotherapist was just sending a victim of cramp on his way, and took immediate care of Melanie.

"It might be something to do with the tracking of the patella," she said after a brief examination, "but you'll have to get a proper diagnosis when you get home. I may be able to help a little. Also, try running in the middle of the road if you can. The camber on the right may be aggravating your problem."

In very little time the physiotherapist had applied an analgesic gel, had worked to stretch Melanie's quadriceps, had strapped her leg in the region of the knee and sent her on her way, bandaged like a wounded soldier. With Bill in attendance, Melanie managed to commence jogging again. She did feel somewhat better for the treatment, and the crowd still lining both sides of the road gave her double encouragement, for her female beauty and for her bandages.

Shortly after they had left busy little Camperdown behind them, Melanie and Bill were caught by Sylvia, who had continued to make steady progress, and who jogged with them for a while. She listened to their story and offered encouragement.

"We still have time to finish," she said. "Is there anything I can do?"

There was not. They moved along together and chatted for a while. Then they came to a steep little downhill and Melanie was forced to walk. Sylvia moved on ahead of them.

Sylvia continued to make satisfactory progress. Like so many around her she could not sustain a level of speed and effort that would take her into oxygen debt, so she ran aerobically and her head was relatively clear. She was able to think quite well, and could and did easily speak to those around her. However, her mind seemed to be floating along on top of a bundle of pain and weariness. Her body, and especially her legs, was tired and stiff and sore. She dared not stop, and vetoed frequent suggestions from her brain that she sit and rest for a while. She feared that if she once stopped and sat down she would not be able to coax her stiff legs into movement again. So she kept on keeping on.

With the heat of the day, and her growing fatigue, she found that her pace was slowing just a little. To keep herself from falling too much off her planned pace, she concentrated on her running technique, making good use of the downhills, and on her rhythm. For long periods she almost mesmerised herself by silently chanting in time with the rhythm of her running Tony's "re-laxed flu-ent rhy-thm re-laxed flu-ent rhy-thm…" So she kept her mind off being tired and sore, and urged herself to try to relax and run rhythmically.

Sylvia also had her difficult moments of doubt and questioning. She nearly always had a number of other runners close to her, so she could not say she was ever lonely in those places where there were no crowds of spectators to urge the competitors on and distract them from themselves. However, there were times when the runners tended to withdraw into themselves and run in dogged silence, as they sensed the heat, the never-ending road and the dry open countryside. It was then easy to feel alone with one's own vulnerability and to question the wisdom of undertaking this enormous test of endurance.

It was beyond anything that Sylvia had ever attempted. However, she had wanted to be involved with Tony and the others in this great race, and here she was. Already it had been a memorable experience, she had run much further than she had ever done before, and she was determined to see it through to the end. Her mind was strong, and she refused to contemplate that anything would stop her from finishing. She would prove that she could climb this Everest. In doing so, she would show that Tony's methods worked, and that the doubters, including those who had said that she would not be able to do Comrades, were wrong. She loved Tony, and she was running as much for him, or even more, than for herself.

As she began to climb Ashburton Hill, she knew that she had time in hand for a finish. Her determination remained, but her confidence and optimism grew. She saw a pair of White Waters club mates walking up the hill ahead of her. She continued to run, albeit slowly, and soon drew level. They were Johan and Simon, looking very tired and dejected. She greeted them.

"Sylvia, has this hill got a name? Is it Polly Shorts?" asked Simon.

"This is Ashburton, or Little Pollys," replied Sylvia. "Polly Shorts is the next one. Good luck!"

Sylvia moved ahead. Inwardly she questioned what kind of preparation the pair had done if they knew so little about the course. *And well done, Tony!* she thought. *These are two who wouldn't train with us because they wanted to do 'real' training.*

She paused at the Hadedas' table to drink, to exchange hurried greetings and news, and to express thanks for their support and patience. They told her that Tony had gone through hours ago looking good. She told them about Melanie's injury.

67

Sipho was having a wonderful race. He was thoroughly enjoying himself. He had looked back a few times after leaving Josh on Inchanga, but once he had turned the first bend in the road he had not seen him again. Sipho hoped that Josh would be all right, for he knew how important it was for Josh to complete the race. From time to time Sipho almost involuntarily looked around and searched the runners behind him for the familiar, tall, bearded figure, even though he knew that Josh was now probably a long way back. Nonetheless, Josh was never far from Sipho's thoughts.

The day grew hot, and Sipho knew that he was running a little slower than he had done in the first half of the race. However, he did not worry too much about time. He ran according to the terrain and how he felt, as he had run as a youngster in KwaZulu. He knew that he must be running well by the number of other runners he was passing.

Sipho had no serious doubts along the way. He was simply glad to be there on a beautiful day. Yes, he was growing tired, but he had never before run so far, or for so long. He never doubted that he would finish the race, and he marvelled that he, who not long ago had had nowhere to live and had not known where his next food would come from, was helping to raise money to build a church.

Sipho worked his way up Ashburton Hill. He was as delighted to see his support team (he, Sipho, with a support team!) as they were to see him. He beamed at them, with shining eyes and brilliant white teeth, as he gratefully took his cold drink from Mary. He sailed down to the bottom of Polly Shorts and hauled himself up that big climb with only two or three short walking breaks. Race time was 8:56 when he reached the top. He had more than two hours for the last six and a half kilometres or so. He set out confidently into Pietermaritzburg.

Josh was not doing nearly as well as Sipho. He continued to struggle with periodic bad patches when he felt ill and lethargic for no apparent reason. However, he kept himself moving forward towards Pietermaritzburg, making reasonable progress, although at a much slower pace than in the first half of the race. He would finish well outside his original target time, but the most important thing was for him to finish. He believed sincerely that anything that was undertaken in God's name should be done to the very best of one's ability, but today for some reason he was not doing as well as he should. That worried him, but perhaps the Lord was testing him, to see whether he could overcome the unforeseen difficulties he was facing and still succeed.

Whenever Josh began to feel a little despondent, he focussed his mind upon the church he would build. If he could finish the race, the money and resources they needed would finally be available, and the building would commence. He dared not think of the consequences if he did not finish this race. The Comrades Project would fail, and at best there would be long delays and a further struggle to raise sufficient funds. He prayed for the strength and determination to keep going until the end, and so to succeed in this his mission.

Josh was cheered by the team at the Hadedas' table at Ashburton, and by the news that Sipho had gone through some time before, looking good. Josh walked up much of Polly Shorts, noting that he was far from alone in that, as many of those on the now busy stretch of road also walked from time to time. However, he grew more optimistic as he neared the top, and he even smiled as he stopped to drink at the refreshment station there. Race time was 9:20. He had more than enough time to finish. The race was virtually over!

It was crowded around the refreshment station. Josh walked forward to one of the water troughs beside the road. As he stretched his arm out to dip his sponge into the trough, he was jostled as someone urgently stretched across him to do the same. In the tangle, Josh turned his ankle on the little step between the edge of the tar road and the gravel verge, and twisted it sharply as he crashed to the ground. He lay there groaning in pain, looking helplessly at legs and coloured shorts above him as his world suddenly fell apart.

As the afternoon wore on, and the time ticked away unrelentingly towards the finish of the race at five o'clock, or race time of eleven hours, the countdown in the runners' minds grew ever more frantic. Watches were consulted more frequently and more urgently, and tired minds tried to calculate the time available to finish the remaining distance, and exhorted weary bodies to keep going a little faster for a little longer.

Sylvia's calculations were still favourable, so she was still fairly relaxed as she finally made her way up the long Polly Shorts Hill, that she had heard so much about. At that stage of the race there were more than sixty runners passing the refreshment station at the top of the hill every minute, so the road was crowded. As Sylvia looked ahead on the long, steep, straight section, she saw an unbroken stream of bobbing figures, spread out across the road. Some were running, some were walking purposefully, while others moved listlessly, or limped in obvious difficulty. They wore a multitude of colours, with vests and shorts a kaleidoscope of reds, yellows, greens, blues, orange, brown, black and white, arranged in a variety of combinations, including stripes and hoops and initials and names.

Sylvia decided to tackle the hill in stages, alternately running slowly and then walking. Many of those around her did the same, so there was much passing and re-passing as the column moved slowly and erratically towards the top of the hill. The mood was generally cautiously cheerful, with competitors encouragingly reminding one another that this was the last major struggle of the race, and that they still had more than enough time in which to finish. Only amongst the limping injured was there a feeling of quiet desperation as they kept moving forward, but with countless others continually streaming past them.

At race time 9:34 Sylvia reached the top of Polly Shorts with a feeling of relief and quiet confidence. She drank and sponged and began to run slowly again towards Pietermaritzburg. At 9:37 she came to a stop as she suddenly saw next to her, in the sky blue of White Waters, a tall thin figure with dark hair and a beard, and a lean face hideously distorted with pain and despair. Josh's right foot was swathed in bandages and he was limping very badly.

"Josh, what's wrong?" asked Sylvia.

"I fell and sprained my ankle. Just as I thought the race was over. Stupid pride before a fall! They took me to the physio tent where they bound up my foot to give it some support. They were very good to me. They advised me not to carry on, because I have a bad injury and I might do more damage. I told them I had to finish because I have a church to build, which they thought was strange. I've lost so much time, and now I can hardly walk. Oh, Sylvia, I must at least try."

As he spoke, the two of them were moving slowly forward with other runners streaming past them. Josh could obviously not put much weight on his right foot, and was also in pain, so he relied heavily on his left leg, levering himself forward on it and hobbling off the right one as quickly as possible every time it touched the ground. His movements were grotesque, but Sylvia could only admire him for trying to keep going.

“What can I do to help?” she asked, but she knew that there was nothing. On her exhausted legs it was difficult enough to keep herself going. It would be foolish even to try to support someone else. Reluctantly, she could only wish him well, and, at his bidding, she moved ahead to continue her own race.

At 9:42 Josh reached the ‘6km to go’ sign. He had 78 minutes left, which meant that he had to try to complete the rest of the course at thirteen minutes per kilometre. He tried to quicken his rhythm and not to notice the pain.

68

Sipho's watch read 9:38 as he turned off Alexandra Road towards the Jan Smuts Stadium. Just before he left the main road he looked back and searched the busy column of runners stretching away behind him, but could not see Josh. As his own race appeared to be coming to a successful conclusion, Sipho's thoughts had turned more and more towards his benefactor, whom he had left nearly five hours before on Inchanga. Sipho felt uneasy. Should he have left Josh behind? What if he was struggling and needed help? How would he, Sipho, feel if Josh needed him and he was not there?

Sipho turned into the stadium and went over the ramp and onto the grass track. All around him there were dozens of runners, covering the last two hundred metres to the finish to the encouragement of a very large crowd. Sipho came out of the last bend and looked up the final straight. There it was! The finish at last, with a huge banner stretched across the track and a big clock just changing the minutes to show 9:40. Sipho should have been elated, like so many others around him. He was very satisfied with his performance, but he was strangely worried about Josh. Somehow he had a feeling that Josh might be in trouble and might need him. He decided that he would finish the race and then go back and find him. Then he stopped halfway up the final straight to think. Runners streamed past him.

"Hey, don't stop!" from voices in the crowd. "The finish is further on. You've done well. Come on. Get going. Don't stop now."

Sipho knew that competitors could assist each other, but that outside help could lead to a runner's disqualification. Would he be counted as a participant, or as an outsider, if he had already finished and then went to help Josh? Better not take the chance. Sipho looked towards the finish only fifty metres away. Then he turned around and started to go back along the course, against the stream of finishing runners, in search of Josh.

"I wish I'd had that injection," said Melanie, as she and Bill jogged painfully up Ashburton Hill.

"You'll have far more satisfaction when you finish without it," said Bill.

They had continued to make slow progress, but progress it was. They had now settled into a determined mode, resolved to keep moving forward whatever happened. As the injured one, Melanie set the pace, and Bill was there in support. They jogged when they could, they walked when they had to, and, despite their resolve, they had to stop occasionally when the pain became too much for Melanie. She kept the stops brief, telling herself that they must keep going, and reminding herself that she had always thought that women could endure pain better than men. There were other competitors around them all the time. Many were walking or hobbling and some were swathed in bandages. They encouraged each other, especially when Melanie and Bill jogged past some that were walking, and then were themselves later overtaken as the others jogged while they in turn had to walk for a spell.

They were glad to see the Hadedas' table near the top of the hill, and took comfort from the friendly, anxious faces there. As the pair reached the table, Mary and Maria handed them drinks, which they swallowed gratefully before resuming their painful journey.

Fred came through soon after Bill and Melanie, and he caught them on the way up Polly Shorts, soon after they began to jog again after the long downhill.

"You're limping worse than me," said Fred. "What's wrong?"

They told him about their problems and their fears of not being able to finish in time.

"You've got one-and-a-half legs haven't you?" asked Fred. "No reason why you can't finish. Only just over seven K's to go. Just hang in there. I know of someone who finished with a partly artificial leg. Also a chap with one lung, and another with one kidney. There are a lot of other stories. No reason for you not to finish."

He told them about his own run, and how his left foot was now so swollen that he would not be able to put his shoe on again if he were to take it off. It helped Melanie and Bill to have Fred with them, and together the three walked and jogged their way to the top of Polly Shorts. Race time was 9:54. There were only 6.6km to go and they had 66 minutes left to do them in. It seemed as though they were winning their struggle, but only if they could keep pressing on.

"Hey! You're going the wrong way!"

"Haven't you had enough?"

"Are you running all the way back to Durban?"

Sipho was becoming used to the calls from the stream of runners as he worked his way back along the course. He ran on the right-hand side of the road, so he did not impede the runners, and from where he could see them coming towards him. Anxiously his eyes searched for Josh. Perhaps he was being stupid, but he still worried that Josh might be in trouble. The further he went the more worried he became. Surely Josh should have come past by now if he were all right? Had he missed him? He did not think so, but he was afraid that Josh might go past, unseen by him in the middle of a bunch of runners.

"Sipho! What's wrong? Why are you going back?"

At 9:58, somewhere between two and three kilometres to go, Sylvia saw Sipho running towards her on the other side of the road. She moved out of the stream to talk to him.

"Sylvia, I'm looking for Mister Josh. I'm worried about him. Have you seen him?"

"I passed him just after Polly Shorts. He's sprained an ankle and can hardly walk. I don't know if he can finish, Sipho."

"I knew something was wrong. I'm going to find him. Thank you, Sylvia."

Sipho continued his search, now even more worried than before. Would he even be able to help if he did find Josh?

At 10:08, at four kilometres to go, Sipho at last saw the tall figure of Josh bobbing unevenly in the stream of runners as he heaved himself forward over his left leg, and then tried to put as little weight as possible onto the right one. Sipho ran across the road towards him.

"Mister Josh, Mister Josh!"

Josh was astounded at the apparition of Sipho coming towards him.

"Sipho! What on earth are you doing here? I thought you must've finished long ago."

"I got almost to the finish, but came back to help you. I thought something was wrong."

He fell into step beside Josh, who told him what had happened. Josh wondered that, after running eighty-eight kilometres, someone could have been so concerned about him that he had run all this way back to find him.

"I don't know how to thank you, Sipho, but this makes me even more determined to finish. I don't know if I can do it, and I do not know why the Lord is testing me in this way. I must do each kilometre in thirteen minutes, and I have just managed to do that for the last two. But as you see, it is difficult. I can't put much weight on my right foot. It is painful, and has very little strength in it."

Sipho tried to support Josh as he walked, but they soon realised that that was impracticable. Sipho was simply not strong enough on his own legs, which had already done more than ninety-two kilometres that day, and which would have to do almost another four in order to finish the race. So he talked to Josh, and helped to keep his spirits up as he struggled on with fierce determination.

69

Sylvia's satisfaction grew quietly into joy as she closed in on the finish at the Jan Smuts Stadium. For some time now she had been confident of a good finish, barring any unforeseen circumstances, and she decided to make sure that she enjoyed the last part of the race. She was relatively relaxed and was in fact running better than at any stage of the race, despite her tired legs. She continued to take in the busy scenes around her and filed them away in her memory, to be recalled in later years.

At last she eased herself carefully down the ramp and ran onto the grass with only two hundred metres to go. It was strange to have green grass under her feet. The way was crowded as runners were finishing at a rate of more than one every second. In their various colours, and in varying states of elation and exhaustion, they were spread out across the track. The sun was now low and the shadows were long. She seemed to be running in slow motion on her weary legs as she moved with the tide around the final bend and into the finishing straight. The crowd lined both sides of the track, and was clearly huge as it was swelled by the arrival of thousands of runners and their loved ones who had come to meet them. Sylvia glimpsed the sky blue of the White Waters tent and moved wide to her left, looking for Tony. She could not see him, but she heard him scream her name above the general roar around them. The progress of the last hundred metres felt like a victory parade, and she did indeed feel victorious as she crossed the line under the clock at 10:19.

With her medal in her hand, Sylvia turned towards the White Waters tent in search of Tony. He fought his way through the crowd to come to meet her, and he found her, despite the crush of so many people.

"Oh, Tony!" she exclaimed, as they fell into each other's arms, oblivious to everything around them. They hugged one another tightly for long seconds, not needing to speak and not wanting to let go of each other.

"Well done, Sylvia! I'm proud of you."

He realised that Sylvia was crying quietly with her head pressed to his shoulder.

"It's all right," he said gently. "You've been wonderful."

"I'm just so happy," she said, looking into his eyes. "Oh, Tony, I knew we could do it. I knew we could show them, and we have."

70

10:21. Josh knew that he and Sipho should be at the '3km to go' mark by then in order to keep to their minimum target of thirteen minutes per kilometre. There it was, just about twenty metres ahead. They had lost a little time over the previous kilometre. He tried to increase the pace.

Fred closed in on the unlikely pair and drew level with them as they reached the '3km to go' mark. Fred was running slowly and unevenly, but was still a little bundle of determination. He rapidly assessed the situation as he approached Josh and Sipho, but asked no questions.

"Keep going!" he said as he overtook them. "You can still make it. Just don't stop!"

Josh and Sipho wished Fred luck as he went by. *That's a good lad*, thought Fred, realising that Sipho was shepherding Josh towards the finish. *I hope they make it, but they're very slow.*

10:28. Somewhere between two and three kilometres to go, Melanie and Bill found Josh and Sipho struggling painfully. The four exchanged hasty greetings and explanations, and walked together for a few seconds. It was a strange sight: four figures in sky blue, two of them limping badly but with their escorts in attendance.

They all wished each other well as Melanie and Bill went ahead. Somehow Melanie's troubles seemed less after she had assessed Josh's situation. He was moving very slowly and was obviously badly injured. *She will keep her promise,* thought Josh, *but will I keep mine?*

He watched Melanie's lovely but limping figure, and her hair glowing with golden red highlights as the low sun touched it into life. Josh tried to increase his pace and keep her in sight for as long as possible, but all too soon she was lost amongst the other runners.

10:34. Josh and Sipho were ten metres past the '2km to go' mark. They had made up about thirty metres over the last kilometre. They were on target, but only just. Sipho was encouraging Josh all the time.

"Come on, Mister Josh! The Lord wants that church. He will help you."

Whenever Josh appeared to be slowing, Sipho moved a metre ahead of him, trying to draw him forward, willing him to increase his pace.

"Come on. If you can build a church, you can do the Comrades Marathon. You must finish Comrades so you can build that church. Come on!"

Josh tried all he could to keep with Sipho, who, he realised, was drawing him on if he showed any sign of slowing. The sun was low in the sky. At one point Josh noticed a few clouds in the west. The sky was all orange and mauves and dove grey. Surely darkness would not overtake them before they reached the end of their journey? Sipho was just ahead of him, urging him on. Josh prayed silently as he tried to move a little faster.

10:40. Fred began to relax a little as he turned into the stadium. He was almost there after his long struggle. It seemed an eternity since he had been forced to stop at

Tollgate. He would have to take plenty of time to recover from this run after the way he had abused his heel. He no longer needed to worry about beating the finishing gun. He had time to crawl to the end if he had to.

Running felt different on the grass after so many hours on the hard road. The little stooping figure with the green number was almost lost in the crowd of runners as he rounded the last bend, limping as he ran slowly towards the finish. There was the banner across the track ahead of him. The clock turned over to 10:42.

Fred crossed the line, and at last he allowed himself to smile. Medal number twenty-six was in the bag!

10:42. Melanie and Bill were approaching the stadium at last. As their confidence had grown that they would reach the finish in time, Melanie had become more and more emotional. She still kept herself moving forward as best she could, and she was aware of the stream of runners in which they moved. There were also the spectators along the way, fewer than earlier in the day, but still willing the runners on ever more urgently as the race cut-off time came closer and closer. However, Melanie now thought more and more of David, who would have loved so much to be here, and in whose memory she had struggled so long and so hard. She often touched her race number and pressed David's to her chest. Did he, or could he, know that she was nearing the end of their tenth Comrades Marathon? It would be a tenth with no green number at the finish, for David would have had to be here to earn and receive that himself, but it was their tenth nonetheless.

They went over the ramp, and then quickly adjusted to the soft, thick grass under their feet. Melanie took Bill's hand and held it tightly as they struggled around the last bend. When the finish came into sight, at the end of the final straight, Melanie took David's yellow race numbers out of their pocket at her breast, where they had travelled all the way from Durban. She held them out in front of her, one in each hand, showing them to the world, and sobbing, “David, my dear David!” Bill moved a metre or two to one side, allowing her the moment, but still watching over her.

At 10:45 Melanie and Bill crossed the line. They turned to one another and hugged closely, oblivious of the officials trying to keep the press of finishers moving on to avoid congestion in the finishing area. Melanie still sobbed, “David, David”, as she held onto Bill.

“We did it!” she said, looking up. “Thank you for helping me to keep my promise.”

“Thank you for helping me when I thought I could go no further.”

“Perhaps we’ll make a good team after all.”

“I think we will.”

71

10:47. Josh and Sipho had just passed the '1km to go' sign. They had gained a few metres, but it was still uncertain whether they would be able to reach the finish before the eleven-hour cut-off at five o'clock. Sipho knew, of course, that he himself could do it, but was determined to stay with Josh and see him home in time if possible.

They continued to struggle. The remaining spectators beside the road knew that time was now of the essence. They could see Josh's struggle, his pain and his slow pace. They frantically urged him on to greater efforts. Sipho kept calm, but he was very worried, and still tried to keep Josh up to the pace they needed. Josh struggled on. Sometimes he felt they were gaining time. Sometimes he felt that they were slowing and tried to speed up. He tried to see before him a beautiful church building rising from the ground, the vision pulling him forward, but he was alternately haunted by the thought of an upraised gun firing to signal the close of the race.

10:53. Tony and Sylvia were sitting on the crowded bank near the White Waters tent watching the runners still streaming out of the final bend and past them along the finishing straight. The flow had lessened slightly, but there were still around fifty runners finishing every minute. The scene was a very busy one, the atmosphere was electric and the support of the spectators grew more and more noisy and frantic as the seconds and minutes ticked away to the end of the race. The whole finish was now in shadow and the temperature had dropped.

Sylvia absorbed the details of the scene, even as they scanned the field for Josh and Sipho, whom they awaited anxiously and who were the only two of their little band still to finish. The runners came in all shapes, sizes and complexions, male and female, young and old. The colours of dozens of clubs were still there on the track. Sylvia noted the black and white of Savages, the white and burgundy of RAC, the red, white, yellow and black of Wanderers, the green and white stripes of Celtic Harriers, and many, many more.

Most of the competitors jogged wearily to the finish, some found the energy for a delighted last minute surge on the final straight, while some walked or hobbled along knowing they would beat the cut-off. Sylvia saw one individual crawling the last few metres on hands and knees as cramps had struck his legs so badly that he could not stand up again. There were couples walking or jogging hand-in-hand. Small groups linked arms as the finish came into view, and larger ones who had run together in 'buses' now celebrated with arms upraised or in song or in mutual congratulation. Some were helping teammates, or others who had been complete strangers at the beginning of the day, supporting them, arms around shoulders. There were even four carrying a club mate bodily down the final stretch. Some came in with flags or banners or funny hats, either carried along the road or collected from supporters just outside the stadium.

There were those who ran joyfully through the finish, and those who stopped just over the line and simply stood there or leant on their knees in utter weariness. Some knelt and kissed the ground, or gave thanks for the strength and endurance to have completed the race. Others collapsed over the line, to be helped up, or carried away to the medical tent by tired and busy stretcher-bearers. The officials had their hands full keeping the finishing area clear for those still streaming in.

There was still no sign of Josh and Sipho.

10:56. A smartly dressed Mick Winn, Chairman of the Comrades Marathon Association, took up his position next to the finishing line, on the inside of the track, pistol in hand. Soon he would turn his back, so that he could not see the last runners coming in, and would fire the pistol as the clock showed eleven hours.

10:57. The flow of runners coming to the finish was slowing to about one every two seconds. The participation of the crowd grew to a crescendo as they assessed the finishing chances of each new competitor that came into view, and seemingly lived every painful step with them as they came down the track.

Josh and Sipho were struggling over the ramp. They had gained a little time, but then lost a few precious seconds as Josh found the ramp's awkward up and down slopes difficult to negotiate. He struggled round the final bend with Sipho in anxious attendance. They were still being overtaken by others frantically racing to beat the cut-off.

10:58:30. "There they are!" Sylvia and Tony shouted simultaneously, as Josh and Sipho came into view at the start of the home straight. Josh was desperately heaving himself forward in ungainly fashion. His face was distorted with pain, but he kept on. He could now see the clock. The seconds seemed to pass at a terrifying rate.

"Come on, Mister Josh!" cried Sipho anxiously taking Josh by the right hand and trying to pull him along faster. The cry was taken up by the spectators who heard him, and then by others in the crowd as they saw the struggle and realised that it would be a close one.

"Come on, Mister Josh! Come on, come on!"

Desperately Josh quickened his pace. With thirty seconds to go, he was sure that they would make it. With barely fifteen seconds to go and ten metres from the line, Josh's left leg suddenly cramped. The strain had been too much.

Somehow Sipho held onto Josh and kept him upright, but he was not strong enough to move him forward. Despairing, he looked around and called for help. Two or three runners went past them, wrapped up in their own struggle for the line. Sipho saw a black runner in Durban Athletic Club colours approaching at speed and looked pleadingly at him.

"Help! Siza! Sicela usisize!"

The runner took in the situation in an instant. Hardly breaking his stride he took hold of Josh's left arm and together they heaved him and themselves across the line. Josh collapsed in a heap. Two other finishers fell on top of him as they threw themselves over the line an instant before the gun was fired.

Officials drew a tape across the finish to stop anyone else from crossing the line. Some competitors who arrived just too late were guided to the side of the official finishing area. They had given their all, but it had not been quite enough on the day. A sponsor's towel was put over the shoulders of the last finisher as a television interviewer hovered to speak to her.

Sipho knelt worriedly next to Josh as the little pile of last second finishers disentangled themselves, and as helpers bearing stretchers came to their aid. Josh lay on his back and looked at Sipho's anxious face.

"Sipho! Oh, Sipho! You have been a blessed gift indeed. Thank you! Thank you! Now we can build God's church. We will build it together, and it will never be closed to any one of God's people."

Epilogue

Josh realised his dream, and they built a beautiful church to the glory of God and for the use of his congregation. It was indeed open to all people of all races, and, perhaps to Josh's surprise, few if any left the congregation to worship elsewhere. On the contrary its numbers continued to grow.

Sylvia and Tony were married by Josh, one lovely sunny highveld afternoon, in one of the first weddings to be held in the new church building. Those who came to the service were greeted by a broadly smiling Sipho, standing at the entrance to the church in a smart dark suit, welcoming them and handing them hymn sheets.

Melanie and Bill were married in the same church a few weeks later, secure in their relationship and in the knowledge that Bill now had a permanent job and a promising career.

The financial markets did not recover quickly, and Nigroup and Nilife had to be rescued by Enduring Bank. In the wreckage, many thousands of people lost at least some part of their savings, and many hundreds lost their jobs. Andy was forced out of his position and retired into relative obscurity. Nora fell with him, though she continued with her legal work. Andy's borrowings proved to be far greater than Nora could have imagined, but with her earnings, and the "golden parachute" Andy was paid on the premature termination of his contract with Nigroup, they manage well enough. They have still not married. As Nora has bided her time, some have wondered whether she has perhaps been assessing the relative chances of Andy's profitable return to business or of a better prospect emerging.

Mandla has become well known and respected as an excellent runner. He was given the job he wanted so much in Terry's speciality running shop and has been making the best of this opportunity to learn the business.

Fred recovered from his injury and has since added to his impressive tally of Comrades medals.

The Comrades Marathon continues to be held each year, and, if possible, to grow in stature. After all, it remains one of the finest races in the world and one of the greatest challenges for both elite and ordinary runners.